C000270291

Uhland, Ludwig

Ernst, Herzog von Schwaben

Trauerspiel in fünf Aufzuegen

Uhland, Ludwig

Ernst, Herzog von Schwaben

Trauerspiel in fünf Aufzuegen

Inktank publishing, 2018

www.inktank-publishing.com

ISBN/EAN: 9783747796818

All rights reserved

This is a reprint of a historical out of copyright text that has been re-manufactured for better reading and printing by our unique software. Inktank publishing retains all rights of this specific copy which is marked with an invisible watermark.

G
u 31e

𝔓itt 𝔓ress 𝔖eries.

ERNST, HERZOG VON SCHWABEN,

TRAUERSPIEL IN FÜNF AUFZÜGEN

VON

LUDWIG UHLAND,

WITH A

BIOGRAPHICAL AND HISTORICAL INTRODUCTION,
ENGLISH NOTES, AND AN INDEX,

BY

H. J. WOLSTENHOLME, B.A. (LOND.)

LECTURER IN GERMAN AT NEWNHAM COLLEGE, CAMBRIDGE.

EDITED FOR THE SYNDICS OF THE UNIVERSITY PRESS.

ℭambriⅾge:
AT THE UNIVERSITY PRESS.

London: CAMBRIDGE WAREHOUSE, 17, PATERNOSTER ROW.
Cambriⅾge: DEIGHTON, BELL AND CO.
Leipⅼig: F. A. BROCKHAUS.

1882

[*All Rights reserved.*]

4

PREFACE.

THOSE persons who take up a modern language with the immediately practical purpose of using it in conversation and correspondence, or in the perusal of technical works, will of course confine their attention to modern prose, and will rather avoid poetry as of little use for their purpose, and as tending to interfere with their acquisition of a correct prose style. The school or college however, as an institution for education and culture, cannot so restrict itself; and probably few private students of German will be willing to exclude themselves from the enjoyment of its fine poetical literature. If it be granted then that modern languages are to be learnt with an aim that includes along with practical knowledge and mental training also an acquaintance with literature, it is obviously necessary that the learner should be taught to distinguish current modern prose from what has become obsolete, and especially from a diction that is peculiar to poetry or the *style soutenu*, which with its licences and archaisms must otherwise tend to give to his own prose style an incorrect and often grotesque character. This principle has long been recognised with regard to Latin and Greek; as applied to German and French it only receives added weight from the fact that these are languages still written and spoken. It may be said, that the student should learn his prose style only from prose writers, and be warned not to imitate what he meets with in poetry. But in every work that is really studied, a considerable mass of material must deposit itself in the student's mind, and suggest itself to him in his own composition. In this there can be nothing but gain, provided only there be that careful discrimination of style which is also necessary to the full appreciation of what is read.

A foreign language learnt at home can be thoroughly acquired only by a process of analytical examination, and a constant attention to principles reached by systematic generalisation, which it is not necessary to apply to the same extent in acquiring a mastery of the native language. This method of study must be applied even to the poetical literature; although we shall naturally choose, where it is possible, to delay the study of the great authors until the learner is so far advanced that he does not need to be unduly drawn away from the appreciation of them as literature by elementary work upon the structure and idiom of the language.

In preparing the present edition of a German poetical drama, an endeavour has been made to supply an introduction into German poetical literature which may meet the wants, so far as it is possible to do this by books, and in the narrow limits of a commentary on a single work, of those who have as yet read only prose. It will however probably contain but little that is superfluous even to such as may already have read, but without close study, one or two poetical dramas, or a selection of shorter poems. The notes are intended for the *student*, and it has been endeavoured so to frame them, that he may be induced by their help to pursue that close analytical study, and comparison of passage with passage, which alone can lead to exact knowledge. It is hoped however at the same time, that with the omission of the notes or parts of notes which are addressed to those who are already somewhat versed in the study of language, it may be found to render suitable help to younger pupils, and to readers whose time does not admit of, or whose purpose does not require, a close and deliberate study.

Mere "translation notes" have been but sparingly given, from a conviction that they are apt to do more harm than good. The aim of the notes is to place the student in a position to work out for himself the exact meaning of what he reads, and to understand it *in the original.* He will then in ordinary cases find it to be no more than good practice in the exercise of his own resources to make out for himself the translation which, if given to him ready made, would be very likely to prove an inducement to him to deal too superficially with the original.

This little volume may be regarded as a continuation of the attempt, explained in the preface to the edition of Gutzkow's *Zopf und Schwert*, which formed the last volume of the Pitt Press German Series, "to apply to a modern language, to some extent at least, and with suitable modifications, principles which have long been recognised in the study of Greek and Latin." The first success of such an attempt, which is comparatively new, and for which but little material lies ready to hand, must almost necessarily be imperfect. Any suggestions or criticisms from persons engaged in the teaching or study of languages will be gratefully received.

I have to acknowledge some obligation to the work of Dr Weismann on *Uhland's Dramatische Dichtungen;* I am however still more indebted to several friends in Germany for help most kindly rendered, and to the Rev. J. W. Cartmell, Fellow and Tutor of Christ's College, for valuable criticism and assistance in the revision of the MS. and the proofs.

H. J. W.

CAMBRIDGE,
    December, 1881.

INTRODUCTION.

JOHANN LUDWIG UHLAND was born April 26th, 1787, in the
university town of Tübingen in Württemberg, where
his father afterwards occupied the post of secretary
to the university. He received his first education at the
grammar-school of his native town, but was according to a
then prevalent custom enrolled at an early age in the university,
receiving here and through private tuition the necessary preparation for his university course proper, which he did not enter
upon until his eighteenth year. He was a lively, rather wild
lad, fond of open-air sports, but intelligent and quick to learn.
He was especially fond of acting in play with his comrades
scenes from the chivalry of the middle ages, towards which
his tastes were thus early turned. As he grew older, he became
more retiring and reserved, even to excess ; so that as a youth
and a man he was often regarded, by those who did not know
his modest integrity and real kindness of heart, as obstinately
taciturn and morose. Though he early showed a marked
facility in Latin verse, and pursued his classical studies with
zeal, he appears to have been influenced in his own poetical
development less by the classical literature than by that of
his native country, and less by modern than by mediæval
literature, and the poetry of the North. At the university it
was necessary that he should take up a professional study,
and external circumstances rather than his own tastes led
to the decision in favour of jurisprudence. After completing
his course and taking his doctor's degree, he invested the

savings from his university *Stipendium*, or scholarship, in a journey to Paris, where however his time was less given to the study of the Code Napoléon, the ostensible object of his visit, than to that of the treasures of Old French and Middle High German poetry in the Imperial library. On his return he published a valuable essay embodying some of the fruits of his researches. After serving for a year and a half in the Ministry of Justice in Stuttgart, without salary and without the promised promotion, he established himself as a practising lawyer in the same town.

In the Wars of Liberation and the momentous events of the years 1813-15 Uhland took the deepest and warmest interest. He was prevented indeed by the condition of affairs in Württemberg, where the king remained at heart a partisan of Napoleon, and by his own family and personal circumstances, from serving his country in the field, as he appears at one time to have wished. Nor were many of his patriotic songs called forth by the great final struggle against Napoleon, in which Rückert, Arndt, and other of his contemporaries gave expression, in their more fiery strains, to the national spirit of warlike enthusiasm. No German was ever more loyally and disinterestedly patriotic than Uhland; in no German poet is true national sentiment a more pervading element. But he was a man of deep and true, rather than of enthusiastic feeling; and his patriotism found its congenial sphere rather in the labours of peaceful political development than in the scenes of war. The greater number of his *vaterländische Gedichte* were occasioned by the constitutional struggle in Württemberg which followed the peace of 1815. King Frederick had on assuming the royal title in 1806 arbitrarily annulled the old constitution, and had ruled since then as an absolute monarch. Early in 1815 he called an assembly of the Estates, and offered a new and in some respects liberal constitution. This however they steadily refused to accept as a gift of royal favour. The old constitution of Württemberg, it was maintained, though indeed in many respects obsolete and in need of revision, rested on the inviolable foundation of a contract between ruler and people;

and a firm demand was made that it should be restored before any further negotiations could take place. This demand for the restoration of " das alte, gute Recht" forms the burden of most of Uhland's " patriotic poems," which, printed on single leaves, were scattered through the land, and exercised a considerable influence both upon the minds of the people and upon the practical issue of the struggle. Some of them possess considerable poetic merit, and all show strong and warm, if occasionally rather narrow patriotic feeling. The poem entitled *Nachruf,* beginning "Noch ist kein Fürst so hoch gefürstet," breathes a bold and manly spirit of liberty, and shows clearly that Uhland, in resisting with all his strength, as a poet and a politician, the introduction of a constitution greatly superior to the old one, was animated solely by fidelity to a principle upon which he felt that the liberties of a people were based, and by the surrender of which any immediate advantages would be dearly purchased. Of his readiness to make great personal sacrifices to his convictions he gave proof in his steadfast refusal to seek or accept any post, which would necessitate his taking an oath to a king who was ruling in defiance of the fundamental conditions of his office. But the history in detail of Uhland's part in the struggle, and of his later activity as a politician, seems to show that he was deficient in some of the qualities most essential to a statesman. Like so many of the learned men of his nation, he was too much a theorist to recognise duly the conditions and requirements of practical and public life. He had moreover in his own character too much of simple straightforwardness and of stern unbending loyalty to conviction and duty, to be able to reconcile himself to diplomacy and compromise. The result of the conflict was the hurried acceptance in 1819, at the time of the Karlsbad Decrees, of a constitution which was indeed based on the principle of contract between prince and people, for which Uhland and his party had so persistently contended, but which was in many points inferior both to that first offered by King Frederick, and to a second one proposed by his more liberal successor, William I. The introduction of the new constitution was celebrated by a representation in the Stuttgart *Hoftheater* of Uhland's *Herzog Ernst*, for which occasion the prologue was composed by special request.

Uhland was at once elected by the town of Tübingen into the second chamber of the *Landtag* or parliament thus established, of which he was for many years one of the most active and influential members, the advocate of liberal reforms and the watchful guardian of civil liberties and popular rights. His patriotic and democratic sentiments, and the devotion with which he strove to serve the interests of his country, both as a representative of the people in Württemberg and later as a member of the short-lived German Parliament in Frankfurt, contributed perhaps no less than his poetical productions to the great popularity throughout Germany which he enjoyed in the latter part of his life. But neither legal nor political pursuits were really congenial to Uhland, and in the inevitable disappointments and discouragements of a time which brought so much disappointment to German patriots, he often longed for quiet and leisure for his studies in mediæval literature and popular poetry. In 1826 he declined re-election ; in 1830 he was appointed to a professorship of German Literature, the prospect of which had been long held out to him, in the University of Tübingen. But in this congenial sphere he was not long left undisturbed. The liberal and national movement in Germany had been stirred up anew by the Paris Revolution of July, 1830, and Uhland considered it his duty to respond to the appeal made to him to resume his parliamentary activity. When in 1833 the government, displeased with his liberal opposition, refused him the necessary leave of absence from his professorial duties to attend the Landtag, he at once sacrificed his professorship, and returned to his political pursuits. In 1838 he again declined re-election, and resumed his literary labours, from which he was but once more called away, when in 1848 he was sent to Frankfurt, first by the ministry in Württemberg as one of the seventeen *Vertrauensmänner*, and afterwards by the district Tübingen-Rottenburg as a member of the National Assembly. After the failure of this ill-directed and unfortunate attempt at German unity, he retired to Tübingen and lived henceforth uninterrupted in the pursuit of his favourite studies until his death. He was an esteemed correspondent and a valued friend of some of the first German scholars of his time, but he avoided as far as possible, with the same retiring modesty which had always characterized him, the admiring homage his countrymen were eager to render him, and declined several public distinctions of a very flattering character that were pressed upon him. In personal appearance he was a very ordinary, almost insignificant looking man, in dress scrupulously neat, but exceedingly plain, in speech not fluent, in general intercourse ever ready to listen rather than to speak, and shrinking from anything that might look like a parade of his own opinions or performances. Of his kindly nature and tenderness of heart his biographers narrate several traits ; his unobtrusive helpfulness and charity, and the thoughtful consideration even for the lower animals which would make him often rise from reading to open the window for a foolish moth seeking its death in the flame of the candle. He was fond of children and young people, and many a student was helped by him through his university course ; many a young would-be poet received from him the most considerate advice and kindly warning. His habits of life were regular and simple, and he enjoyed robust and vigorous health even in his old age, until shortly before his death, which took place Nov. 13th, 1862.

Uhland began his literary career in connection with the so-called " Romantic School," in its later development,
Works. though he never fell into the fantastic extravagance and unreal sentiment which characterized many of its members. The Romanticists had turned away in disgust from the real life of the cheerless present, and had taken refuge in the study and revival of the middle ages, their poetry, art and religious feeling. Some of them had turned to the older German and Scandinavian popular poetry and heroic legend, which however they but imperfectly understood, and in imitating often only caricatured. The brothers Grimm did much, by their scholarly researches and the disquisitions founded upon them, and next to them no

one did more than Uhland, both as a poet and a scholar, to give a healthy direction and a basis of reality to this interest in mediæval life and literature, and in the popular poetry and mythology of earlier times. It has already been mentioned how this mediæval lore had taken hold of him while yet a boy, and influenced from the beginning the direction taken by his early developed poetic talent. He became the centre of a group of young poets, most of them countrymen of his own, and hence generally known as the *Schwäbische Dichterschule.* His own poetical production however became intermittent at a comparatively early period, and gave place almost entirely, while he was yet hardly past middle life, to his literary and antiquarian pursuits. His interests were chiefly directed to researches into the legend and mythology of the North, and the connection between legend and history, to the older heroic poetry, and especially to the German *Volkslieder,* of which he published a valuable collection. Most of his tours throughout Germany, continued until late in life, were largely directed towards the gathering of the material, derived either from ancient literary monuments, or from still living tradition, and the study of localities and people, which he embodied in his contributions to the history of antique poetry and legend. Eight volumes of *Schriften zur Geschichte der Dichtung und Sage* were collected and published after his death.

Uhland's poetry derives its chief inspiration from communion with nature, and from ancient story. Both in language and style, and in the character of the thoughts and sentiments, it is marked by great simplicity, the simplicity of perfect naturalness. Uhland is one of the few highly educated poets who have written songs which have struck the tone and attained the popularity of the true *Volkslied.* Some of his lyrics show a considerable resemblance, in simple charm, in melody and directness of effect, to those of Goethe, and deservedly rank very near to these in popular esteem. It was however as a lyric-epic poet, by his *Balladen und Romanzen,* that Uhland won his chief and most enduring fame. Some of the poems which he placed under this head have too slight a basis of incident to be

Poems.

classed as ballads, but among these chiefly lyrical romances are to be found some of the gems of his poetry, *Das Schloss am Meere, Der Wirthin Töchterlein, Der gute Kamerad,* and others. Among his ballads properly so called are many, such as *Des Sängers Fluch* and *Bertran de Born,* which will probably be as lasting in popularity as those of Schiller and Goethe, while others such as *Der Waller* and *Die verlorene Kirche* will always be highly esteemed by the lovers of exquisite poetry. The life which Uhland depicts, whether of outward event or of inward feeling, is indeed neither wide in range, nor prevailingly of a very stirring character. But the scenes and incidents of his poems show a fine tact in selecting from the story of the past only what has an abiding human interest, and rejecting whatever is merely accidental, and would now be felt to be disturbing; and are portrayed with the skill of a painter who with a few chaste touches puts before us a picture complete in tone and outline. There is a great charm in the expressive brevity of his musically flowing lines, and the sentiment is always warm and true, and not seldom of a winning tenderness and grace.

Of Uhland's dramas, only two of which, *Ernst, Herzog von Schwaben,* and *Ludwig der Bayer,* were completed,
Dramas. several others remaining unfinished, it is unnecessary to say much. They are distinguished by the same excellences as his shorter poems, already characterized, but they are lacking in true dramatic life. The onward movement of the action is too slow, and too much interrupted by long passages of narrative and reflection. Their general tone is more epic and lyrical than dramatic; they are rather dramatised pictures of a bygone time than dramas suited for the stage, on which they have never attained success. Uhland has failed here as Goethe also to a great extent failed; but his failures, like Goethe's, are from the broader point of view of literature better than most men's successes. The classical simplicity of style and the nobleness of tone, which make Goethe's *Iphigenie* one of the purest pearls of German literature, have perhaps never found a nearer,—if still a distant—parallel in a German poet than in Uhland.

Our play, *Ernst, Herzog von Schwaben*, was written in 1816-
17, in the midst of the political agitations mentioned
Herzog above, and of the unhappy reaction which followed up-
Ernst.
on the national rising in the Wars of Liberation. The
prologue shows how Uhland, while drawing a picture of times
long past, found in them a parallel with the present. What gives
unity to the piece is the moral idea it is intended to illustrate
and exalt, that of *mutual fidelity*[1] *in friendship*, unwavering in
life and death. The plot is taken from a story already familiar
to the people in a legendary form. For the background we have
a period of mediæval history characterized by a tenacious
struggle[2] between imperial ambition on the one hand, which
combined the aim of self-aggrandisement with that of establish-
ing a strong and united empire as the protector of civil order ;
and on the other, the spirit of ungoverned freedom and im-
patience of any central authority, among the princes who ruled
the various provinces or duchies of the empire. Konrad repre
sents one side ; Duke Ernest, and still more his vassal and
friend Werner, the other. The imperial power wins the day ;
the action and the catastrophe assume a tragic character because
the ruin of Ernest and Werner is the result of a conflict between
their loyalty as friends and their duty as subjects.

Uhland's chief historical authority, whom he has for the most
part closely followed, is Wipo's Life of Konrad II.[3]
Authorities. Wipo or Wippo, probably a Burgundian by birth, was
Wipo.
chaplain and at the same time an influential statesman
at the court of Konrad II. and afterwards of Henry III. He
was a man of considerable culture, and endeavoured to mould
his Latin style after classical models, especially Sallust, mixing
with it however something of the style of thought and language
of the Christian fathers. His last editor, Bresslau, does not rate
the value of his work so highly as Pertz ; but it is written in a
style that inspires confidence in the person of the author, and is
probably on the whole fairly impartial and reliable. He omits

---

[1] Cf. in the play, ll. 436 ff.   [2] *Ib.*, ll. 301—2.
[3] Wiponis *Gesta Chuonradi II. Ex Monumentis Germaniae His-
toricis recusa.* Recognovit Hen. Bresslau. Hannoverae, 1878.

indeed, or passes over lightly, some things which might not have pleased his patron Henry III., and he is not in all points equally well informed, as he was often withdrawn by illness from the scenes he had to narrate. It will be convenient to give in brief connected narrative the historical material, drawn from Wipo or elsewhere[1], of which Uhland has made use, or which may be needful to make clear the connection of events and the references in the drama, where the notes do not afford a fitter place.

The Emperor Henry II., called the Pious, the last of the Saxon line, died in 1024, just when a hard-won success was crowning his efforts for the re-establishment of unity and order in the empire. No arrangement with regard to the succession had been made during his lifetime, and it was much feared that in the struggle for election to the imperial dignity the dissensions and divisions of a time but shortly past would return. But these fears soon proved to be groundless. The great nobles of the empire, and the rival peoples occupying its various provinces, sank their differences and private ambitions in the general desire to select for the empire a worthy head. An elective assembly of all the freemen of the empire, that is, the princes and nobles with their trains of followers, came together at Kamba, in the valley of the Rhine, near Mainz. At first a few were chosen out of the many, and from these few the choice was reduced to two Frankish nobles, sons of brothers, and bearing the same name, Kuno or Konrad. The elder Konrad, afterwards called the Salian[2],

Historical Introduction. Election of Konrad II.

---

[1] The chief work here consulted, besides Wipo's monograph, has been Giesebrecht's *Geschichte der deutschen Kaiserzeit*, 2. Aufl. 2. Bd. 1860. Weismann's summary has also been found useful.

[2] The name Franks was applied early in the third century to a number of Germanic tribes collectively, which were afterwards divided into the Salian Franks, those on the Lower Rhine, and the Ripuarians, who occupied the right bank of the Middle Rhine, with stretches of territory further south. It was the Salians who founded the great Frankish kingdom, which reached its height under the Emperor Charles the Great. At the period with which we are concerned, after the final break up of Charles' dominion, *Franken* or Franconia was the name borne by the

U.   2

had by his marriage with Gisela, the widow of Duke Ernest I. of Swabia, acquired a considerable addition to his own possessions in Franconia and on the Rhine. This union had excited much opposition against him, and led the Emperor Henry II. to remove Gisela's son Ernest, whom he had invested with the duchy of Swabia after his father's death, from the guardianship of his mother to that of his uncle, Archbishop Poppo of Trier. The church was also scandalised at Konrad's marriage with a princess who was related to him (Gisela was the sister of Konrad's aunt by marriage), and who had been so short a time a widow. But Konrad possessed all the qualities felt to be at that time required for the preservation of order and the protection of existing rights. He was a man of firm will, generous but prudent, possessed of skill in dealing with men, and adorned with all knightly virtues. The majority inclined to him, but feared to stir up enmity and disunion, so long as they did not know the mind of the rival candidate and of the princes who supported him. The elder Konrad approached his cousin and conferred with him ; the people in the distance saw by their brotherly embrace that they were in friendly agreement. Aribo of Mainz gave the first vote for the elder Konrad, and was followed first by the other ecclesiastical princes, then by the younger Konrad and the rest. Only the nobles of Lorraine had gone away in discontent that the choice had not fallen upon the younger Konrad, who was the stepson of Frederick, Duke of Upper Lorraine. Konrad the Salian was accordingly elected

most important of the duchies into which Germany was divided. Franconia occupied the centre of the empire ; to the north lay the Saxons and Thuringians, with Slavonian tribes to the east of them; on the east and south-east were the *Baioarii* or Bavarians ; to the south lay Swabia, on the west and north-west were Upper and Lower Lorraine, which then formed a province much larger than the modern Lorraine. The eastern part of Franconia was called *Ostfranken*, the western at one time *Rheinfranken*. Though some tribes and individuals still called themselves ' Salic,' this designation no longer referred to a distinct part of the Frankish territory, and must have been assumed either because the famous Salic Code was in force among them, or because they were proud to trace their descent from the race which had brought glory to the Frankish name. (Cf. Waitz, *Deutsche Verfassungsgeschichte*, 5. Bd., 162—4.)

with loud acclamation, received the insignia from Kunigunde, the widow of Henry II., who had held the reins of the empire since his death, and went on the same day in festive procession to Mainz, where he was crowned. Archbishop Aribo however refused to crown with him his wife Gisela, whose marriage he regarded as unlawful. She was afterwards crowned at Cologne by Archbishop Piligrim.

The Empress Gisela was the sister of Duke Hermann III. of Swabia, and by her mother the niece of King Rudolf III. of Burgundy. By her second husband, Ernest, Margrave of Austria, she had two sons, Ernest and Hermann. On the death of her brother in 1012 the Emperor gave Swabia in fief to her husband, who however ruled only three years, being killed in the chase by an arrow shot by one of his own knights, according to the chronicler Thietmar "rather accidentally than of purpose." The same authority relates that his dying message to his wife was "to preserve her honour and not to forget him." Gisela's marriage with Konrad took place however in the following year, 1016. Her son Ernest, then a minor, was at the time of Kónrad's election in full possession of his duchy, and is mentioned as the fourth voter among the dukes. Her claims to the succession of Burgundy Gisela had formally transferred to Henry, her only son by the marriage with Konrad.

The Empress Gisela.

Rudolf III., the old and feeble king of Burgundy[1], being without direct heirs, and in need of support against his turbulent vassals, had in 1006 appointed the Emperor Henry II., the son of his eldest sister, as his successor, and had given up to him the city of Basel as a pledge. On the death of Henry, Rudolf reclaimed Basel,

The Burgundian succession.

---

[1] This kingdom of Burgundy was formed by the union, in A.D. 937, of two kingdoms, called respectively the kingdom of Provence or Burgundy, including Provence, Dauphiné, the southern part of Savoy, and the country between the Saone and the Jura, and the kingdom of Trans-Jurane Burgundy, including the northern part of Savoy, and all Switzerland between the Reuss and the Jura. Bryce's *Holy Roman Empire*, pp. 447—8.

2—2

asserting that the contract had been made with Henry as a private prince, and his next of kin, not as emperor. Konrad however took the opposite view, urging that Henry would not as a private prince have employed imperial forces and means in order to effect the occupation of Basel, and to secure to himself the succession, in face of the opposition of the Burgundian nobles. To his chief claims as Emperor, Konrad also added a further claim as the husband of Rudolf's niece. He repossessed himself of Basel, and thus gave clearly to understand that he intended to hold fast what he regarded as his established right to the reversion of Burgundy.

But Konrad's stepson Ernest held himself to be through his mother Gisela the rightful successor of his uncle.

Ernest's first rebellion. In order to establish his claims he joined in revolt with Count Odo of Champagne, himself a nephew of Rudolf and a claimant to the succession, with King Robert of France, the Dukes of Lorraine, the younger Konrad, and others. The Emperor however succeeded by prompt and energetic measures in breaking up the alliance; Duke Ernest made his submission, and through the intercession of his mother and his brother Henry, was pardoned and again received into favour. Konrad now marched to Italy, to subdue the disturbances which had broken out there immediately upon the death of Henry II. Before doing so he caused his son Henry, a boy eight years old, to be nominated, with the consent and guarantee of the princes of the empire, as his successor to the imperial throne. Henry was then given in charge to Bishop Bruno of Augsburg, to whom also was entrusted the conduct of imperial affairs in Germany during Konrad's absence. The Emperor took Ernest with him to Italy, but after a brief service invested him with the abbey of Kempten, and dismissed him with honour to his Swabian territories, hoping that his presence would help to keep the peace in Germany. In March, 1026, Konrad received the crown of Lombardy at Milan; at Easter, 1027, he was crowned with his consort Gisela at Rome, and soon afterwards returned home, after restoring peace throughout Italy.

During his absence Ernest had again risen in rebellion, supported by Count Werner[1] of Kiburg, and by Count Welf, a powerful Swabian noble at that time in violent feud with Bishop Bruno of Augsburg, who had just left for Italy to join the Emperor. While Welf fell upon the territories of his enemy Bruno, Ernest invaded Alsace, destroying there several castles belonging to Count Hugo of Egisheim, a relative of the Emperor, and then made an inroad into Burgundy. Meeting however here with resistance from Rudolf, who feared to receive an open enemy of the Emperor, he withdrew to the neighbourhood of Zürich, where he took up a fortified position, making it the centre for plundering expeditions, in which especially the monastery of Reichenau and the abbey of St Gall suffered severely.

Second rebellion.

On the Emperor's return a Reichstag, or general assembly of the nobles of the empire, was convened at Ulm, July, 1027. Duke Ernest came among the rest, not however to tender his submission, or in any way to humble himself, but relying upon the support of his vassals to enable him to make advantageous terms with the Emperor, or this failing, to withdraw in safety. But when he conferred with his followers, and exhorted them to stand true to their liege lord, the Counts Frederick and Anshelm gave answer for the rest, that they had indeed sworn fealty to him, but as free men and vassals of the Emperor; against all other enemies they were his loyal followers, but against the Emperor, as their highest lord, and the protector and guarantor of their freedom, they might not do him service. Finding himself thus forsaken, Ernest surrendered unconditionally, and was banished to the castle of Gibichenstein, situated on a rocky eminence by the river Saale, near to Halle. Konrad marched through Alamannia[2], and reduced those who had joined in the rebellion to

Reichstag of Ulm.

---

[1] So he is called by most chroniclers; Wipo calls him Wezelo, and also in the Volksbuch he bears the name Wezel. Wezelo or Wezilo is the diminutive form of Werinhari or Werner. Weismann.

[2] The names Alamannia and Swabia (*Alamanni, Suevi,* collective names for a number of allied tribes) were at this time used interchange-

obedience. The government of the duchy he seems for the time to have taken into his own hands. Count Welf made his submission, and was compelled to make full restitution to the bishopric of Augsburg. After a short imprisonment he was set free and restored to his fiefs and dignities[1]. Count Werner was put to the ban of the empire, but succeeded in making good his escape, after being besieged for three months in his strong castle of Kiburg, near to Zürich.

On his way from Alamannia to Franconia, Konrad was met by Rudolf of Burgundy, and a conference of the two monarchs took place at Basel. Chiefly through the mediation of the Empress Gisela, a definite and final agreement was arrived at, by which the compact made with Henry II. was renewed with Konrad, to whom the succession to Burgundy was thus secured, a share in the government being at once conceded to him. After Rudolf's death Burgundy was to become a constituent and inseparable part of the empire.

Settlement of the Bur- gundian ques- tion.

In Franconia the Emperor received the submission of the younger Konrad, who had secretly instigated and abetted Duke Ernest in his rebellion. He was now kept for a time a prisoner at large, but was finally restored to his honours and possessions. Some years afterwards[2] he received from the Emperor the possessions of Adalbero, Duke of Istria and Carinthia, who had been vehemently denounced as a traitor by the Emperor, and with his two sons banished from the empire. From this time forth the younger Konrad remained faithful to the Emperor.

ably. The Duchy of Alamannia formed the south-west portion of Germany, including Alsace and the eastern part of the present Switzerland. It was bounded on the north by East and West Franconia, on the west and south-west by Upper Lorraine and Burgundy, and on the east by Bavaria, including however a strip from the south-western portion of the present kingdom of that name.

[1] Uhland (l. 917) represents him as banished from the empire, connecting his name with that of Adalbert or Adalbero of Carinthia.

[2] Wipo in Chap. 21 says "Paulo post," but in Chap. 33 he again mentions the banishment of Adalbero, giving its right date as 1035. Uhland (918, 261 ff.) places it before Ernest's release from imprisonment, and represents it as following upon defeat in war.

In the year 1028 Konrad caused his youthful son Henry, with the concurrence of the princes of the empire, to *Coronation of Henry II.* be crowned at Köln as German King[1]. This was the first considerable step towards the goal of his ambition, the establishment in his own family of the hereditary right to the imperial dignity.

In May, 1029, Duke Ernest was at the intercession of his *Release of Ernest. Outlawry.* mother released from his imprisonment, and Konrad bestowed upon him the Duchy of Bavaria in place of his own Swabian territories, which on account of their neighbourhood to Burgundy it was not considered prudent to restore to him, more especially as Werner of Kiburg was still free and living a wild and roving life. Ernest however never came into actual possession of Bavaria, and Konrad made up his mind to reinstate him in his own duchy. In the following year the Emperor celebrated Easter at Ingelheim in the Palatinate. Here he declared himself willing to restore his stepson Ernest to the Duchy of Swabia, in compensation for the loss of his hopes with regard to Burgundy, on condition of his taking an oath to pursue as a foe of the empire his vassal and former intimate friend, Werner of Kiburg. Upon Ernest's indignant refusal to do this, he was pronounced a public enemy of the Emperor, and left the court, accompanied by a few followers. Konrad now gave the Duchy of Swabia to Ernest's younger brother Hermann, placing him under the care of Warmann, Bishop of Constance. With the assent of a general assembly of the princes Konrad put Ernest to the ban of the empire, and caused him and all his followers to be excommunicated by the assembled bishops, at

---

[1] In the middle ages it was not uncommon for the heir to a throne to be crowned during his predecessor's lifetime, in order that on the death of the latter he might at once step without dispute into his possessions. Many Emperors and German Kings thus caused their successors to be elected and crowned during their own lifetime, not however surrendering to them any part of their authority. Henry VI., and all who after him were thus elected and crowned during the life of the Emperor, took the title of "King of the Romans," a style first adopted by Henry II. before he had gained the right to the imperial title by coronation at Rome at the hands of the Pope.

the same time declaring forfeit all their possessions. Even the Empress Gisela now gave up her misguided[1] son, and took a public and solemn oath not to take vengeance or to bear malice on account of any treatment he might receive.

Ernest was joined by his sole remaining friend and faithful vassal, Werner of Kiburg. With him and a few other
The final struggle.
followers he fled to his cousin Odo of Champagne, who like himself had been disappointed in his hopes of Burgundy. But Odo either would not or dared not give him any consolation or encouragement against the Emperor, and he returned to Swabia, in the last hope that his presence might re-awaken the sympathy and loyalty of his former vassals. Here also he found himself disappointed, and was finally obliged to retreat to the wildest districts of the Black Forest, where for some months he found refuge in the fortified castle of Falkenstein, the ruins of which, not far from Schramberg, may still be seen. After supporting himself for a time by plundering expeditions ("praeda miserabili"), he was at length hemmed in on all sides by imperial troops ; and finding escape cut off, he did not await the attack, but sallied forth, "holding an honourable death to be better than a shameful life." He soon came upon a camp just forsaken by Count Mangold, a vassal of Konrad's, who had been entrusted by him and by Bishop Warmann with the duty of protecting the neighbourhood against the outlaws. Eager for vengeance, Ernest and his little band of followers now pursued their pursuers ; they soon met, and a fierce struggle began. The Duke's men, caring nothing for their lives, rushed into destruction ; Ernest himself, "sparing none, was not spared," and fell covered with wounds. With him fell Count Werner, for whose sake all this had come to pass ; also two noblemen, Adalbertus and Werin, and many others. On the other side fell Count Mangold himself, and many of the Emperor's men. Ernest's body was taken to Constance and there buried, after the removal of the ban of excommunication. When

---

[1] "Filium inconsultum sapienti marito postponens." Wipo.

the Emperor received the news, he is said to have quoted the proverb,

"Raro canes rabidi foeturam multiplicabunt."

The tragic end of Duke Ernest made a great impression upon the minds of the people, who were always inclined *The Volks-buch.* to regard any resistance against high-handed authority as a struggle in the cause of freedom, and were stirred to admiration and sympathy by his fidelity in friendship, and his manly courage. His conflict with the Emperor became the subject of popular songs and ballads, which were interwoven with those already current concerning the earlier and somewhat similar struggle between the Emperor Otto I. and his son Liudolf. The mingling of the two gave rise to a heroic poem, in which Ernest and Liudolf became one person, and the historical elements were confused, and mixed up with mythical stories of adventure in the Crusades and with oriental fable. Thus arose the *Volksbuch* "Herzog Ernst," which in the most various forms and versions remained for centuries one of the most popular legends in German mythical literature.

Uhland has deviated in but few points, except where the economy of the drama required it, from the historical *Deviations from history in the play.* facts as above related. Henry's coronation, Ernest's release from imprisonment, the offer of reinstatement, and the pronouncing of the ban of the empire and of excommunication, are all grouped together in the year 1030, and are all made to take place at Aachen. Ernest is represented as having been still under guardianship at the time of Konrad's election; and the vague hint of a chronicler has served as the foundation for a story of young love and bitter separation. The parts assigned to Mangold von Veringen, Adalbert von Falkenstein, and Warin, are with the exception of the slight historical facts mentioned above, the free invention of the poet. The characters of Gisela and of Ernest himself are also freely treated according to the exigencies of the poet's plan. It still remains for us briefly *Later events woven into it.* to mention the facts of history which, really occurring after Ernest's death, have been anticipated by Uhland, and woven into his story. King Rudolf of Burgundy, called *der Träge*, died in 1032, having first commissioned one of his nobles to deliver into the hands of Konrad the crown, the spear of St Maurice as representing the banner of his realm, and the other insignia of the kingdom. Count Odo of Champagne however again asserted his claims and invaded Burgundy. Konrad concluded an alliance with Henry I., the young King of France, which was sealed by Henry's betrothal to the Emperor's little daughter Matilda, who however died two years later. Supported by the French alliance, Konrad succeeded in reducing Odo to submission, and in 1034 the subjugation of Burgundy was complete. In 1037, while the Emperor was engaged in subduing in Italy the disturbances raised by Bishop Aribert of Milan, Odo again rose in rebellion, and invaded Lorraine. Aribert had offered him the crown of Lombardy, and he cherished the ambitious hope of being able to unite upon his head three crowns. But he was defeated and slain by Duke Gozelo of Lorraine, who caused his head to be severed from his body, and sent it to the Emperor as a trophy, together with the banner of Champagne. In Italy Konrad's success was considerably furthered by the fidelity of the Margravine Bertha of Susa, as a reward of which he invested his stepson Hermann, Duke of Swabia, who had married Bertha's daughter Adelheid, with the Mark of Susa. But the homeward march had been too long delayed, the hot season came, and with it the plague in the German camp, of which Hermann died with a great part of the army. His body could not be brought to Constance, and was buried at Trent.

It has already been said that Uhland's dramas are not suited for actual representation. The few occasions on which "Herzog Ernst" has been put upon the stage have been called forth by patriotic feeling, and affectionate regard for one of the most national of German poets, who has celebrated in verse the "Deutsche Treue," which Germans are proud to regard as a national virtue. The whole of the first act indeed, and some parts and situations in the others, are really dramatic, and would be effective on the stage. The plot is clear, and is carefully and consistently worked out. The characters are well conceived;

and if they do not all possess a very strongly marked individuality, they are drawn with many fine traits and touches that to the reader give them interest and life. But in the play as a whole, dramatic movement is wanting; the plot presents too few salient points to bear extension over five acts, and the passages of narrative and sentiment, whatever beauties they may have of their own, impede too much the course of the action, and are themselves fully appreciated only when a repeated perusal gives us leisure to do them justice. We cannot help feeling too that Werner rather than Ernest is the real hero. Ernest is too much crushed by misfortune, and his heroism is through the greater part of the play of too passive a nature and too much tinged with melancholy for him not to suffer somewhat as a dramatic hero by contrast with the more stout-hearted Werner. Nor can it fail to affect to some extent our enjoyment of the drama that when we turn aside for a moment from our admiration of the loyalty of the two friends to each other, we are unable to sympathise freely and warmly with either party in the struggle which forms the background of the piece. However we may admire the personal qualities of our heroes, we cannot give our approval to the wilfulness and selfishness, but thinly concealed, which characterize the striving of the princes after personal independence and arbitrary power, at the cost of the unity and well-being of the empire. On the other hand there can be little enthusiasm in our approval of the issue of the struggle in the triumph of the imperial cause. This is indeed the triumph of order and of national consolidation, but it is also that of the personal ambition of a man whose character inspires respect, but does not kindle sympathy, a triumph too that has been won by the ruin and tragical death of men towards whom our feelings have warmed with enthusiastic admiration.

In spite however of all the defects which candid criticism may reveal, Uhland's "Herzog Ernst" will still remain, after the great classical dramas of Goethe and Schiller, one of the best dramatic poems in German literature, and one of those works which no true German can read in his youth without a quickening interest, or will turn to in later life without a kindly remembrance. A fair and appreciative judgment may be briefly expressed in the words of Otto Jahn, when he says, "Uhland's dramas are among the most precious pearls of our literature ; they will indeed hardly produce a thrilling effect upon the stage, but their many beauties will assure to them the lasting favour of all who read them."

Ernst, Herzog von Schwaben.

Trauerspiel
in
fünf Aufzügen.

Prolog.

Ein ernstes Spiel wird euch vorübergehn.
Der Vorhang hebt sich über einer Welt,
Die längst hinab ist in der Zeiten Strom,
Und Kämpfe, längst schon ausgekämpfte, werden
Vor euern Augen stürmisch sich erneun.   5

Zween Männer, edel, bieder, fromm und kühn,
Zween Freunde, treu und fest bis in den Tod,
Preiswerthe Namen deutscher Heldenzeit,
Ihr werdet sehn, wie sie geächtet irren
Und, in Verzweiflung fechtend, untergehn.   10

Das ist der Fluch des unglückſel'gen Landes,
Wo Freiheit und Gesetz darniederliegt,
Daß sich die Besten und die Edelsten
Verzehren müssen in fruchtlosem Harm,
Daß, die fürs Vaterland am reinsten glühn,   15
Gebrandmarkt werden als des Lands Verräther
Und, die noch jüngst des Landes Retter hießen,
Sich flüchten müssen an des Fremden Herd.
Und während so die beste Kraft verdirbt,
Erblühen, wuchernd in der Hölle Segen,   20
Gewaltthat, Hochmuth, Feigheit, Schergendienst.
Wie anders, wenn aus sturmbewegter Zeit
Gesetz und Ordnung, Freiheit sich und Recht
Emporgerungen und sich festgepflanzt!
Da drängen die, so grollend ferne standen,   25
Sich fröhlich wieder in der Bürger Reihn,

Da wirket jeder Geist und jede Hand
Belebend, fördernd für des Ganzen Wohl,
Da glänzt der Thron, da lebt die Stadt, da grünt
Das Feld, da blicken Männer frei und stolz;   30
Des Fürsten und des Volkes Rechte sind
Verwoben, wie sich Ulm' und Reb' umschlingen,
Und für des Heiligthums Vertheidigung
Steht jeder freudig ein mit Gut und Blut.

Man rettet gern aus trüber Gegenwart   35
Sich in das heitere Gebiet der Kunst,
Und für die Kränkungen der Wirklichkeit
Sucht man sich Heilung in des Dichters Träumen.
Doch heute, wen vielleicht der Bühne Spiel
Verwundet, der gedenke, sich zum Troste,   40
Welch Fest wir wahr und wirklich heut begehn!
Da mag er sehn, für was die Männer sterben.

Noch steigen Götter auf die Erde nieder,
Noch treten die Gedanken, die der Mensch
Die höchsten achtet, in das Leben ein;   45
Ja, mitten in der wildverworrnen Zeit
Ersteht ein Fürst, vom eignen Geist bewegt,
Und reicht hochherzig seinem Volk die Hand
Zum freien Bund der Ordnung und des Rechts.
Ihr habt's gesehen, Zeugen seid ihr alle;   50
In ihre Tafeln grab' es die Geschichte!
Heil diesem König, diesem Volke Heil!

Personen.

Kunrad der Zweite, römischer Kaiser.

Gisela, seine Gemahlin.

Heinrich, Kunrads und Giselas zwölfjähriger Sohn.

Ernst,
Hermann, } Söhne der Gisela erster Ehe.

Warmann, Bischof von Konstanz.

Odo, Graf von Champagne.

Hugo von Egisheim, Graf im Elsaß.

Werner von Kiburg,
Mangold von Beringen, } Grafen in Schwaben.

Adalbert von Falkenstein,
Warin, } schwäbische Edle.

Geistliche und weltliche Reichsstände. Kriegsleute. Volk.

Die Handlung fällt in das Jahr 1030.

ARGUMENT TO ACT I.

Sc. I. The Emperor Konrad II., having secured the election of his young son and heir Henry (afterwards the Emperor Henry
III.) as German King, and consequently his successor in the empire,
is about to celebrate Henry's coronation at Aachen; an event
which he regards as a decisive step achieved in his cherished endeavour
to make the imperial dignity hereditary in his own family. The Empress Gisela seizes the opportunity to intercede for her son by a former
marriage, Ernest II. Duke of Swabia, who, having twice risen in rebellion against Konrad, in defence of his claims to the succession to Burgundy (his mother being the niece of the old and childless King Rudolf),
has been deprived of his duchy, and has already suffered three years'
imprisonment. Konrad himself claims Burgundy as falling to him
through his predecessor, the Emperor Henry II., who was the son of
Rudolf's eldest sister, and whom Rudolf had appointed heir to his
kingdom,—whether however as emperor, to be succeeded by following
emperors, or only as his nearest kinsman, is the point in dispute. Konrad
declares himself willing once more to pardon Ernest, but makes Gisela
swear that if he revolt a third time, refusing to abide by the conditions
imposed by emperor and empire, she will not help him, nor revenge
what may be done to him, nor further petition in his behalf. Konrad
has anticipated Gisela's wishes, and Ernest appears, broken by imprisonment into repentance and submission. All now proceed to the
ceremony of the coronation.

Sc. II. In the hall of the Assembly of the Empire a conversation
takes place between Count Mangold of Veringen, one of the vassals of
Duke Ernest who forsook him at the Diet of Ulm, and went over to the
side of the emperor in the Burgundian dispute, and his uncle, Bishop
Warmann of Constance, who has had in charge the conduct of affairs in

U.   3

Swabia, and who has just been drawing up a new deed of enfeoffment for Duke Ernest.　Mangold, rewarded by the imperial favour, has cherished still more ambitious hopes, which are now frustrated by Ernest's restoration to his duchy; he is also moved to compunction and self-reproach by the wan and haggard appearance of his former liege lord, to whom he has been so faithless.　Warmann reproves Mangold for his faintheartedness, and expresses his distrust in the reconciliation between the high-handed emperor and his stepson, and his belief that the old antagonism between imperial ambition and the self-willed spirit of independence among the princes must soon lead to a fresh outbreak, and thus open up to Mangold the way to honour and power.　Konrad appears in the midst of the princes and magnates of the empire, and declares his purpose to reinvest Ernest, who has formally renounced all claims to the Burgundian succession, with the Duchy of Swabia.　He demands however as a condition, that Ernest shall not suffer the outlawed Count Werner of Kiburg, the former instigator and associate of his revolt, within his dominions, but shall promise to seize and deliver him up, if discovered there, to the imperial power.　Ernest pleads indignantly against this demand, and steadfastly refuses to betray his loyal vassal and faithful friend.　Konrad consequently adjudges the duchy to Ernest's younger brother Hermann, and formally pronounces upon Ernest the ban of the empire, which is approved and confirmed by the assembled princes.　Warmann follows in the name of the bishops of the empire with the curses of excommunication, and Ernest goes forth a doomed outlaw, but unshaken in his resolution never to give up his friend.

Erster Aufzug.

Erste Scene.

Saal im Palaste zu Aachen. Auf beiden Seiten Eingänge, in
der Mitte eine Flügelthür.

Kaiser Kunrad tritt von der Rechten auf, seinen Sohn Heinrich an
der Hand führend, beide festlich geleitet.

Kunrad.

Die Sonne, die sich strahlend dort erhebt,
Sie führet einen folgeschweren Tag
Für mich und dich, geliebter Sohn, herauf.
Geweihet sollst du werden und gekrönt
Zu Aachen hier, der alten Krönungsstadt,   5
Als deutscher König; Erbe sollst du heißen
Des Thrones, der vor allen herrlich steht.
So stellt sich mir die große Hoffnung fest,
Daß mein Geschlecht, der sal'sche Frankenstamm,
Begründet sei als Deutschlands Herrscherhaus.   10
Noch faſſeſt du die volle Deutung nicht;
Jedoch geziemt es dir, an solchem Fest
Dich würdig zu benehmen, achtsam, ernst,
Denn reiche Zukunft schwebt ob deinem Haupt.

3—2

Heinrich.

Wohl glaub' ich, deine Rede zu verſtehn.   15
Mein Lehrer und Erzieher, Biſchof Bruno,
Hat mir geſagt, daß Gott uns auserwählt,
Neu aufzurichten Karls des Großen Reich.
Doch ſieh! die Mutter wandelt dort heran;
Wie ſchön geſchmückt! Doch traurig iſt ihr Gang.   20

Die Kaiſerin Giſela tritt von der Linken auf.

Giſela.

Mein Herr und mein Gemahl! du biſt bereit,
Dahinzugehn in feierlichem Zug
Zum hohen Dome, zu der Krönung Feſt.
Da werden, wie du ſchreiteſt durch die Stadt,
Der Armen viel' und der Unglücklichen   25
Hilfſlehend faſſen deines Mantels Saum,
Denn Gnade blüht an ſolchem Freudentag.
Laß mich der Flehenden die erſte ſein,
Laß mich die erſte faſſen dein Gewand;
Iſt doch mein Leiden auch das letzte nicht!   30

Kunrad.

Nicht mein Gewand ergreife, nimm die Hand;
Sag' an, was dieſe Hand vollführen ſoll!
Nichts je gebeten hat mich Giſela,
Was zu gewähren mir nicht rühmlich war.
O zögre nicht! Wo alles Volk ſich freut,   35
Soll ich bekümmert ſehn die Königin?

Giſela.

Ob ich in Purpur, ob in ſchwarzer Tracht
Erſcheinen ſolle, zweifelte mein Herz,

Darin die Freude ringet mit dem Leib.
Indeß der Sprößling unsres Ehebunds   40
Der Königskrönung hier entgegengeht,
Und drob das Herz mir schwillt von Mutterstolz,
Indeß verzehrt ein Andrer, auch mein Kind,
Der frühern Ehe erstgeborner Sohn,
Der einst der Schwaben Herzogsfahne trug,   45
Vom Vater, meinem Gatten, ihm vererbt,
Verzehrt im Kerker seiner Jugend Kraft;
Drei Jahre sitzt er auf dem Gibchenstein
Und horchet auf der Saale Wellenschlag,
Die unter seinem Gitter rauscht entlang.   50

Heinrich.

Auch mich verdroß es, wenn ich's sagen darf,
Als jüngst ein Edelknabe zu mir sprach,
Du habest darum Ernsten eingesperrt
In einen tiefen und sehr finstern Thurm,
Damit ich desto reicher werden soll.   55
Drum bitt' ich, lieber Vater, laß ihn los!

Kunrad.

Ward Herzog Ernst entsetzt und eingekerkert,
Nicht unverschuldet litt er solche Schmach,
Und nicht durch meinen, durch des Reiches Spruch.
Aufrührer war er, seines Königs Feind.   60
Begnadigt nach so frevelhafter That,
Empört' er gleichwohl sich zum zweiten Mal
Und setzte so der Gnade selbst ein Ziel.

Gisela.

Rudolf, der Schattenkönig von Burgund,
Mein Oheim, dessen ich mich nie gerühmt,   65

Ein Greis, der niemals Jüngling war noch Mann,
Erzitternd vor dem meisterlosen Trotz
Unbändiger Vasallen, wandt' er sich
An seiner Blutsverwandten mächtigsten,
An Kaiser Heinrich, der vor dir geherrscht.   70
Damit er diesen sich verpflichtete,
Ernannt' er ihn durch bündigen Vertrag
(Denn ohne Sprößling war der dürre Stamm)
Zum Erben des burgund'schen Königthums.
Doch Gottes heil'ger Rathschluß fügt' es so,   75
Daß Kaiser Heinrich zu den Vätern gieng,
Indeß der Greis noch auf dem Throne schwankt.
War Heinrich als des deutschen Reiches Haupt
Thronerbe von Burgund, so tratest du,
Der neue Kaiser, in den Anspruch ein;   80
Schloß er als Blutsverwandter den Vertrag,
So blühte jetzt des Erbes Anwartschaft
Dem Schwesterenkel Rudolfs, meinem Sohn.
Darob entspann sich Hader zwischen euch
Und, als nun Rudolf selbst zu feige war,   85
Sich auszusprechen, wie er es gemeint,
Ergriff mein Sohn, in jugendlicher Hast
Und aufgeregt durch schlimmer Freunde Rath,
Ergriff die Waffen. Und urtheile nun,
Wenn du es nochmals prüfend überschaust: 90
Hatt' er nicht einen Schein des Rechts für sich,
Den Schein, der leicht ein junges Herz verführt?

                        Kunrad.

Ein Vorwurf liegt in deinem milden Wort,
Ich fühl' ihn, aber nicht verdien' ich ihn.

Als du nach Herzog Ernsts unsel'gem Tod   95
Die Hand mir gabest zu beglücktem Bund,
Da übernahm ich und beschwor die Pflicht,
Der zugebrachten Söhne jederzeit
Zu pflegen, wie ein rechter Vater soll.
Und als mich drauf der Fürsten und des Volks   100
Einstimm'ge Wahl zum Kaiserthron berief,
Da steckt' ich mir nach wohlermeßnem Recht
Die scharfen Grenzen meines Wirkens aus.
Burgund gehört dem Reiche, Schwaben bleibt
Bei deinem Stamme; darnach handelt' ich.   105
Weil Ernst nicht lassen wollte von Burgund,
Mußt' ich ihn strafen, als des Reiches Vogt;
Weil Schwaben deinem Hause bleiben soll,
Ließ ich das Herzogthum bis jetzt erledigt.
Die Jugend Hermanns, deines zweiten Sohns,   110
Gestattete mir nicht, ihn zu belehnen,
Damit nicht, gleich dem Bruder, ihn die Macht
Verleitete zu übermüth'gem Thun;
Dem klugen Bischof Warmann übertrug
Ich unterweilen die Statthalterschaft,   115
Den Deinen blieb das Herzogthum bewahrt.

Gisela.

Nicht ziemet mir, erlauchtester Gemahl,
Das Urtheil über deinen Herrschergang,
Die kräftige Verwaltung deines Amts.
Doch, was ich sagte, wirst du gern verzeihn;   120
Der Kinder Fehle zu entschuldigen,
War doch von je der armen Mütter Recht.

Kunrad.

Man rühmet, Gisela, von dir, du seist,
Gleich wie an Würden die erhabenste,
So auch die weiseste der deutschen Fraun,   125
Und oft schon warest du Vermittlerin
Von Zwiespalt, welcher unversöhnlich hieß.
Auch zwischen mir und deinem Sohne, der
Mit meinen schlimmsten Feinden sich verschwor
Und wider mich des Aufruhrs Fahne schwang,   130
Hast du Versöhnung einst herbeigeführt;
Bestätiget in seinem Herzogthum,
Nahm ich ihn mit auf den ital'schen Zug,
Vertraut' ihm meiner Schaaren Führung an.
Belehnt mit Kemptens stattlicher Abtei,   135
Entließ ich ihn und lud durch diese Gunst
Auf mich den Haß gekränkter Geistlichkeit;
Doch kaum hat er die Alpen überstiegen,
Indeß im fernesten Apulien ich
Mir die Normannen nehm' in Lehenspflicht,   140
Ruft er die alemann'sche Jugend auf,
Verheert das Elsaß und bedrängt Burgund.
Hat, wie du sagst, der Jugend Ungeduld,
Hat böser Freunde Rath ihn irregeführt,
So war ihm jetzt im einsamen Verließ   145
Zu reiflicher Besinnung Zeit gegönnt.
Und wenn ich jetzo, deinem Wunsch gemäß,
Von neuem gänzlich ihn begnadigte,
Und gleichwohl ungebessert, unbeschämt,
Er wieder sich auflehnte gegen mich: 150
Sprich! könntest du nach deinem weisen Sinn
Auch dann noch ihn rechtfert'gen, könntest du

40

Zum dritten Mal verlangen....

Gisela.

                    Wie? du willst?
Mein banges Flehen hat dein Herz gerührt?
O sprich es aus! Gieb mir Gewißheit!   155

Kunrad.

                              Eins
Vernimm zuvor! Wenn jetzt zum dritten Mal
Dein Sohn mir trotzig sich entgegenstemmt;
Wenn er den nöthigen Bedingungen,
Die ihm das Reich vorschreibt, sich widersetzt:
Dann hab' ich meine Vaterpflicht erfüllt,   160
Dann bin ich der Vollstrecker des Gerichts,
Das furchtbar über ihn ergehen muß.
Du aber leg' die Finger auf die Brust
Und schwöre mir mit einem theuren Eid,
Daß du alsdann ihm nicht zur Hülfe sein,   165
Daß du nicht rächen wirst, was ihm geschieht,
Und daß du selbst nicht bittest mehr für ihn!

Gisela.

Ich schwöre das bei dem wahrhaft'gen Gott.
Gieb mir den Sohn! Für ihn verbürg' ich mich.

Kunrad.

Zuvorzukommen jedem deiner Wünsche,   170
War stets mein Trachten, und so hab' ich auch,
Vorahnend, was du jetzt von mir begehrst,
Nach dem Gefangnen zeitig ausgeschickt.
Sein Bruder Hermann hat ihn abgeholt,
Und angekommen sind sie diese Nacht.   175

41

Geh, Heinrich, führe deine Brüder her!
Durch dieses freudenreiche Wiedersehn
Verherrliche sich uns dein Ehrentag!

(Heinrich durch die Mittelthür ab.)

Gisela.

Nimm meinen Dank, den heißen Herzensdank,
Den Dank, der aus dem vollen Auge quillt!   180
Die Thräne, die den Purpur mir benetzt,
Sie ist der reichste, königlichste Schmuck,
In dem ich könnt' an deiner Seite gehn.

Ernst, Hermann und Heinrich treten auf.

Heinrich.

Hier ist er.

Ernst.

Meine Mutter!

Gisela.

O mein Sohn!
Bist du's, mein Ernst? Wie hager, o wie bleich!   185

Hermann.

Das Reisen durch die Nacht hat ihn verstört.

Ernst.

Wohl war es eine lange, kalte Nacht.

Gisela.

Die braunen Locken sind ihm halb ergraut.

Ernst.

Das ist der Reif von jener kalten Nacht.
Hier athm' ich Morgen. Mutterliebe, dir   190
Ist aufgethauet dies erstarrte Herz.

Gisela.

Wohlthätig wirkt der Freiheit reine Luft,
An innrer Heilkraft ist die Jugend reich;
Auch du wirst neu aufleben, theurer Sohn!

Kunrad.

Die trüben Bilder der Vergangenheit,   195
Die Spuren trauriger Erfahrungen,
Laßt sie verschwunden und vergessen sein!
Der heitern Zukunft öffnen wir den Blick,
Die mit dem heut'gen Tage sich erschließt!
Schon rufet uns der Glocken Feierklang,   200
Die Krone harret dieses Jünglinges.
Hernach in offner Reichsversammlung wird
Mit Schwaben neu belehnet unser Ernst.

Ernst.

Erhabner Kaiser, deine Huld an mir
Soll dir in deinem Sohn vergolten sein.   205
Ihr aber, meine treugeliebten Brüder,
In frischer Jugendblüthe steht ihr da;
Ich stehe frühgealtert zwischen euch,
Dem Laube gleich, das vom vergangnen Jahr
Am frischbegrünten Zweige hängen blieb.   210
O nehmt an mir ein Beispiel, Jünglinge,
Daß eure Jugend euch beglückter sei!
Du wirst, mein Hermann, zu dem ersten Kampf
Hinabziehn in Italiens Waffenfeld:
O mögen schönre Kränze dir erblühn,   215
Als meiner Jugend Kämpfe mir gebracht!
Und du, mein Heinrich, der du heute wirst
Zum Erben eines hohen Throns geweiht:

O streu' in deinem Volke solche Saat,
Daß beßre Früchte dir gedeihn, als mir!   220.

Heinrich.

Dank deinem Wunsche!

Hermann.

              Dank und Bruderkuß!

Gisela.

Ihr theuren Söhne, Segen über euch,
Ihr meine Hoffnung, meine Lust, mein Stolz!

Kunrad.

Laßt uns vereint zum Krönungsfeste gehn,
Und alles Volk erfreue sich, wenn es   225
So schön verbunden sieht sein Königshaus!

(Sie gehen durch die Mittelthür ab, der Kaiser mit Heinrich, Gisela
mit Ernst und Hermann.)

Zweite Scene.

Saal der Reichsversammlung.

Bischof Warmann und Graf Mangold von Veringen treten von
verschiedenen Seiten auf.

Mangolb.

Dich sucht' ich, Oheim!

Warmann.

              So erregt, so heiß!

Was ist geschehn?

Mangold.

Du weißt es nicht?

Warmann.

Was denn?

Mangold.

Du haſt nicht das Geſpenſt geſehen, das
Am hellen Tag, im vollen Krönungszug   230
Gewandelt durch die Straßen dieſer Stadt?

Warmann.

Nicht hatt' ich Muße zur Geſpenſterſchau;
Beſchäftigt war ich auf beſonderen
Befehl, an des erkrankten Kanzlers Statt
Zu fertigen den neuen Lehensbrief   235
Für Herzog Ernſt von Schwaben.

Mangold.

Hat dir nicht
Die Hand gezittert?

Warmann.

Sprich mir deutlicher!

Mangold.

Dort bei den Marmorſäulen des Palaſts
Stand ich mit der geſammten Ritterſchaft,
Zum Krönungszuge feſtlich aufgeſchmückt.   240
Da ſtiegen ſie die hohen Stufen nieder:
Der Kaiſer, an der Hand den jungen Sohn,
Hernach die Kaiſerin; zur Rechten ihr,
Im Fürſtenmantel, aber blaß und hager,
Wie aus dem Grab erſtanden, Herzog Ernſt.   245

Er wankt' an mir vorüber, und ein Blick
Aus seinem hohlen Auge fiel auf mich,
Ein Blick, nicht strafend, doch von solcher Macht,
Daß er mich ausschloß von der Festlichkeit,
Daß ich geheftet an der Säule stand,   250
Als schon der lange Zug hinabgewallt
Und das Geläute längst verhallet war.
Wie selig könnte dieser Tag mir sein,
Der schönste meines Lebens, wenn ich treu
Geblieben wäre! Wie viel anders nun!   255
Dich muß ich drum verklagen, deinem Rath
Hab' ich gefolgt, als auf dem Tag zu Ulm
Ich mit den Andern von dem Herzog wich.
Von dir nun fordr' ich, richte du mich auf
Aus der Vernichtung! Denn sie ist dein Werk. 260

Warmann.

Verwöhnter Sohn des Glückes! sprachst du so,
Als jüngst in Kärnthen auf dem Siegesfeld
Der Kaiser dankend dir die Rechte bot,
Dir selbst umgürtete das Ehrenschwert
Und dich mit Lehen reich begnadigte?   265
Damals erkanntest du, daß meine Hand
Aus des Empörers unfruchtbarem Dienst
Zu lohnesreichem dich emporgeführt.

Mangold.

Du mahnst mich glücklich an das Feld der Schlacht.
Ich sehe Rettung, nach Italien ruft   270
Die Heerfahrt, neuer Lorbeer grünet dort
Für die entehrte Stirne.

Warmann.

Thöricht Herz,
Das Sieg und Ehre mißt nach dem Erfolg
Des Augenblicks, des ewig wechselnden!
Als Herzog Ernst im Kerker schmachtete,   275
Da warst du freudig in des Kaisers Dienst;
Nun Herzog Ernst zu Gnaden wieder kam,
Gleich wähnst du dich verstoßen und entehrt.
Du weißt, wie eine Reiterschaar sich schwenkt,
Noch aber kennst du nicht den Lauf der Welt.   280
Wohl wahr, es kommen Augenblicke, wo
Die kampfbewegte Welt mit einem Schlag
Zum sel'gen Paradies verwandelt scheint:
Der Wolf hat sich zum Lamme hingestreckt,
Der Geier nistet mit der frommen Taube,   285
Die Schlange, die vom Apfelbaume lauscht,
Sie schlüpft in das Gezweige scheu zurück,
Und in der alten Unschuld tritt der Mensch
Aus dem Gebüsch, worin er sich versteckt.
So waltet heut im kaiserlichen Haus   290
Vertrauen, Liebe, Segnung. Und gewiß,
Wenn wir feindsel'gen Sinns verdächtig sind,
Geziemt es schweigend uns zurückzustehn.
Doch oft am Abend noch des klaren Tags,
Des wolkenlosen, steigt Gewitter auf   295
Mit aller Elemente wildem Kampf.
Sieh, Jüngling, nicht von gestern ist der Groll,
Und wenig trau' ich der Beschwichtigung.
Dem Herzog wurmt es ewig um Burgund;
Vertrauen sog er nicht im Kerker ein.   300
Des Kaisers Herrschsucht und der Stände Trotz

Sind ein uralter, nie verſöhnter Zwiſt.
Nicht brauchſt du ihn zu ſchüren; aber feſt
Mußt du dich ſtellen, mußt auf das nur baun,
Was in der menſchlichen Natur beruht,   305
In der Gewalten ew'gem Gegenſaß,
Der unter allen Formen wiederkehrt.
Selbſt wenn du augenblicklich tiefer ſtehſt,
Wenn fremde Regung den Gebieter faßt,
Wenn neue Neigung einmal dich verdrängt,   310
Bleib unermüdlich nur in deinem Dienſt!
Die Herzensregung, die Begeiſtrung weicht,
Das ewige Bedürfniß kehrt zurück:
Du wirſt hervorgerufen, und bewährt
Biſt du in deiner Unentbehrlichkeit.   315
Drum, iſt auch heut nicht unſer Ehrentag,
Noch kommen Tage, wo man nach uns fragt,
Wo man begehret deines tapfern Arms.

Mangold.

Was hör' ich?   Hieher wälzet ſich der Zug.

Warmann.

Der Herzog wird belehnt in dieſem Saal.   320

Mangold.

Soll ich entfliehen? ſoll ich bleiben?

Warmann.

Bleib!
Sieh! dieſe Rolle, dieſes Pergamen,
Es iſt der Gnadenbrief für Herzog Ernſt,
Von mir verfaßt, beſiegelt, eben jeßt;
Und dennoch kann aus dieſer Rolle noch   325

So manches sich entfalten, was du nicht
Erwartet und ich selber kaum geahnt.

Der Kaiser, Gisela, Heinrich, Ernst, Hermann, geistliche und weltliche
Reichsstände ziehen auf. Kunrad läßt sich auf dem Throne nieder, Gisela zu
seiner Rechten, Heinrich zur Linken, neben Gisela die geistlichen, neben Heinrich
die weltlichen Stände. Hinter den Schranken Volk.

Kunrad.

Erlauchte Fürsten, eurer Gegenwart
Bei unsrem heut'gen Feste seid bedankt!
Die Krönung ward vollbracht nach eurer Wahl,   330
Und so verhoffen Wir, ihr werdet jetzt
Die Treue, die ihr rühmlich Uns bewährt,
Auch Unsrem vielgeliebten Sohne weihn.
Ein andres Geschäft von Wichtigkeit
Versammelt hier uns in dem Saal des Reichs: 335
Auf öfteres Ersuchen Unsrer Frau,
Der Kaisrin Gisela, und Unsres Sohns,
Des jetzt gekrönten Königes, sowie
Nach dem zuvor mit euch gepflognen Rath,
Am meisten doch nach Unsres Herzens Drang   340
Beschlossen Wir, mit Unsrem Stiefsohn Ernst,
Der nach des Reiches Spruch gefangen lag,
Uns wieder zu befrieden, ihn durchaus
In Würden und in Ehren herzustellen;
Und darum haben Wir den heut'gen Tag,   345
Als einen freudenreichen, auserkiest,
Dem Fürsten das verwirkte Fahnenlehn
Des Herzogthums von Schwaben neuerdings
Vor offner Reichsversammlung zu verleihn.
Der Anlaß früherer Mißhelligkeit,   350

U.   4

Der Zweifel wegen des burgund'schen Erbes,
Fiel weg, nachdem der König Rudolf sich
Entschieden und den alten Erbvertrag,
Den er mit Kaiser Heinrich abgeschlossen,
Auf Unsere Person bestätigt hat.   355
Da ihr, mein Sohn, bei dieser Abkommniß
Euch zu beruhigen Uns angelobt
Durch förmlichen, besiegelten Verzicht,
So haben Wir willfährig Unsrerseits
Den Lehensbrief auf Schwaben ausgestellt   360
Und nehmen jetzo, wenn es euch geliebt,
Sogleich die feierliche Handlung vor.

Ernst.

Ich trete vor den kaiserlichen Thron
Und bitte nach Gebühr, daß eure Huld
Von neuem mit des Reiches Fahnenlehn,   365
Dem Herzogthum von Schwaben, mich belehne.

Kunrad.

Aus kaiserlicher Machtvollkommenheit
Ergreif' ich Schwabens Herzogsfahne, die
Nach altem Recht und Kriegsbrauch in den Schlachten
Des deutschen Reichs das Vordertreffen führt,   370
Damit du Ernst, der Zweite dieses Namens,
Belehnet werdest mit dem Herzogthum
Sammt Zugehörden und Gerechtsamen.
Nach Unsrem und gesammter Fürsten Schluß
Hast du auf dieses herzogliche Banner   375
Zu dem gewohnten Eid der Lehenstreu'
Uns zu beschwören ein Gedoppeltes.

Ernst.

Laßt mich vernehmen, was ich schwören soll!

Kunrad.

Fürs Erste sollst du schwören, daß du nicht
An irgend einem, Freien oder Knecht,　　　　　380
Dich rächest, der zu deinen Gegnern hielt,
Zumal an keinem deiner Mannen, die
Von dir getreten auf dem Tag zu Ulm.

Ernst.

Nicht Rache dürstend kehr' ich in die Welt;
Versöhnung, Ruhe nur ist mein Begehr:　　　385
Drum bin ich diesen Schwur zu thun bereit.

Kunrad.

Fürs Zweite sollst du feierlich beschwören,
Daß du den landesflücht'gen Grafen Werner
Von Kiburg, der zum Aufstand dich gereizt,
Der noch zur Stunde nicht sich unterwarf　　390
Und als des Reiches Feind geächtet ist,
Daß du nicht diesen, noch die mit ihm sind,
In deines Herzogthumes Grenze dulden,
Vielmehr, wenn er sich drin betreten läßt,
Ihn greifen wollest zu des Reiches Haft.　　395

Ernst.

Das soll ich schwören? Nein, erlaßt mir das!

Kunrad.

Du zögerst?

Gisela.

Gott, es geht mir furchtbar auf!

4—2

Ernst.

Ich war nach Ulm gekommen auf den Tag,
Mit euch zu unterhandeln um Burgund.
Nicht als ein Flehender erschien ich dort,   400
Nein, an der Spitze meiner Lehnsmannschaft,
Auf deren Treu' und Kraft ich sicher gieng.
Da traten Anshelm vor und Friederich,
Die beiden Grafen, und erklärten laut,
Sie seien mir zu Dienste nicht verpflichtet   405
Entgegen ihrem Herrn und Könige,
Der ihrer Freiheit höchster Schirmvogt sei.
Mit diesen stimmte die gesammte Schaar:
Verlassen stand ich plötzlich da; mein Schwert
Warf ich zur Erde; schmählich, unbedingt   410
Mußt' ich mich übergeben, und hinweg
Ward ich geführt zum Felsen Gibchenstein.
In jener Noth, in jener tiefen Schmach
Blieb einzig nur Graf Werner mir getreu,
Der meiner Jugend Freund und Führer war.   415
Auf Kiburg warf er sich, sein festes Schloß,
Und wurde dort von euch, erhabner Herr,
Drei Monden lang belagert und bedrängt.
Als man zuletzt die gute Veste brach,
Entkam er selber mit genauer Noth   420
Und irrt seitdem geächtet durch die Lande.
Sollt' ich nun den verleugnen, der so fest
An mir gehalten? Nein, verlangt es nicht!

Kunrad.

Du bist in großer Täuschung, wenn du meinst,
Daß Werner das um deinetwillen that;   425

Du warst nur stets das Werkzeug seiner stolzen,
Gefährlichen Entwürfe.

Ernst.

Ja, ich weiß,
Mit großen Dingen trägt sich dieser Mann,
Doch nicht mit strafbarn noch gefährlichen.
Was er für mich, was ich für ihn gethan,   430
Es war ein Bund der Redlichkeit und Treu'.

Kunrad.

Je eifriger du sprichst, je klarer wird's,
Wie eng der Meutrer dich umgarnet hat,
Und um so weniger darf dir der Schwur,
Den Wir von dir begehrt, erlassen sein.   435

Ernst.

Die Treue sei des deutschen Volkes Ruhm,
So hört' ich sagen und ich glaub' es fest,
Trotz allem, was ich Bitteres erfuhr.
Ihr selbst, o Kaiser, höchstes Haupt des Volks,
Das man um Treue rühmet, habt noch jüngst,   440
Was von Verrath ihr denkt, so schön bewährt:
Als Misiko, der junge Polenfürst,
Gedrängt von eurer Waffen Ungestüm,
Zu Odelrich, dem Böhmenherzog, floh,
Und dieser, um den Zorn, den ihr ihm tragt,   445
Zu sühnen, euch den Flüchtling anerbot,
Da wandtet ihr euch mit Verachtung ab.
Was ihr vom Feind, vom Fremdlinge verschmäht,
Könnt ihr's verlangen von dem eignen Sohn,
Vom deutschen Fürsten? Nein, ihr könnt es nicht. 450

Kunrad.

Vom Sohne heiſch' ich, daß er nicht dem Feind,
Dem bitterſten, des Vaters ſich geſelle;
Vom deutſchen Fürſten, daß er nimmermehr
Die Friedensſtörer heg' in ſeinem Land.
Was ich verlang', iſt dir zwiefache Pflicht,   455
Und ſehr mit Unrecht nennſt du es Verrath.

Ernſt.

Nennt's, wie ihr wollt, doch iſt es Treue nicht;
Es iſt nicht Freundſchaft, iſt nicht Dankbarkeit,
Nichts, was begeiſtern könnt' ein edles Herz.

Kunrad.

Noch einmal frag' ich: Schwöreſt du den Eid,   460
Den Wir bedungen, oder ſchwörſt du nicht?
Antworte nicht zu raſch, erwäg' es reiflich!
Es handelt ſich nicht bloß ums Herzogthum,
Nicht bloß um fernere Gefangenſchaft:
Des Kerkers biſt du ledig, aber was   465
Ich mühſam abgelenkt von deinem Haupt
Damals, da man zu Ulm dich richtete,
Jetzt hängt es unabwendbar über dir:
Die Acht des Reiches und der Kirche Bann.

Giſela.

Erbarmen meinem Sohne!   470

Kunrad.

        Muß ich dich
Des Schwurs erinnern, Giſela?

Warmann.

Mein Fürſt!
Vernehmet, was die Kirche zu euch ſpricht!
Als ihr euch ungehorſam, undankbar
Erhobet gegen euren Herrn und Vater,
Damals habt ihr, vom böſen Geiſt geſpornt,   475
Selbſt nicht geweihtes Eigenthum verſchont:
Der heil'ge Gallus und das fromme Stift
Von Reichenau erſeufzten eurem Drang.
Schon war der Bannſtrahl über euch gezückt
Und nur die kaiſerliche Fürſprach' hielt   480
Den Arm zurück, der noch gehoben iſt:
Deß warnet euch die Kirche mütterlich.

Giſela.

Warnt eine Mutter ſo?

Kunrad.

Und jetzt biſt du
Gemahnet.   Jetzt antworte mit Bedacht:
Beſchwörſt du die Bedingung oder nicht?   485

Ernſt.

Die Luft des Kerkers, die ich lang gehaucht,
Hat abgeſpannt die Sehnen meiner Kraft.
Wohl bin ich mürbe worden, doch nicht ſo
Bin ich herabgekommen, nicht ſo ganz
Zerbrochen und zernichtet, daß ich den   490
Verriethe, der mir einzig Treue hielt.

Kunrad.

Genug.   Die Pflicht des Vaters iſt erfüllt.
Auch ſoll der jüngre Bruder keineswegs

Entgelten, was der ältere verbrach:
Dem Hermann fällt das Herzogthum anheim;   495
Er führe nach Italien mir das Heer!
Mit reiner Hand erheb' ich dieses Schwert
Und spreche so den Spruch der Reichesacht:
Aus kaiserlicher Macht und nach dem Schluß
Der Fürsten steh' ich und erkläre dich,   500
Vormals der Schwaben Herzog, Ernst den Zweiten,
Als Feind des Reichs, als offenbaren Ächter.
Vom Frieden setz' ich dich in den Unfrieden,
Dein Lehen theil' ich hin, woher es rührt,
Dein eigen Gut gestatt' ich deinen Erben,   505
Erlaube männiglich dein Leib und Leben,
Dein Fleisch geb' ich dem Thier im Walde preis,
Dem Vogel in der Luft, dem Fisch im Wasser.
Ich weise dich hinaus in die vier Straßen
Der Welt und, wo der Freie wie der Knecht   510
Fried' und Geleit hat, sollst du keines haben.
Und, wie ich diesen Handschuh von mir werfe,
Wie dieser Handschuh wird zertreten werden,
Sollst du verworfen und zertreten sein!

Die Fürsten.

Sollst du verworfen und zertreten sein!   515

Warmann.

Im Namen sämmtlicher des Reichs Bischöfe
Verbann' ich dich, vormal'gen Herzog Ernst,
Sammt allen, die dir helfen und dich hegen,
Aus unsrer heil'gen Kirche Mutterschooß
Und übergebe dich dem ew'gen Fluch.   520
Verflucht seist du zu Haus und auf dem Feld,

Auf offnem Heerweg, auf geheimem Pfad,
Im Wald, auf dem Gebirg und auf der See,
Im Tempel selbst und vor dem Hochaltar!
Unselig sei dein Lassen und dein Thun,   525
Unselig, was du issest, was du trinkst
Und was du wachest, schlummerst oder schläfst:
Unselig sei dein Leben, sei dein Tod!
Verflucht seist du vom Wirbel bis zur Zeh'!
Verflucht sei der Gedanke deines Hirns,   530
Die Rede deines Munds, des Auges Blick,
Der Lungen Odem und des Herzens Schlag,
Die Kraft des Armes und der Hände Werk,
Der Lenden Mark, der Füße Schritt und Tritt,
Und selbst der Kniee Beugung zum Gebet!   535
Und wie ich dieser Kerzen brennend Licht
Auslösch' und tilge mit des Mundes Hauch,
So aus dem Buch des Lebens und der Gnade
Sollst du vertilget sein und ausgelöscht!

Die Bischöfe.

Sollst du vertilget sein und ausgelöscht!   540

Ernst.

Hin fahr' ich, ein zwiefach Geächteter,
An meine Ferſen heftet sich der Tod,
Und unter Flüchen krachet mein Genick:
Vom Werner laß' ich nicht!

ARGUMENT TO ACT II.

The outlawed Duke Ernest, wandering in the neighbourhood of Basel, overhears the discourse of the Counts Odo of Champagne and Hugo of Egisheim, as they are returning from an assembly of the turbulent Burgundian nobles. Odo (who as the nephew of Rudolf of Burgundy had asserted joint rights with Ernest, and had been his associate in his first insurrection), had on hearing of Ernest's recent restoration been minded again to make common cause with him in supporting their claims against the emperor by force of arms, but forsook and disowned him on the news of his outlawry, and is now cherishing secret hopes of conquering Burgundy for himself. Hugo is just parting from him with words of reproach and of warning. Ernest approaches and appeals to him for help, but is repulsed with bitter reviling and contempt by Odo, who would have eagerly welcomed him on his entry into Burgundy at the head of an army, but will have nothing to do with a beggared outlaw, who for the sake of an exiled friend has ruined himself and disappointed his allies. In departing, Odo refers him with an angry sneer to his own unwelcome counsellor Hugo. Ernest had before his imprisonment been betrothed to Hugo's daughter Edelgard, and he now learns that after at first devoting herself wholly to works of charity, she has since his outlawry taken conventual vows. After Hugo's departure Ernest is discovered by his friend Werner of Kiburg, who cheers him up by his own stoutheartedness, though he is himself an outlaw, and inspires him with new courage. Werner explains his own unbroken spirit and dauntless bearing by the inspiring memory of the great day of the imperial election, the story of which he narrates at length, when the liberty and majesty of the German people showed itself in vigorous and united action. He knows indeed that the bright prospects then opened up have not been realised, that Konrad, at first so wise and moderate, has shown himself arbitrary and imperious, ambitious of absolute rule and hereditary empire. Still he does not despair of Ernest's cause, which he proposes to promote by endeavouring to stir up the loyalty of his former vassals and adherents in Swabia.

Zweiter Aufzug.

An der Heerstraße.

Ernst, in geringer Tracht.

Dort hebt der Dom von Basel sich empor;   545
Nicht darf ich's wagen, der Landflüchtige,
Ins Thor der Stadt, das gastlich offen steht,
Hineinzuschreiten wie ein andrer Mann.
Der breite Heerweg ziehet sich hinauf,
Ich aber darf gebahnte Straßen nur   550
Durchkreuzen wie ein aufgescheuchtes Wild,
Das quer hinüber nach dem Walde flieht.
Zween Herren reiten mit Gefolg heran,
Am Kreuzweg halten sie, sie steigen ab,
Sie wandeln hieher nach dem Schattensitz.   555
Er ist's, er ist's, Graf Odo, ja er ist's,
Und auch den Andern sollt' ich kennen, ja:
Wie schlägt mein Herz, der Vater Edelgards!

Ernst tritt in das Gebüsch zurück, während die Grafen Hugo von Egisheim
und Odo von Champagne auftreten.

Hugo.

Ich bat euch abzusteigen, werther Graf!
Wir trennen uns an diesem Scheideweg;   560
Euch führt die Straße links nach der Champagne,
Mich jene rechts zum kaiserlichen Hof.

Damit nun diese Scheidung unsrer Bahn
Nicht eine Trennung sei für immerdar,
Vergönnt ein wohlgemeintes Abschiedswort!   565
Es ist in vor'gen Zeiten wohl geschehn,
Daß ihr den ältern Freund um Rath befragt;
Vergebt ihm, wenn er ungebeten jetzt
Mit seinem Rath erscheinet!

Odo.

Sprecht, Herr Graf!

Hugo.

Ihr habt in Basel selbst euch überzeugt   570
Von der burgund'schen Großen Wankelmuth;
Ihr saht die stürmischen Versammlungen
Herüber und hinüber wogen.

Odo.

Nun?

Hugo.

Als erst gemurmelt ward, daß Herzog Ernst
Entlassen sei aus seiner Kerkerhaft   575
Und hergestellt in herzogliche Macht,
Da war es all vergessen, daß man jüngst
Dem Erbvertrag einhellig beigestimmt,
Den Rudolph mit dem Salier neu beschwor.
Um euch, den Blutsverwandten Ernsts, den gleich   580
Betheiligten, erhob sich das Gedräng',
Die Losung: Ernst und Odo.

Odo.

Und wozu

Mir dieses jetzt?

Hugo.

Als aber bald darauf
Der Bann, die Ächtung Ernsts verlautet war,
Da wechselte der Wind.   585

Odo.

Erlaßt mir das!

Hugo.

Die Losung: Kunrad.

Odo.

Graf, gehabt euch wohl!

Hugo.

Noch nicht, mein Freund! Das eben macht mir Sorge,
Daß ihr so feindlich, mit verbißnem Groll
Nach Hause kehret.

Odo.

Wißt ihr das gewiß?

Hugo.

Noch ist mein Auge nicht so alterschwach,   590
Daß ihm der Blicke Zorn, der Lippen Trotz
Und jeglicher Bewegung Hastigkeit
An euch verborgen bliebe. Theurer Freund,
Nicht in vereinter Kraft mit Herzog Ernst
Wär's euch gelungen, noch viel weniger   595
Könnt ihr's allein erzwingen. Hofft es nicht!
Unbeugsam steht des Kaisers Wille, groß
Ist seine Macht. Vermeidet seinen Grimm!
Verzehren würd' er euch. O schleudert nicht
Die Fackel in das unglücksel'ge Land,   600

Das noch vom alten Kriegesbrande raucht!
Ihr werdet nicht; gebt mir darauf die Hand!

(Ernſt tritt hervor und faßt ten Mantel des Grafen Odo.)

Odo.

Ein Bettler zerrt mich hier und einer dort.
Was bettelſt du?

Ernſt.

Das Erbe von Burgund.

Odo.

Ernſt!   605

Hugo.

Herzog Ernſt!

Ernſt.

Nicht er, ſein Schatten nur,
Sein irrer Geiſt, der auf dem Kreuzweg ſpukt.

Odo.

Wahnwitziger!

Ernſt.

Wär' ich wahnſinnig worden,
Wen dürft' es wundern? Doch ich bin es nicht.
Noch weiß ich gut, daß du Graf Odo biſt,
Mein Vetter und Miterbe von Burgund.   610
Dir laur' ich an den Straßen auf, von dir
Begehr' ich Hülf' in meiner tiefen Noth.

Odo.

Zur böſen Stunde biſt du mir genaht,
Wo mir's im Buſen kocht, im Hirne brennt,

Wie du ſo ſchmählich, ſchmählich mich getäuſcht.   615
Als Herzog hoch zu Roß, an Heeresſpitze
Einziehend in Burgund, mein Kampfgenoß,
So hab' ich dich erwartet und es ſtand
In deiner Macht. Für einen Landsverwieſnen
Betrogſt du mich und läufſt nun ſelbſt daher,   620
Ein weggejagter Bettler, und verlangſt,
Ich ſoll die nackten Lenden dir mit Purpur
Bekleben, ſoll dir auf dein ſtruppig Haar
Die Krone ſtoßen, ſoll auf meinen Schultern
Thronan dich ſchleppen. Nein, du kennſt mich falſch;   625
Nicht will ich an Geächtete mich ketten,
Frei will ich ſchreiten an mein hohes Ziel.
Gelüſtet's dich nach Kronen, frage nur
Den Alten hier! Der weiß für alles Rath.
                    (Abgehend.)
Mein Roß!   630

                    Ernſt.
        O Schmach! o racheloſe Schmach!
Auch du biſt ehrlos, herzogliches Schwert,
Und keines Freien Klinge kämpft mit dir.

                    Hugo.
Unglücklicher!

                    Ernſt.
        Du fühleſt Mitleid noch,
Und ungetröſtet ſoll ich nicht von hier.
Du ſiehſt dich ſorglich um: ſei ohne Furcht!   635
Wir ſind hier unbehorcht, kein Lauſcher wird's
Verrathen, wenn du den Verbannten hörſt.
Ich will dir ferne ſtehen, daß mein Hauch
Dich nicht berührt noch mein Gewand dich ſtreift.

Hugo.

Könnt' ich dir Troſt gewähren, o wie gern!   640

Ernſt.

Ehrwürd'ger Greis, wenn die Erinnerung
Vergangner Tage dich nicht ganz verließ,
So wirſt du dich entſinnen, daß ich einſt,
In ſchönrer Zeit, um deine Tochter warb.
Nicht will ich die Bewerbung jetzt erneun;   645
Ich wär' ein unglückſel'ger Bräutigam.
Wollt' ich zur Kirche führen meine Braut,
Kein hochzeitlich Geleite trät' uns nach,
Vor meinem Anblick kreuzte ſich das Volk,
Kein Feſtklang tönte von dem Glockenhaus,   650
Noch die Poſaune von des Thurmes Kranz;
Und, wollt' ich mit ihr nahen dem Altar,
So ſchwiege Chorgeſang und Orgelſchall,
Der Prieſter höbe dräuend ſeine Hand
Und ſpräche Fluch ſtatt Segen über uns.   655
Nein, werben darf ich nicht um Edelgard,
Auch hab' ich's um dich ſelber nicht verdient;
Drei feſte Burgen hab' ich dir zerſtört,
Weil du zum Kaiſer, deinem Vetter, hieltſt.
Nur eines bitt' ich, ſag' es mir zum Troſt: 660
Hat deine Tochter, wenn einmal von mir,
Von meinem Mißgeſchick die Rede ward,
Hat ſie, ich meine nicht, um mich geweint,
Nein, ob das Aug' ihr flüchtig überlief,
Nur, wie ein leichter Hauch den Spiegel trübt;   665
Ob ſie, geſeufzet nicht, nein, tiefer nur
Geathmet, wie man oft im Traume pflegt.

Hugo.

Von Thränen und von Seufzern merkt' ich nichts,
Nur, daß sie ernster, feierlicher ward.
Mildthätig, hülfreich war sie schon zuvor,   670
Jetzt gab sie gänzlich sich der Armuth hin.
Wie fromme Witwen pflegen, spendete
Die jungfräuliche Witwe jeden Tag
Almosen, war der Kranken Wärterin,
Erquickte Pilger und Gefangene ...   675

Ernst.

Gefangene!

Hugo

      Bis nun die Botschaft kam,
Daß du mit Acht belegt und Kirchenbann;
Da bat sie freundlich eines Morgens mich,
Sie zu geleiten zum Ottilienberg.
(Du kennst das Kloster, das von seiner Höh'   680
Das schöne Elsaß weithin überschaut.)
Als sie vom Zelter dort gestiegen war
Und in der Hand den Ring der Pforte hielt,
Da sprach sie: „Wohlgelegen ist dies Stift.
Man sieht von seiner Schwelle weit umher   685
Die Städt' und Burgen, Fluß und Feld und Hain
Und allen Reichthum dieser schönen Welt
So freundlich und so blühend hingelegt,
Daß, wem nicht alles Erdenglück erstarb,
Wem nicht die Hoffnung ganz entwurzelt ist,   690
Hier an der Pforte noch umkehren muß."
Mit diesem trat sie in der Mauern Kreis.
Und dort im Hofe quillt ein heil'ger Born,

   U   5

Ein wunderkräft'ger, der die Augen ſtärkt
Und ſelbſt der Blindheit nächt'ge Binde löſt;   695
Damit benetzte ſie der Wimpern Saum.
„Mein Aug' iſt trübe worden," hub ſie an,
„Und wohl bedarf ich, daß ein Himmelsthau
Zur ew'gen Klarheit mir den Blick erſchließt."
So ſagte ſie dem Irb'ſchen Lebewohl.   700

(Ab.)

Ernſt.

Auch du hinab, du goldner Liebesſtern,
Der meiner Jugend Pfade ſchön erhellt,
Der tröſtend in mein Kerkergitter ſchien!
An dieſes Weibes liebevoller Bruſt
Hätt' ich geneſen können. Vieles noch   705
Und Härtres hätt' ich auszuſtehn vermocht,
Wenn ſie mir blieb. Noch kannt' ich keine Schmach,
Kein Drangſal, keine Wunde, keinen Schmerz,
Dafür nicht ſie der ſüße Balſam war.
Ja, ſie erquickte mich Gefangenen;   710
Sie hätte dem erſchöpften Pilgersmann
Noch einſt den friſchen Lebenskelch gereicht.
Nun muß ich wandern meinen rauhen Pfad
Einſam, umnachtet, ewig herberglos.

(Er will abgehen, ein Kriegsknecht vertritt ihm den Weg.)

Kriegsknecht.

Halt!   715

Ernſt.

Wer da?

Kriegsknecht.

Halt!

Ernſt.

Zurück! ich ſag' zurück!
Du biſt gedungen, mich zu morden. Ja,
Schon lang verfolgſt du mich.   Heb dich hinweg!
Noch wehr' ich um mein elend Leben mich,
Noch bin ich Mördern kampfgerecht.

Kriegsknecht.

Stoß zu!
Triff dieſes Herz!   720

Ernſt.

Mein Werner! o mein Werner!

Werner.

Dein Werner und der Deinige ſo ganz
Und ſo mit jedem Athemzug, mit jedem
Blutstropfen . . .

Ernſt.

Jetzt bin ich geborgen.   Gott
Verließ mich nicht.

Werner.

O du getreuer Freund!
Du edles Herz! du lauteres Gold!   725

Ernſt.

Halt ein!

Werner.

Wie viel, wie viel haſt du für mich gethan,
Geduldet! Nie vergelt' ich dir's.

Ernſt.

Du haſt
Voraus vergolten.

67

Werner.

Nichts hab' ich gethan.
Du bist der einzig Treue.

Ernst.

Laß uns hier
Im Schatten ruhn! Ich bin vom Wandern müd'. 730
Die Eiche breitet uns ein wirthlich Dach.
Mir ist, als ob ich wieder Herzog sei,
Als wären wir an einem schönen Tag
Hinausgeritten auf die Falkenjagd
Und hätten uns zu Mittag hier gesetzt. 735
Erzähle, Werner, wo du warst indeß,
Wie du gelebt!

Werner.

In Frankreich sah ich zu,
Wie dort der König seine Fürsten zähmt;
Da kam von Aachen her mir der Bericht
Durch einen Kriegsknecht, der nach Solde gieng, 740
Daß du aus deiner Kerkerhaft befreit,
Daß du geächtet und gebannet seist
Und zwar um meinetwillen. Augenblicks
Riß ich dem Knechte seinen Mantel ab
Und gürtete sein kurzes Schwert mir um 745
Und lief nach deinen Fährten, edles Wild,
Und habe dich ergriffen.

Ernst.

Werner, sprich!
Auf dir auch lastet Acht und Kirchenfluch:
Wie hast du es gemacht, daß du so fest,

So aufrecht bliebest? Höher, kräftiger   750
Erscheinst du mir, als ich dich je gekannt.

Werner.

Es heißt, die Saat gedeih' im Wetterschein:
Vom Bannstrahl, glaub' ich, wuchs auch mir die Kraft.

Ernst.

Mir dünkt es, deine Treue hat's gethan.

Werner.

O! macht' uns Treue kräftig und gesund,   755
Dann müßtest du wie eine Rose blühn.
Woraus mein Leben seine Nahrung zieht,
Was mich erhält und was mich kräftiget,
Ist die Erinnrung eines großen Tags,
An dem die deutsche Freiheit mir erschien   760
In offnem Wirken, in lebend'ger Kraft.
Dies Angedenken trug ich auf der Flucht
Mit mir als ein gerettet Heiligthum,
Und unter dieser hohen Eiche hier,
Uralt, doch grünend wie die Freiheit selbst,   765
Stell' ich mein wunderthätig Bild dir auf,
Daß es gerad' im Abgrund unsrer Noth
Erhebend sich beweise dir und mir.

Ernst.

Wenn etwas noch mich aufzurichten taugt,
Ein Wort aus deinem Munde muß es sein.   770

Werner.

Nicht bloß, daß in der Stunde der Geburt

Der Sterne Wechſelſtand geheimnißvoll
Die menſchlichen Geſchicke vorbeſtimmt:
Noch mitten oft ins Leben tritt ein Tag,
Der unſrem Weſen erſt den Vollgehalt,   775
Der unſrer Zukunft, allem unſrem Thun
Die unabänderliche Richtung giebt.
Auch mich ergriff ein Tag für alle Zeit; ·
Vollkommen klar bin ich mir deß bewußt:
Der fromme Kaiſer Heinrich war geſtorben,   780
Des ſächſiſchen Geſchlechtes letzter Zweig,
Das glorreich ein Jahrhundert lang geherrſcht.
Als nun die Botſchaft in das Reich ergieng,
Da fuhr ein reger Geiſt in alles Volk,
Ein neu Weltalter ſchien heraufzuziehn;   785
Da lebte jeder längſt entſchlafne Wunſch
Und jede längſt erloſchne Hoffnung auf.
Kein Wunder jetzo, wenn ein deutſcher Mann,
Dem ſonſt ſo Hohes nie zu Hirne ſtieg,
Sich, heimlich forſchend, mit den Blicken maß: 790
Kann's doch nach deutſchem Rechte wohl geſchehn,
Daß, wer dem Kaiſer heut den Bügel hält,
Sich morgen ſelber in den Sattel ſchwingt!
Jetzt dachten unſre freien Männer nicht
An Hub- und Haingericht und Markgeding,   795
Wo man um Eſch und Holztheil Sprache hält:
Nein, ſtattlich ausgerüſtet, zogen ſie
Aus allen Gauen, einzeln und geſchaart,
Ins Maienfeld hinab zur Kaiſerwahl.
Am ſchönen Rheinſtrom, zwiſchen Worms und Mainz, 800
Wo unabſehbar ſich die ebne Flur
Auf beiden Ufern breitet, ſammelte

Der Andrang sich, die Mauern einer Stadt
Vermochten nicht, das deutsche Volk zu fassen.
Am rechten Ufer spannten ihr Gezelt   805
Die Sachsen sammt der slav'schen Nachbarschaft,
Die Baiern, die Ostfranken und die Schwaben;
Am linken lagerten die rhein'schen Franken,
Die Ober= und die Niederlothringer.
So war das Mark von Deutschland hier gedrängt, 810
Und mitten in dem Lager jeden Volks
Erhub sich stolz das herzogliche Zelt.
Da war ein Grüßen und ein Händeschlag,
Ein Austausch, ein lebendiger Verkehr!
Und jeder Stamm verschieden an Gesicht,   815
An Wuchs und Haltung, Mundart, Sitte, Tracht,
An Pferden, Rüstung, Waffenfertigkeit,
Und alle doch ein großes Brüdervolk,
Zu gleichem Zwecke festlich hier vereint!
Was jeder im Besondern erst berieth,   820
Im hüllenden Gezelt und im Gebüsch
Der Inselbuchten, mählich war's gereift
Zum allgemeinen, offenen Beschluß.
Aus vielen wurden wenige gewählt,
Und aus den wenigen erkor man zween,   825
Allbeide Franken, fürstlichen Geschlechts,
Erzeugt von Brüdern, Namensbrüder selbst,
Kunrade, längst mit gleichem Ruhm genannt.
Da standen nun auf eines Hügels Saum
Im Kreis der Fürsten, sichtbar allem Volk,   830
Die beiden Männer, die aus freier Wahl
Das deutsche Volk des Thrones werth erkannt
Vor allen, die der deutsche Boden nährt,

Von allen Würdigen die Würdigſten
Und ſo einander ſelbſt an Würde gleich,   835
Daß fürder nicht die Wahl zu ſchreiten ſchien,
Und daß die Wage ruht' im Gleichgewicht;
Da ſtanden ſie, das hohe Haupt geneigt,
Den Blick geſenkt, die Wange ſchamerglüht,
Von ſtolzer Demuth überwältiget.   840
Ein königlicher Anblick war's, ob dem
Die Thräne rollt' in manchen Mannes Bart.
Und wie nun harrend all die Menge ſtand,
Und ſich des Volkes Brauſen ſo gelegt,
Daß man des Rheines ſtillen Zug vernahm   845
(Denn niemand wagt' es, dieſen oder den
Zu küren mit dem hellen Ruf der Wahl,
Um nicht am Andern Unrecht zu begehn,
Noch aufzuregen Eiferſucht und Zwiſt):
Da ſah man plötzlich, wie die beiden Herrn   850
Einander herzlich faßten bei der Hand
Und ſich begegneten im Bruderkuß.
Da ward es klar, ſie hegten keinen Reid
Und jeder ſtand dem Andern gern zurück.
Der Erzbiſchof von Mainz erhub ſich jetzt: 855
„Weil doch" ſo rief er „einer es muß ſein,
So ſei's der Ältre!" Freudig ſtimmten bei
Geſammte Fürſten und am freudigſten
Der jüngre Kunrad; donnergleich erſcholl,
Oft wiederholt, des Volkes Beifallsruf.   860
Als der Gewählte drauf ſich niederließ,
Ergriff er ſeines edeln Vetters Hand
Und zog ihn zu ſich auf den Königsſitz.
Und in den Ring der Fürſten trat ſofort

Die fromme Kaiserwitwe Kunigund,   865
Glückwünschend reichte sie dem neuen König
Die treubewahrten Reichskleinode dar.
Zum Festzug aber schaarten sich die Reihn,
Voran der König, folgend mit Gesang
Die Geistlichen und Laien: so viel Preis   870
Erscholl zum Himmel nie an einem Tag.
Wär' Kaiser Karl gestiegen aus der Gruft,
Nicht freudiger hätt' ihn die Welt begrüßt.
So wallten sie den Strom entlang nach Mainz,
Woselbst der König im erhabnen Dom   875
Der Salbung heil'ge Weihe nun empfieng.
Wen seines Volkes Ruf so hoch gestellt,
Dem fehle nicht die Kräftigung von Gott!
Und als er wieder aus dem Tempel trat,
Erschien er herrlicher, als kaum zuvor,   880
Und seine Schulter ragt' ob allem Volk.
Das ist der große Tag, der mich ergriff,
Der mich in allem Drangsal frisch erhält.

Ernst.

Ein großer Sinn faßt große Bilder auf,
Ein andrer andre. Dazumal, als du   885
Dem freien Vaterland ins Auge sahst,
Erglänzte mir der ersten Liebe Huld
In eines Mägdleins minniglichem Blick.
Ich war ein Jüngling, stand in Vormundschaft
Von meinem Ohm, dem Erzbischof von Trier,   890
Und noch war mir des Reiches Sache fremd.
Wohl kamen andre Zeiten, strengere,
Die mich gerüttelt aus dem Liebestraume.

Werner.

O nicht vergeß' ich's: mit dem alten Welf
Von Altdorf und mit andern schwäb'schen Herrn   895
War ich geritten auf das Maienfeld;
Wir tränkten eben unsre Pferd' im Rhein,
Da kamest du den Strom herabgeschifft
Auf einer leichten, buntverzierten Jacht,
Du selbst im Fürstenschmuck, zur Seite dir   900
Graf Hugo mit der schönen Edelgard,
Und schwebend auf dem Schiffesrande saß
Ein Sänger, der die Harfe lieblich schlug;
Des Stromes Klarheit aber spiegelte
Die glänzenden Gestalten.   905

Ernst.

Schöne Zeit!
Wie ist das alles längst den Strom hinab!

Werner.

Auch was vor mir so groß und herrlich stand,
Es ist nicht mehr, nur im Gedanken lebt's.
Der Mann, den wir zum König uns gewählt
Und der so demuthsvoll das Haupt geneigt,   910
Er hat's emporgeworfen; ihn verlangt
Nach Unbeschränktheit, nach Alleinherrschaft
Und nach der Erblichkeit in seinem Stamm.
Die ihn erwählten, tritt er in den Staub.
Den Kunrad, den er jenes Mal geküßt,   915
Hat er genöthigt, nach dem Schwert zu greifen;
Des Reichs verwiesen ist der graue Welf;
Der Herzog Adalbert von Kärnthen irrt
Mit seinen Söhnen heimathlos umher.

Und du, mein Herzog, o wie hat er dich   920
Vom Anbeginn verfolgt, beraubt, zerknirscht!
Ich bin dir zugethan durch Lehenseid,
Der Freundschaft heilig Band verknüpfet uns;
Doch, wär' ich nicht dein Mann und nicht dein Freund,
Dein Banner hätt' ich dennoch aufgesucht,   925
Damit ich ihn bekämpfe, dem auch ich
Einst zugerufen auf dem Feld der Wahl.

Ernst.

Wohl wittert jedes Wesen seinen Feind;
Drum hegt auch dir der Kaiser wildern Haß
Und unversöhnlicheren, als mir selbst.   930

Werner.

Von diesem Haß, den ich allein verwirkt,
Mußt du, Unglücklicher, das Opfer sein.
Nicht ich bin elend, denn mich treibt die Gluth,
Die ich an jenem Tag in mich gesaugt;
Du aber hast nach Frieden dich gesehnt   935
Und mußt nun so unendlich friedlos sein
Und hast für all die Treue keinen Dank
Von mir, als daß ich schadenfroh und stolz
Auf dich hinblicke, wie du nun so ganz
Verlassen dastehst und so ganz entblößt,   940
Und wie nun ich dein einz'ger Lehensmann,
Der Einz'ge bin, der dich noch Herzog nennt,
Und wie nun mir allein die Ehre bleibt,
Dir Dienst zu leisten bis zum letzten Hauch.

Ernst.

Gewaltiger, was neigst du dich vor mir?   945

Werner.

O wahrlich, nie in deinem Fürſtenglanz
Erſchienſt du mir ſo herrlich, ſo erlaucht,
So würdig jeder tiefſten Huldigung,
Als wie du jetzt in freierkorner Schmach,
In deiner Selbſtverbannung vor mir ſtehſt!   950
Doch nein, ſo ganz vergeſſen biſt du nicht.
In Schwaben, wo dein Vater Herzog war,
Wo ihn und dich ein biedres Volk geliebt,
Wo mancher jetzt auf ſeiner Veſte hauſt,
Der unter deinem Banner einſt gekämpft,   955
Dort muß von dir noch ein Gedächtniß ſein.
Dorthin ſei unſer irrer Pfad gelenkt,
Des Schwarzwalds dichter Schatten nehm' uns auf!

Ernſt.

Dir folg' ich, und wenn alles mich verſchmäht,
Du wirſt mich nie verlaſſen.   960

Werner.

                                Siehſt du hier?
Der Handſchuh, den ich aus dem Koller zieh',
Er ward vom Kaiſer in den Staub geſchleudert,
Daß er verſchmähet und zertreten ſei.
Der Kriegsknecht hob ihn auf und gab ihn mir,
Und dieſer Handſchuh liegt an meiner Bruſt.   965

                                (Beide ab.)

ARGUMENT TO ACT III.

Count Hugo of Egisheim is about to return to Burgundy, sent thither by Konrad to prevent any new outbreak: and Gisela, bound by her oath not to help Ernest, nor to plead for him, begs Hugo to do all he can to confirm the weak King Rudolf in adherence to the contract by which Burgundy has been assigned to the empire, to restrain Odo from his bold and ambitious plans, and to quiet and conciliate the turbulent vassals, that Ernest may not gain new adherents and again rise in active revolt. In this way she hopes that peace may be established, and that the Emperor may then be inclined to remove the sentence of outlawry from her son's head. But fresh news has just been brought to the Emperor by Count Mangold, that Swabia is again in revolt, that Ernest and Werner are ranging the Black Forest at the head of a small band of followers, and that a legendary tale has sprung up among the people about their wonderful adventures during the years when Ernest was really in prison, a story of which Gisela makes a figurative application to the actual vicissitudes of Ernest's fortunes. Konrad forthwith despatches Mangold to quell the rebellion, promising quickly to follow in person. Gisela, contemplating Mangold's sword, about to be drawn against her son, appeals in agony to the Mother of Sorrows. Moved to charity by her own trouble, she calls to her a pilgrim standing near, who reveals himself as Adalbert of Falkenstein, a Swabian noble who in the excitement of the chase had slain her former husband, Ernest I. of Swabia. Adalbert has wandered about for years as a pilgrim, doing penance, but nowhere finding peace; he believes that the murdered man still haunts him, because his last wish, conveyed by Adalbert, that Gisela should preserve her widowhood, has not been carried out. He reproaches her with the unhappy consequences to her son of her marriage with Konrad, and calls upon her to renounce it. Gisela explains and justifies her remarriage, pointing with dignified pride to the sphere of usefulness and benevolence that she fills; and indignantly shows him that the true way to deliver himself from the curse is to cease from his vain and worthless penance, and to do his duty as a knight, a father, and the loyal vassal of an exiled lord. Her words rouse him to energy and enthusiasm; he resolves to expiate his guilt towards the father by devoting himself, even to death, for the son.

Dritter Aufzug.

Palast zu Aachen, wie am Anfang des Stücks.

Gisela und Graf Hugo im Gespräch.

Gisela.

Ihr kehrt zurück nach Basel, edler Graf?

Hugo.

Dem Kaiser melbet' ich den neusten Stand
Der Angelegenheiten in Burgund. Er will,
Daß ich dort wieder gegenwärtig sei
Und mit unausgesetzter Wachsamkeit   970
Vorbeuge jedem neuen Friedensbruch.
Noch fehlt mir euer Urlaub, hohe Frau!

Gisela.

Befürchtet nicht, wie ihr zu fürchten scheint,
Daß ich mit Auftrag euch behellige,
Der dem, was euch der Kaiser anbefahl,   975
Entgegen wäre! Nein, ich bitt' euch selbst,
Verwendet euer Ansehn, euern Rath
Allwärts zur Söhnung und Beruhigung!
Mein Oheim, König Rudolf, schätzt euch hoch.
O haltet sein geschwächtes Alter fest,   980
Daß er nicht wieder wanke dem Vertrag!
Und wie ihr biesen stärket und erhebt,
So stillt und sänftiget am andern Theil

78

Die gährenden Vasallen, dämpft den Muth
Des stolzen Odo, der Verwegnes sinnt,   985
Und hütet überall, daß nicht mein Sohn
Verbindung knüpft und neuen Anhang wirbt!

Hugo.

Verehrend ahn' ich eurer Worte Grund.
Indeß ihr gegen den Geächteten
Zu wirken scheinet, seid ihr überzeugt,   990
Sein Heil zu fördern; ist Burgund nur erst
Durchaus beruhigt und dem Reich gewiß,
Dann wird der Kaiser auch geneigter sein,
Die Acht zu nehmen von des Herzogs Haupt.
Ich aber gehe freud'ger ans Geschäft,   995
Da ich, dem Kaiser dienend, euch zugleich
Und eurem Sohne frommen darf.

Gisela.
Noch eins!

Wenn ihr jetzt wieder das Otilienstift
Besucht, und Edelgard ans Gitter tritt,
Grüßt sie von mir!   1000

Hugo.
Huldreiche Kaiserin!

Gisela.

O! schöne Hoffnungen sind mir zerknickt!
Die einz'ge Tochter, die mir Gott geschenkt,
Ein holdes Kind, in zarter Jugend schon
Dem Könige von Frankreich anverlobt,
Nicht sollt' ich sie zum Traualtar geleiten;   1005
Die Todtenkrone statt des Hochzeitkranzes

Mußt' ich ihr flechten in das blonde Haar.
Und wieder hofft' ich, daß mein Älteſter
Mir eine Tochter brächte zum Erſatz.
Denn wie des Vaters Stolz darin beſteht,   1010
Den Sohn gekrönt zu ſehn mit Ruhm und Macht,
So iſt der Mutter Wonne, wenn der Sohn
Einhertritt mit der jugendlichen Braut,
Der liebenden, die ihm das Leben ſchmückt.
Umſonſt hab' ich die Arme aufgethan   1015
So ſeligem Empfang.   Lebt wohl, Herr Graf!

(Graf Hugo ab.   Indem Giſela abgehen will, tritt von der antern
Seite der Kaiſer mit dem Grafen Mangold auf.)

Kunrad.

Verweile, Giſela, wenn nicht zu ſehr
Dich anderen Berufes Eile drängt!

Giſela.

Auf dich zu hören, gehet jedem vor.

Kunrad.

Aus Schwaben iſt mir Botſchaft zugekommen,   1020
Sehr unerfreuliche, womit ich gern
Dein Ohr verſchonte, wenn ſie anders dir
So unerwünſcht, wie mir, zu hören iſt.
Der Überbringer dieſer Kunde ſelbſt,
Graf Mangold, melde dir, was dort geſchehn!   1025

Mangold.

Erlauchte Frau, laßt es den Boten nicht
Entgelten, wenn die Botſchaft euch mißfällt!
Indeß der Ungar deutſche Mark bedräut,
Und wider ihn das Aufgebot ergeht,

Indeß erhebt von schwäb'schen Gauen her   1030
Sich innre Gährung. Durch den Schwarzwald streift
Unheimlich eine kriegerische Schaar,
Die man zuerst für Räuber achtete
(Denn ihre Zehrung holt sie mit Gewalt),
Bis man hernach an ihrer Spitze sah   1035
Den Fürsten Ernst und Wernern, seinen Freund.
Noch werden sie auf fünfzig kaum geschätzt,
Noch sind sie unberitten, schlecht bewehrt,
Noch öffnete sich ihnen keine Burg,
Noch lagern sie in Wald und Felsgeklüft;   1040
Und doch ist dumpfes Harren überall,
Und mancher, der die Klinge schon geputzt,
Um mit dem Heer nach Ungarn auszuziehn,
Erwartet, was daheim geschehen will.

Gisela.

Schreckt nicht die Reichsacht und der Kirchenbann, 1045
Womit mein Sohn belegt ist, jeden ab?

Mangold.

Ein sonderbarer Glaube herrscht im Volk:
Sie wollen's nicht begreifen, daß ihr Fürst
So lang gesessen in der Kerkernacht;
In wundervolle Reisen wandeln sie   1050
Die öden Jahre der Gefangenschaft
Und geben sein Ergrauen vor der Zeit
Dem scharfen Strahle fremder Sonnen schuld.

Gisela.

Ich selber hab' es immer nicht gefaßt,
Wie, der so jung sei und so lebensfroh,   1055

U   6

Im Kerker modern könne, und noch jetzt
Erſcheint er mir im Traume anders nie,
Denn friſch und blühend, wie er ſollte blühn.
Die Mutter, die ihn unterm Herzen trug,
Kann nicht vergeſſen, was ſein Alter iſt.   1060
Doch laßt mich weiter hören, was man ſpricht!

Mangold.

In Indien und im ganzen Morgenland
Hat er der Abenteuer viel beſtanden.
Durch eines finſtern Berges Eingeweib'
Riß ihn auf ſchwankem Floß ein wilder Strom,   1065
Der rieſ'ge Greif entführt' ihn durch die Wolken;
An dem Magnetberg fuhren ſeinem Schiff
Die Nägel aus, daß es in Trümmer gieng;
Mit Völkern von unmenſchlicher Geſtalt
Hat er gekämpft und manchen Sieg erlangt.   1070
Was je ein Pilger Seltſames erzählt,
Das wird auf eures Sohnes Haupt gehäuft,
Und dieſer Schein des Wunderbaren zieht
Leichtgläubige Gemüther mächtig an.

Giſela.

Wohl fuhr mein Sohn durch einen finſtern Berg, 1075
Ein furchtbar Schickſal rafft' ihn durch die Luft,
Die Nägel ſeines Schiffes löſten ſich,
Die ungetreuen, daß es ſcheiterte,
Und auf den Scheitern treibt er noch umher.
Weh ihm, wenn ſich das edle Menſchenbild   1080
Zu wilden Mißgeſtalten ihm entſtellt!

Kunrad.

Graf Mangold, diese Rede kränk' euch nicht!
Ihr habt gethan, was Ehr' und Pflicht gebot,
Und mein Vertrauen lohnet euch dafür.
Dies Schwert hat meine Hand euch umgehängt,   1085
Nicht um darauf zu ruhn (den Todten nur
Legt man die Schwerter unters müde Haupt):
Zur fernern That bezweckt' ich euch zu weihn,
Und wenn ich vom ital'schen Heereszug
Zurück euch hielt, so war die Absicht die,   1090
Daß ich mir einen wohlerprobten Arm
Bewahrte für die heimische Gefahr.
Der Augenblick ist da: der Aufruhr gährt;
Ihr sollt ihn mir vertilgen in der Brut.
Und wie ich eures Oheims klugem Sinn   1095
Der Staatsgeschäfte Leitung anvertraut,
So übergeb' ich eurer Tapferkeit
Die Kriegsmacht mit vollkommener Gewalt.
Nur rasch zum Werk!   Der Rücken werd' uns frei!
Der Ungarn Andrang, den die Meuterer   1100
Zu nützen hofften, leidet nicht Verzug.
Mit nächstem werd' ich selbst in Schwaben sein,
Um nachzusehn, was euer Schwert vollführt.

Mangold.

Geblendet von so hellem Gnadenschein,
Von plötzlicher Erhebung überrascht,   1105
Versagt mir jeder Ausdruck meines Danks
Und meiner treuesten Ergebenheit.

Kunrad.

Die Vollmacht langt ihr bei dem Kanzler ab.
Dich, Gisela, gemahn' ich deines Eids.   (Ab.)

6—2

Giſela.

Herr Graf, vergönnt mir, euer Schwert zu ſehn! 1110
(Sie nimmt es.)

Und iſt nun das die mörderiſche Spitze,
Die nach dem Blute meines Sohnes lechzt?
Nicht kann ich Schwerter ſchmelzen und nicht darf
Ich Menſchen rühren, doch zum Himmel noch
Darf ich mich wenden in der Seelenangſt: 1115
O gnadenreiche Mutter, der ein Schwert
Durchs Herz gegangen, als du thränenvoll
Aufblickteſt zu dem Kreuze deines Sohns,
Dich fleh' ich an, geſtatte du es nicht,
Daß dieſer kalte Mordſtahl meinem Kind   1120
Die Bruſt durchbohre und die meine mit!
(Sie giebt das Schwert zurück.   Mangold ab.)

Ein Pilger ſtehet dort im Säulengang;
Er ſah mich beten und gefaltet hält
Auch er die Hände. Segne Gott den Mann,
Der mein ſchmerzvolles Flehen unterſtützt!   1125
Tritt ein! Die Thore dieſes Hauſes ſind
Jedwedem offen, der nach Hülfe geht.

Pilger.

Wer mir kann helfen, muß ein Meiſter ſein.

Giſela.

Dein Blick iſt finſter, deine Stirn' gefurcht;
Ein tiefer Kummer, nicht von geſtern her,   1130
Hat dich getrieben auf die Pilgerfahrt.

Pilger.

Das Angedenken einer grauſen That
Verfolgt mich.

Gisela.

Rede, wenn ich's wissen soll!

Pilger.

Ich war ein Ritter, nein, ein Jäger nur.
Mich trieb die unbarmherz'ge Lust, das Thier   1135
Zu hetzen auf das Thier; mich rührt' es nicht,
Wenn mich die Hindin, blutig und zersetzt,
Bethränten Auges bat um ihren Tod.
Wär' mir, wie einst dem heiligen Hubert,
Das Kreuz erschienen auf des Hirsches Haupt,   1140
Ich hätt' ihm doch den Pfeil ins Herz geschnellt.
Nun kam der Herzog einst, (ihr werdet bleich,
Erlauchte Frau?) er kam in meinen Forst,
Als eben dort ein Zwanzigender strich.
Welch beßre Kurzweil hätt' ich ihm gewußt,   1145
Als ihn zu laden zu so edler Jagd?
Auf schweißbeträuften Rossen rannten wir
Dem Wilde nach; der Herzog hatte schon
Sich mit gespannter Sehne vorgelegt;
Da gönnt' ich ihm den Hauptschuß nicht: ich warf 1150
Querüber meinen Speer; der Hirsch flog hin,
Hin flog das leb'ge Pferd, am Boden lag
Der Herzog, in der Seite meinen Speer.

Gisela.

Weh dir!

Pilger.

Gebüßt war meine Lust.

Gisela.

Warum
Zerreißest du mein Herz, das schon genug   1155

Von Angſt gequält iſt, noch mit Schreckniſſen
Verfloßner Tage? Mörder meines Gatten,
Unſel'ger Abalbert, iſt dir es leid,
Daß dich die Zeit und deiner Schuld Gefühl
Unkenntlich machte? Gerne hab' ich ſtets   1160
Auch Unbekannten hülfreich mich gezeigt;
Warum, wenn irgend Noth zu mir dich führt,
Hebſt du den Vorhang, der wohlthätig mir
Die gräßliche Vergangenheit bedeckt?

Abalbert.

Der Herzog aber richtete ſich auf,   1165
Und ächzend ſprach er: „Komm, dir iſt verziehn;
Komm her, damit ich ſterb' in deinem Arm!"
Und als ich ihn im Arme hielt, da ſchloſſen
Die Jäger einen dichten Kreis umher.
Und wieder ſprach er: „Iſt kein Prieſter hier?   1170
Mich drücken meine Sünden." Drauf begann
Er, uns zu beichten mit gebrochnem Laut.
Sein Letztes war: „Für meine Seele betet!
Sagt meiner Frau, der Giſela, ſie ſoll
Ihr Witwenthum bewahren, ſoll nicht mein   1175
Vergeſſen." Warb's euch ausgerichtet?

Giſela.

Ja.

Abalbert.

Mein Friede war ſeit jenem Tag dahin;
Denn wo ich gieng und wo ich raſtete,
War mir's, als krampfte ſich ein Sterbender
An meine Bruſt, als hört' ich dicht am Ohr   1180

Ein letztes Röcheln. Drum den Pilgerſtab
Ergriff ich, nahm mein Söhnlein auf den Arm,
Nach Sanct Georgen trug ich es hinüber,
Daß es erwachſ' in ſtrenger Kloſterzucht
Und nicht den Jagdſpieß werf' auf ſeinen Herrn.   1185
Zum heil'gen Grabe wallt' ich, betete
So lang und brünſtig dort, daß ich dem Stein
Eindrückte meiner Kniee Spur. Umſonſt!
Kein Friede ſtieg erquickend mir herauf.
Zehn Jahre lang, in harter Sklaverei,   1190
Zog ich am Pfluge wie ein Stier und riß
Der dürren Erde Schollen auf. Umſonſt!
Die Saat gieng auf, kein Segen grünte mir.
Als ich nun wiederkam ins deutſche Land
Mit dem Entſchluß, mir einen finſtern Wald   1195
Zu ſuchen, den, wie meine Seele, nie
Ein Sonnenſtrahl durchdringt, um mir darin
Ein Klausnerhaus zu bauen und mein Grab,
Da fragt' ich erſt, als ich die Straße zog:
„In welchem Kloſter, welcher Siedelei,   1200
In welcher tiefſten Einſamkeit verweilt
Die Witwe des erſchlagnen Herzogs Ernſt,
Um zu beweinen ihres Gatten Tod
Und um zu beten für ſein Seelenheil?"
Da wies man mich des Weges fort und fort,   1205
Bis ich vor dieſem Kaiſerſchloſſe ſtand
Und bis ich trat in dieſes Prunkgemach.
Jetzt weiß ich, warum der Ermordete
Von mir nicht läßt, und jetzt iſt mir es klar,
Daß er von mir nicht laſſen wird, ſo lang   1210
Vergeſſen bleibt, was ſterbend er befahl.

Gisela.

Wenn dies dich quält und mich zu quälen treibt,
So höre denn, mir zur Rechtfertigung
Und dir zum Troste, wie es sich begab!
Ich lebte, wie es Witwen ziemlich ist,   1215
Mit meinen Kindern, einsam und betrübt.
Die Herrn des Landes aber forderten,
Daß meinem Sohne, dem verwaisten Ernst,
Ein zweiter Vater werde, der zum Schutz
Dem Knaben sei und der das Herzogthum   1220
Bevogte bis zu Ernstes Mündigkeit.
Der tapfre Graf in Franken, Kunrad, warb
Um meine Hand und er vor allen schien
Ein tücht'ger Schutzherr meiner Sprößlinge;
Ihn wünschten die Vasallen unsres Lands,   1225
Er ward von meinen Räthen mir gerühmt;
Ich aber blieb dem Witwenstande treu.
Als ich nun eines Morgens vom Gebet
Aus der Kapelle kam, da war der Hof
Mit hochzeitlichen Reitern angefüllt,   1230
Aus deren Reihn der hohe Kunrad trat
Und mich auf einen schmucken Zelter hob;
Die Landesherren aber und das Volk,
Die mich vertheid'gen sollten, jubelten
Der seltsamen Entführung Beifall zu.   1235
So ist's geschehn. Verdamme, wenn du kannst!

Adalbert.

Vermeßner Sinn, der sich zu weise dünkt,
Die Warnung eines Sterbenden zu achten!

Den du den Hort der Deinigen geglaubt,
Er ist ihr Feind, ihr Unterdrücker jetzt.   1240
Du aber stehest mit getheiltem Herzen
Inmitten doppelseitigen Verbands,
Und schon hast du dem erstgebornen Sohn
Durch schnöden Eid stiefmütterlich entsagt.

Gisela.

Willst du mich tödten, wie du den Gemahl   1245
Mir tödtetest?

Abalbert.

Ein Warner komm' ich dir.
Umsonst hat Kaiser Heinrich euch ermahnt,
Den Bund zu lösen, dem die Kirche zürnt,
Weil du des Kunrads Anverwandte bist;
Vergebens zauderte der Erzbischof,   1250
Da er dich krönen sollt' als Königin.
So muß nun ich erscheinen im Palast,
Nicht um, ein Höfling, Weihrauch dir zu streun,
Nein, um zu warnen mit dem letzten Hauch
Des Sterbenden, den ich in mich gesaugt,   1255
Daß du entsagest diesem Ehebund,
Daß du die Wittwe bleibest Herzog Ernsts
Und seinen Kindern eine Mutter seist.

Gisela.

In meinem Heiligsten greifst du mich an.
Du wirfst mir vor, was noch kein Weib ertrug,   1260
Du kränkst mich da, wo auch die Löwin fühlt,
Du reißest an den Banden der Natur.
War meine Einsicht kurz, mein Vorsatz schwach,
Die Liebe doch ist ewig stark in mir;

Hab' ich den Eid geschworen allzu rasch,   1265
So hab' ich tausendfältig drum gebüßt;
Hab' ich den Witwenschleier nicht bewahrt,
Die Kaiserkrone trag' ich unentweiht.
Es segnet mich mein Haus, es segnet mich
Das Volk, soweit man deutsche Zunge spricht.   1270
Der Andacht bau' ich hohe Tempel auf,
Der Krankheit weih' ich Pflegehäuser ein,
Der Armuth spend' ich meiner Kammern Schatz,
Allwärts entblühet Segen meiner Spur
Und, thront der Kaiser mit dem Schwert des Rechts,   1275
So thron' ich mit der Gnade Palmenzweig;
Vermittlerin bin ich, Fürbitterin,
Wie meinen Kindern, so dem ganzen Volk.
Du aber, der du strafend vor mich trittst
Und mir die Krone werfen willst vom Haupt   1280
Und mir das Herz erdrücken in der Brust,
Was thatest du, das dich berechtigte,
Mich zu vernichten, sprich! was thatest du?
Den Stein hast du gehöhlt mit deinen Knien,
Am Pflug hast du gezogen statt des Stiers,   1285
Dich selbst hast du zerfleischet, ob dir gleich
Der, den dein Speer gefällt, so schön verzieh;
Dein Werk ist todt, unfruchtbar all dein Thun.
Und wenn du nun durch deutsche Gaue wallst
Und siehst die Burgen glänzen auf den Höhn   1290
Und siehst die Ritter reiten durch das Thal
Und hörst des Jagdhorns Klänge durch den Wald,
Die wohlbekannten ...

Adalbert.
Weck' nicht diesen Hall!

Gisela.

Und siehst das Feuer brennen auf dem Herd
Und siehst die Kinder spielen vor der Thür;   1295
Mußt du nicht schamroth werden vor dir selbst,
Daß du so leblos durch das Leben gehst?
Warst du nicht selber einst ein Rittersmann?
Hast du nicht einen Forst, nicht eine Burg?
Hast du nicht einen Herd und hast ein Kind,   1300
Das du verlassen so unväterlich?
Und wenn dich nicht die Lust des Lebens lockt,
Weißt du nichts mehr von Ritterpflicht und That?
Ist keine Unschuld mehr bedrängt? Ist kein
Unglücklicher, der tapfern Arms bedarf?   1305
Irrt nicht dein Herzog, dem den Vater du
Erschlagen, irrt er hilflos nicht umher,
Geächtet, ohne Burg und ohne Herd?
O! läge nicht der Eid vor meinem Mund,
Wär' nicht verschüttet mein lebend'ger Quell,   1310
Wär' nicht gebunden meiner Liebe Kraft,
Ich wollte mit dir ringen, finstrer Geist,
Und wie die Sonn' ins Mark der Erde dringt
Und aus dem Boden treibt die grüne Saat,
So wollt' ich dich ergreifen, todtes Herz,   1315
Und bersten sollte mir dein starres Eis.   (Ab.)

Adalbert.

Bin ich verwandelt? Wie ist mir geschehn?
Hat mich ein Zauberstab berührt? Bin ich
In einen Wunderbrunnen eingetaucht?
Was nicht der Oelberg, nicht das heil'ge Grab, 1320
Was nicht des Jordans hochgeweihte Flut

An mir gethan, das hat dies Weib vermocht.
Ja, Gott kann Wunder wirken überall;
Der Schuld, die mich zermalmte, bin ich los,
Das Thor der Gnade schließt sich leuchtend auf,   1325
Dem Hoffnungslosen iſt ein Weg gezeigt.
Nicht das entsühnte meine Mörderhand,
Daß ich sie wund gerungen im Gebet;
Nein, hülfreich sei dem Sohne sie gereicht,
Dem sie den Vater freventlich geraubt!   1330
Soll ich gegeißelt sein, so sei's für ihn!
Mein Blut, für ihn vergoſſen, waſcht mich rein,
Mein Geiſt, für ihn verhaucht, schwebt himmelan,
Und mein Geschlecht, das ich verflucht gewähnt,
Noch kann es blühen; bis ins fernſte Glied   1335
Bin ich gesegnet. Heil sei diesem Weib!   (Ab.)

ARGUMENT TO ACT IV.

Sc. I. Ernest is sleeping in the lap of his friend Werner, at the foot of the Castle of Falkenstein, in the Black Forest. Adalbert appears, and entreats the fugitive but reluctant Ernest not to deny to the unhappy slayer of his father the opportunity of making some atonement to him, by affording to him in his outlawry the shelter and protection of his castle. A body of troops with Warin, a Swabian noble, at their head, approach in mournful procession; they are the remnant of the army with which Hermann, Ernest's younger brother, made Duke of Swabia in his stead, had been sent by Konrad into Italy. After brilliant victory, Hermann with many of his men has died of the plague, first charging Warin, his standard-bearer, to take the banner of the army, the Swabian ducal banner, to his brother Ernest, for whom alone he had accepted it in charge. Warin and his followers beg to be led to battle, before they too are carried off by the pestilence. Under such sombre auspices Ernest resumes his dignity as Duke, and rouses himself to fresh exertion.

Sc. II. Count Mangold is advancing upon the Castle of Falkenstein. He is visited in his camp by Bishop Warmann, who now that Hermann is dead stirs up anew his nephew's hopes of himself receiving the Duchy of Swabia. Werner now boldly presents himself before Mangold (who is a kinsman of his own), reproaches him for having sold his honour and his independence, and urges him to return to the service of freedom and of his rightful lord. Mangold is stirred to shame and compunction, but declares that it is too late to go back, and Werner leaves him with the warning to beware of him when they meet in battle.

Sc. III. Werner returns to the castle with the news that they are encompassed, and that their only choice is between surrender or famine, and a desperate fight, for which they accordingly prepare. Adalbert brings his young son and devotes him to Ernest's cause. Werner, now equipped again as a knight, resumes his place at Ernest's side, and strives to relieve somewhat the gloom of the occasion by telling the story of the Count of Abensberg and his thirty-two sons. Ernest, wearing the mantle his murdered father had worn, and carrying the shield borne by his brother Hermann, is hailed by his followers as their lord, and goes forth to battle.

Vierter Aufzug.

Erste Scene.

Schwarzwald. Auf der Höhe die Burg Falkenstein.

Im Vorgrund Werner, den schlafenden Ernst im Schooße.
Kriegsleute, umhergelagert.

Werner.

Er schläft in meinem Schooß, er schläft so sanft;
Vertrauend hat er sich mir angeschmiegt.
O! nur zu sehr hat er mir stets vertraut!
Die Eiche, die ihm sollte Schutz verleihn,   1340
Hat auf sein Haupt den Wetterstrahl gelenkt.
Sein Leben war so schön, so morgenhell,
Bis ich sein Freund und sein Verderber ward.
Ich bin's, der in den wilden Streit ihn riß,
Ich warf ihn ins Gefängniß, ich hab' ihn   1345
Geächtet, ich sein Liebesglück zerstört,
Mein Werk ist er, wie er hier vor mir liegt.
Doch er ist immer freundlich, immer treu;
Kein andrer Vorwurf ward mir je von ihm,
Als diese Blässe seines Angesichts   1350
Und dieser Schmerzenszug in seinem Schlaf.
O könnt' ich ihn mit diesen Armen weit
Hinübertragen in ein glücklich Land,
Wo Friede wohnet und wo Freude blüht,

Wo dem Erwachenden sein schweres Leid   1355
Verschwunden wäre wie ein böser Traum!

Adalbert tritt auf.

Adalbert.

Da liegt er. Ha! wie er dem Vater gleicht,
Als der Erblaßte mir im Arme lag!

Werner.

Tritt sacht auf, Pilger! Weck' nicht meinen Freund!

Adalbert.

Laß mir die Wacht bei diesem Schlafenden!   1360
Ich hab' ein altes Recht, die Herzoge
Im Arm zu halten.

Werner.

Wunderlicher Mann!
Wenn man dir tiefer in die Runzeln schaut,
Bist du der Adalbert vom Falkenstein.

Adalbert.

Wenn du die Locken von der Stirne streichst,   1365
Bist du der Werner, der von Kiburg stammt.

Werner.

Was willst du hier?

Adalbert.

Den Herzog sucht' ich auf.

Werner.

Weißt du, daß er gebannt, geächtet ist?

Adalbert.

Wer solchen Fluch getragen hat wie ich,

Der bleibt von Acht und Bannstrahl ungeschreckt.   1370
Das eben soll vom Fluche mich befrein,
Daß ich dem Ächter öffne meine Burg,
Den sichern Horst, der dort vom Felsen trotzt.

Werner.

Schon hab' ich angeklopft an ihrem Thor;
Der Burgvogt hat den Einlaß uns versagt.   1375

Adalbert.

Ihm übergab ich meiner Väter Haus,
Als ich hinausgieng auf die Pilgerfahrt,
Und keinem öffnet er, als seinem Herrn.

Ernst (erwachend).

Wer ist der Mann?

Werner.

         Mein Herzog, sei erfreut!
Erhebt euch, ihr Gefährten unsrer Noth!   1380
Gewonnen ist uns heut der erste Sieg.
Noch schweiften wir im Walde wie der Wolf,
Noch kreisten wir umher, dem Geier gleich,
Der sich nicht setzen darf auf wohnlich Dach,
Und nur der Busch, der auch das Wild behegt,   1385
Und nur die Schluft, die auch das Raubthier birgt,
War uns Herberge; dieser Mann zuerst
Eröffnet menschliche Behausung uns,
Die Burg dort oben schließet er uns auf
Und macht uns heimisch in dem schwäb'schen Land.   1390

Ernst.

Wer bist du, der du, selbst ein Pilger, mir,
Dem unstet Wandernden, ein Obdach beutst?

Adalbert.

Ich bin der unglückſel'ge Adalbert,
Der ſeinen Herzog in die Seite warf,
Und der von fünfzehnjähr'ger Pilgrimſchaft   1395
Nur dann entſündiget nach Hauſe kehrt,
Wenn du mit ihm in ſeine Mauern trittſt.
O wende dich nicht ab! Bei dieſem Kreuz,
Das noch der Stätte Denkmal iſt, auf der
Dein Vater ſtarb und ſterbend mir vergab,   1400
Beſchwör' ich dich, verſchmähe nicht mein Haus!
Du retteſt eine Seele.

Ernſt.

Hingebeugt
Auf dieſen Boden, den dein Blut getränkt,
Umfaſſend dieſen moosbedeckten Stein,
Den in der Mitternacht dein Geiſt umſchwebt,   1405
Klag' ich, geliebter Vater, dir mein Loos.
So elend ſiehſt du mich und ſo verwaiſt,
Daß ich zu dem die Zuflucht nehmen muß,
Der dich gemordet.

Werner.

Horch! ein Horn erdröhnt.
Zur Wehr, ihr Männer! Weicht vom Herzog nicht!   1410

Ernſt.

Nicht wie zum Angriff naht ſich dieſe Schaar,
Sie ſchreiten vor in ernſtem Trauerzug;
Umflort iſt ihr Panier, die Schärpen ſchwarz.
Das iſt Warin, der Schwabens Fahne trägt.

V.   7

Warin, an der Spitze einer Kriegsschaar, tritt auf.

Warin.

Wir treten, Herzog, in geringer Zahl,   1415
Doch tapfern und getreuen Muths zu dir.
Hinunter ins ital'sche Schlachtgefild
Hat uns dein Bruder Hermann einst geführt.
Das Banner, das ich trage, wallt' ihm vor
Zu manchem heißen, ehrenvollen Kampf.   1420
Des jungen Helden freute sich das Heer;
Uns Schwaben nur war's auf des Jünglings Stirn'
Ein häßlich Mal, daß er die Würde trug,
Die dir entrissen worden, und ich selbst
Hab' ihm die Fahne mit Verdruß geschwenkt.   1425
Nach wohlerfochtnem Siege zogen wir
Hinauf gen Susa, wo die holde Braut,
Des Grafen Tochter, ihn erwartete.
Da fiel auf uns der Seuche böser Thau,
Die Männer sanken auf dem Weg dahin,   1430
Nicht einzeln, nein, in Schwaben hingemäht,
Und nicht erhielt der besten Ärzte Kunst
Des Herzogs junges Leben: zu Trient
Liegt er begraben; seinen Leib hat so
Das Gift verzehret, daß wir selbst sein Herz   1435
Nicht mit uns brachten in das Vaterland.
Noch in der Stunde seines frühen Tods
Berief er mich und, von mir abgewandt,
Damit mir nicht sein Anhauch tödtlich sei,
Sprach er: „Das Banner, das du trägst, Warin,   1440
Bring meinem Bruder Ernst! Für ihn allein
Hab' ich's genommen und bewahrt, für ihn
Hab' ich's mit Ruhm bekränzt." Dies letzte Wort

Ergriff die Herzen. Trauernd und beschämt
Folgt' ihm zu Grab der Unsern kleiner Rest;   1445
Dann setzten wir, gehorsam dem Befehl
Des Sterbenden, sogleich den Heimzug fort.
Noch unterwegs, noch auf der Alpen Steig
Hat uns der Tod gezehntet; manche Leiche
Ward in das Felsgeklüft hinabgestürzt.   1450
Wir aber bringen dir dein brüderlich
Vermächtniß: nimm dies trauernde Panier!
Führ' uns zum Kampfe, führ' uns rasch voran,
Bevor noch lichter unser Häuflein wird!
Denn der noch jetzo blühend vor dir steht,   1455
Trägt schon vielleicht in sich der Seuche Keim,
Und besser fällt ein Mann in offner Schlacht,
Als daß er auf dem Krankenlager fault.

Ernst.

O herrlich tret' ich in mein Herzogthum!
Des Vaters Mörder öffnet mir das Thor,   1460
Des Bruders Leichenzug ist mein Gefolg.
Komm, Adalbert! Mich schrecket nicht der Mord.
Folg' mir, Warin! Ich scheue nicht die Pest.

(Alle ab.)

Zweite Scene.

Mangolds Lager.

Graf Mangold und der Bischof Warmann treten auf.

Warmann.

Im Lager muß ich, Neffe, dich begrüßen:
Du gehst dein Schloß vorüber, lässest mich   1465

7—2

Zu Konſtanz harren; unaufhaltſam eilſt
Du an der Spitze deiner Kriegsmacht vor.

Mangold.

Mein Auftrag heiſcht ſo ſchleunigen Vollzug.

Warmann.

Und nicht gedenk' ich, dich darum zu ſchmälen.
Durch Regenſchauer und durch Sonnenſchein   1470
Iſt mächtig dir das Glück herangereift;
Selbſt was noch jüngſt im fernſten Gebiet
Der Wünſche lag, was ein bedachter Sinn,
Der Kühnes meidet, ſtill in ſich verſchloß,
Iſt jetzt uns überraſchend nah gerückt   1475
Und will vernehmlich ausgeſprochen ſein.

Mangold.

Die günſt'ge Stunde werd' uns nicht verſäumt!
Was iſt's?

Warmann.

Indeß die kaiſerliche Huld
Das Schickſal Ernſts in deine Hand gelegt,
Indeß der wüſte Friedensſtörer ſchon   1480
Von deinen Schaaren faſt umſchloſſen iſt,
Indeß verkündet jedem ſchwäb'ſchen Gau
Ein dumpf Geläute Herzog Hermanns Tod.
Wer ſoll nun Herzog werden? Wem vertraut
Der Kaiſer? Welches Haus in Schwaben kennt   1485
Er als das treueſte? Für welches ſpricht
Das älteſte Recht, das neueſte Verdienſt?

Mangold.

Daß unsres vom erlauchten Burkhard stammt,
Daß es in Schwaben Herzogswürde trug,
Wohl weiß ich's und du selber schaltest oft   1490
Den kühnen Stolz, den ich darob gezeigt.

Warmann.

Ich schalt, was sich zur Unzeit offen gab.
Doch, wenn du nun den letzten Abkömmling
Des welken Fürstenstammes niederwirfst,
Wenn über dem zertretnen Wappenschild   1495
Du siegreich stehest und den deinen hebst,
Dann ...

Eine Wache tritt auf.

Wache.

Herr, ein fremder Kriegsmann bittet euch
Um Zutritt und um sicheres Geleit.

Mangold.

Bring ihn!

(Die Wache ab.)

Warmann.

Brauch' Vorsicht, Neffe!

Mangold.

Was soll mir
Der einzle Mann?   1500

(Werner tritt auf.)

Wer bist du?

Werner.

Kennst du mich?

Warmann.

Verwegner!

Mangold.

Wenn die Reue nicht dich treibt,
Welch toller Muth führt dich vor mein Gezelt?

Werner.

So ist's doch wahr, was ich nicht glauben wollte,
Bis ich mit eignen Augen es gesehn,
Daß du, Graf Mangold, dem verwandtes Blut 1505
Mit meinem durch die Adern rollt, daß du
Den Herzog, deinen rechten Herrn, nicht bloß
Verlassen hast, nein, daß du ihn verfolgst,
Daß du an der Verfolger Spitze stehst!

Mangold.

Mit welchem Recht du mich zur Rede stellst,   1510
Das möcht' ich wissen.

Werner.

Mit dem Recht des Bluts.
Es rühmen sich die Männer des Geschlechts,
Von dem sie stammen, und ruhmwürdig ist's,
Wenn Kraft und Tugend weithin sich vererbt,
Wenn vor dem Sohn des Vaters Beispiel glänzt, 1515
Wenn unter Brüdern edler Wettkampf brennt,
Wenn jeder eifersüchtig wacht und ringt
Für solchen Adels unbefleckten Glanz.
Und daraus fließt das Recht mir und die Pflicht,
Dich abzumahnen von verkehrter Bahn.   1520

Mangold.

Geziemt es dir, mich abzumahnen, dir,

Dem Landsverwiesnen, dem Geächteten,
Der unsres Stammes Auswurf ist ...

Werner.

Dem du

Ins Auge nicht zu blicken dich erkeckst.
Dein Blut, das ich gemahnt, hat sich empört   1525
Und hat die Wange dir mit Scham gefärbt:
Folg' dieser Regung, laß den bessern Trieb
Dich ganz ergreifen! Sei der Väter werth!
Ja, Mangold, wenn du nicht den Feinden Ernsts
Mit Leib und Seele schon verfangen bist,   1530
Wenn dir zur Ehre noch die Rückkehr blieb,
So tritt zurück, aufrichtig, sonder Scheu!
Die Lehn, die dich verpflichten, gieb sie heim!
Die eitle Gnadenkette, wirf sie ab!
Der schnöden Hauptmannschaft, die dich entehrt,   1535
Die deinen Stamm befleckt, entschlage dich!
Der Dienst der Freiheit ist ein strenger Dienst;
Er trägt nicht Gold, er trägt nicht Fürstengunst,
Er bringt Verbannung, Hunger, Schmach und Tod.
Und doch ist dieser Dienst der höchste Dienst;   1540
Ihm haben unsre Väter sich geweiht,
Ihm hab' auch ich mein Leben angelobt,
Er hat mich viel gemühet, nie gereut.
Für diesen Dienst, Graf Mangold, werb' ich dich:
Du wirst mir folgen.   1545

Warmann.

Halt, Vermessener!

Willst du Verrath hier stiften? Hoff' es nicht!
Die Schaaren, die du rings gelagert siehst,
Sind treu dem Kaiser wie Graf Mangold selbst.

Werner.

Mit diesen Söldnern hab' ich kein Geschäft;
Sie mögen thun, wofür man sie bezahlt. 1550
Auch hab' ich nichts mit dir: du bist ein Mönch,
Du bist ein todter Schößling unsres Stamms;
An dir nicht üb' ich der Verwandtschaft Recht.
Zu Mangold sprech' ich: er vielleicht wird einst
Stammvater eines grünenden Geschlechts; 1555
Drum ziemt es mir zu sorgen, daß er nicht
Verräther zeuge, Schranzen, Miethlinge.

Warmann.

Graf Mangold, kaiserlicher Feldhauptmann,
Zu lange schon hörst du es mit Geduld,
Wie dieser Freche, dieser Rasende 1560
Dich selbst und deines Amtes Würde schmäht;
Zu lange schon mißbraucht er dein Geleit,
Das dem Rechtlosen du nicht schuldig bist.

Mangold.

Von hinnen, Werner! Du erschienst zu spät:
Ich bin geschleudert und ihr seid zermalmt. 1565

Werner.

Ich geh'. Erfüllt hab' ich der Mahnung Pflicht;
Noch eine heischet unser Stamm von mir,
Auch der will ich genügen. Wenn dem Aar
Der Seinen eines aus den Lüften fällt,
So schießt er nieder und vertilgt's: wenn du 1570
Mir in der Schlacht begegnest, sieh dich vor!

(Ab. Mangold und Warmann in das Gezelt.)

Dritte Scene.

Burg Falkenſtein.

Ernſt allein, am Fenſter.

Ernſt.

Es iſt die Zeit jetzt, wo im offnen Land
Das reife Ährenfeld den Schnittern winkt,
Wo in den ſonnigen, belebten Gaun
Allwärts geerntet wird und eingeheimſt.   1575
Ich bin vom Feld der Ernten ausgeſperrt,
Bin eingeſchloſſen in der Wildniß hier
Und blicke von dem Felſen dieſer Burg
Hinunter in den Abgrund, wo der Strom
Durch Trümmer und geſtürzte Föhren toſt;   1580
Die Tannenwälder überſchau' ich, die
Im Winter grün ſind und im Sommer welk.
Mir iſt kein andres Ernteſeſt bereit,
Als wo die Schwerter ſtatt der Sicheln ſind
Und wo ich ſelbſt die falbe Ähre bin.   1585
Der Thürmer bläſt. O möcht' es Werner ſein!
Der Abend dunkelt und mir bangt um ihn.
Er iſt's. Ja, nicht gefangen ſein kann der;
Die Feſſeln ſprängen ab von ſeinem Arm,
Die Schlöſſer klirrten auf vor ſeinem Hauch: 1590
Die Freiheit mögt ihr binden, dieſen nicht.

Werner tritt auf; ter Saal füllt ſich mit Kriegsleuten Ernſts.

Werner.

Herein, herein, ihr Männer! Kommt und hört!
Euch alle gehet meine Kundſchaft an:

Wir sind umzingelt, jeder Weg verbaut,
Und kaum bin ich hieher noch durchgeschlüpft.   1595
Ja, dieser Kaiser schreitet raschen Schritt;
Nichts rettet uns, als schleuniger Entscheid.
Schon weiß ich nicht zu schätzen ihre Zahl,
Und jeder Tag verstärket Mangolds Schaar.
Uns ist der Zuwachs abgeschnitten, wir   1600
Sind unsern Freunden aus dem Blick gerückt!
Die uns erwarten, haben nicht Gewähr,
Ob wir noch stehn, ob wir zertreten sind;
Noch stehn wir und noch ist uns freigestellt,
Zu wählen zwischen Übergab' und Kampf,   1605
Und noch getröst' ich mich der Möglichkeit,
Daß wir in einer heißen, blut'gen Schlacht
Den Feind zernichten und, mit Sieg gekrönt,
Vorbrechen in das Land, das uns erharrt.
Wenn jetzt wir zaudern, bleibt uns keine Wahl,   1610
Als zwischen Übergab' und Hungertod:
Entschließt euch, Männer! Soll's gekämpfet sein?

Warin.

Zum Kampf begehren wir.

Die Andern.

Zum Kampf! zum Kampf!

Ernst.

Ist einer unter euch, dem eine Braut,
Ein Weib, ein Kind das Leben kostbar macht,   1615
Er zieh' in Frieden! Nicht verdenk' ich's ihm,
Nicht heisch' ich so verzweifelten Entschluß.
Ihr schweigt und steht. So ruf' auch ich: Zum Kampf!

Der erste Morgenschein find' uns bereit!
Ein Jeder rüste sich, so gut er kann!   1620
Manch Waffenstück noch hängt in diesem Saal,
Das unser Wirth uns willig überläßt.

Werner.

Du selber, Herzog, bist noch unbewehrt
Und jedem bloßgegeben, der dich sucht;
Laß mich dich wappnen für den heißen Tag! 1625

Ernst.

Ist's eine Sturmhaub', ist's ein Bruststück nur,
Genug, wenn es die Wetterseite schirmt.

Werner.

Die Brünne werd' um deine Brust geschnallt!
Den Kettenpanzer werf' ich über dich,
Den Sturmhut bind' ich unter deinem Kinn,   1630
Dein gutes Schwert häng' ich in diesen Gurt.
Sei dieser Stahl wie unsre Treue stark!
Sei'n diese Ringe fest wie unser Bund!

Adalbert tritt gewappnet aus der Schaar, einen Jüngling an der Hand.

Adalbert.

Zum Ritter umgewandelt, tret' ich jetzt
Vor dich, mein Herzog! Dir verdank' ich es,   1635
Daß mir der Helm die Stirne wieder deckt,
Daß mir das Schwert die Hüfte wieder schmückt.
Wenn auch den Arm die Jahre mir geschwächt,
Verschmäh' nicht meinen Dienst! Als Jüngling auch
Geb ich mich dir: sieh! dieser ist mein Sohn;   1640
Er sei der Deine! Aus dem Klosterzwang
Hat er sich losgerissen, Waffenwerk

Hat er mit Fleiß erlernet. Nimm ihn hin!
Verjüngt empfängſt du mich, unſchuldig noch
Und unbefleckt von deines Vaters Blut. 1645

Ernſt.

Ich nehm' ihn. Füg' es Gott, daß ich ihn dir
Zurück kann geben, wie ich ihn empfieng!

Werner.

Der ich bis jetzt als Kriegsknecht dir gedient,
Gewappnet als ein Ritter tret' auch ich
Dir nun zur Seite, denn ein ſolcher Kampf 1650
Steht uns bevor, wobei es ſich verlohnt,
Im vollen Kriegesſchmucke zu erſcheinen.
Beneiden aber muß ich dieſen Mann,
Der dir ein doppelt Leben widmen darf.
Laß dir erzählen einen luſt'gen Schwank, 1655
Weil jetzt die Zeit iſt, Schwänke zu erzählen!
Als Kaiſer Heinrich einſt zu Regensburg
Aufs Jagen ausritt, gab er den Befehl,
Daß keiner von den Herren ſeines Hofs
Sich folgen laſſe mehr denn einen Knecht. 1660
Gleichwohl kam ihm der Graf von Abensberg
Mit drei und dreißig Reiſigen getrabt,
Ein rüſtig Häuflein, ſauber angethan,
Die Rößlein wohl geſattelt und gezäumt.
Da ſprach der Kaiſer: „Iſt euch unbekannt, 1665
Daß ihr nur einen Diener bringen ſollt?"
Der Graf darauf: „Nur einen bring' ich mit."
„Wer ſind die Andern?" „Meine Söhne ſind's;
Sie alle ſchenk' ich und befehl' ich euch.
Sie ſeien euch im Frieden eine Zier, 1670

Im Krieg ein Beistand! Laß' es Gott gedeihn!"
So sprach der Graf. O wär' ich reich wie er!
O könnt' ich dir so vielfach Leben weihn!
So aber steh' ich einsam auf der Welt;
Von meinem Stamm hab' ich mich losgesagt,   1675
Geschleift ist meiner Väter alte Burg,
Kein Haus hab' ich, kein Weib und keinen Sohn:
Nichts hab' ich dir zu bieten, als mich selbst.
In meines Lebens ungeschwächter Kraft,
Im Stolz der Freiheit, in des Herzens Gluth,   1680
Im Klirren dieser Waffen werf' ich mich
Dir in die Arme, dein bis in den Tod.

Ernst.

Hat je ein Herzog solche Schaar geführt,
So treuergebne, so hochherzige?
Ja, meine Würde fühl' ich; anders nicht   1685
Darf ich euch führen, als in Fürstentracht,
Damit ich, siegend oder sterbend, so
Erscheine, wie es eurem Herzog ziemt.
Erkennen soll man mich, damit das Schwert,
Das mich begehret, keinen trifft von euch.   1690
Ein Scharlachmantel hängt an jener Wand;
Legt mir ihn um! Es ist ein fürstlich Kleid.

Abalbert (indem er Ernsten den Mantel umlegt).
Dein Vater trug's auf der unsel'gen Jagd.
Die Zeit hat es entfärbt.

Ernst.

                    Dies blasse Roth
Ist echte Farbe meines Mißgeschicks.   1695

Warin.

Den Schild hier, drauf das Wappen eures Stamms
Erbleicht ist, trug der tapfre Hermann einst.
Er würd' euch angeboten, gält' uns nicht
Für schlimmes Zeichen solch erloschnes Bild.

Ernst.

Gieb her! Der Letzte meines Stamms, geh' ich   1700
Der Schlacht entgegen, die entscheiden wird,
Ob dieser welke Scharlach neu erblühn,
Dies trübe Wappen neu erglänzen soll.

Werner.

Heil unsrem Herzog!

Die Andern.

Heil dem Herzog Ernst!

ARGUMENT TO ACT V.

Mangold cannot storm the rock-bound castle, and is obliged to wait until the enemy shall be forced by hunger to sally forth. Meanwhile the Emperor is approaching, anxious to end the struggle, being hard pressed in the east by the Hungarians, and in the west by Odo of Champagne, who has again risen in revolt, and is striving for the Italian crown. An outpost announces an attack and an engagement; Mangold orders a retreat to more advantageous ground. Ernest and his friends appear, devote themselves with enthusiasm to death or victory, and rush into the fight; this is viewed from a height by Adalbert, who has been posted there to give guidance and warning. Ernest and his men break through the first rank of the enemy, the second advances; Werner smites like an angel of death; Mangold is wounded, but recovers himself. After a brief rest Ernest's men, with sadly diminished numbers, renew the struggle; they are surrounded, but succeed in effecting a retreat. Ernest appears, leading his wounded friend Werner, who expires in his arms, after which he no longer cares to avail himself of a way of escape which is offered by Adalbert. The rest of his men appear, struggling with their pursuers; Mangold follows, and calls upon him to surrender, as now that Werner is dead he may be pardoned by the Emperor. But Ernest casts mantle and shield over the body of his friend, and engages with Mangold, who falls; he is himself immediately afterwards slain by Mangold's followers. Warin appears, bearing the rescued banner, which he raises with his last dying strength. Konrad and Gisela now arrive and learn what has happened; the ban of excommunication is to be removed from Ernest and Werner, that they may receive a Christian burial. News is brought by Hugo of Egisheim of the death in battle of Odo of Champagne, whose head Duke Gozelo of Lorraine has sent in an urn as a present to Konrad. Hugo is also the bearer, from the deceased King Rudolf, of the insignia of Burgundy; Konrad assigns the hard-won prize to his son Henry, who shudders in receiving it. Gisela finds consolation for her son's tragic death in the assurance that the memory of his devoted loyalty to his friend will live on in the hearts of the people, and that the sacred bond of their friendship is now renewed and perfected in a higher world.

Fünfter Aufzug.

Mangold und Warmann.

Mangold.

Der Kaiser kommt und noch ist nichts geschehn. 1705
Er drängt zu sehr; kaum bin ich angelangt,
Schon blickt er ob der Schulter mir herein.

Warmann.

Das ist das mächt'ge Wirken dieses Manns,
Daß überall mit seiner Gegenwart
Er jedes fördert und im Schwung erhält.   1710
Jetzt muß ihm doppelt angelegen sein,
Daß du den Aufstand schnell und gründlich tilgst,
Seit Odo von Champagne sich erhob
Und selbst nach der ital'schen Krone langt,
Die ihm der Erzbischof von Mailand beut.   1715
Wird Ernst gewaltig hier und Odo dort,
Und bleibt der Ungar forthin ungestraft,
So steht es schlimm mit kaiserlicher Macht.

Mangold.

Und doch, kann ich's erzwingen? Soll mein Volk
Anrennen gegen jene Felsenwand?   1720
Sie halten keinen Mond sich auf der Burg,

Sie ſind verloren, kommen ſie ins Feld,
Gewiß iſt ihr Verderben. Nur die Friſt
Soll er mir gönnen, die nothwendigſte.

Warmann.

Er weiß, wie leicht die Stunde Neues bringt,　1725
Und darum drängt er.

Eine Wache tritt auf.

Wache.

Herr, ein Überfall.
Die Vorwacht iſt im Handgemeng, ſie weicht.
Sie bringen wüthend vor.

Mangold.

Willkommne Mähr'.
Zum Rückzug blaſt das Horn! Dort unterhalb,
Am Schlund des Thales, ordne ſich die Schaar!　1730
Dort wird ſich brechen dieſer tolle Sturm.
Die Zelte laßt! Bald wieder ſind wir hier.
Du, Oheim, gehſt, den Kaiſer zu empfahn;
Sag' ihm, ſein Auftrag ſei vollzogen! Marſch!

(Beide ab mit Gefolge.)

Kampfgetümmel hinter der Scene. Flüchtlinge eilen über die Bühne. Dann erſcheinen Ernſt, Werner, Adalbert, Warin und ihre Schaar, mit ge-zogenen Schwertern.

Werner.

Die Schlacht geht friſch, die Schwerter ſtehn im Saft.
Es kämpft ſich raſch, wo Muth die Feldmuſik,　1736
Verzweiflung das Panier iſt.

Ernſt.

Dorthin ſchaut!

U　　　　　　　　　　　　　　8

Werner.

Ja, dort ist Arbeit, dort ist Heldenwerk;
Lebend'ge Mauern, sechsfach aufgeführt;
Es muß ein starker Strom, ein wilder sein,   1740
Dem man so mächt'gen Damm erbaut. Brecht durch!

Adalbert.

Ein Posten bleib' uns auf dem Hügel hier!
Man übersieht von ihm das ganze Thal;
Im Rücken droht Gefahr.

Ernst.

Du, Adalbert,
Bleib selbst und warne! Keiner kennt wie du   1745
Die Gegend.

Adalbert.

Ist mir nicht das Heil gegönnt,
Für Herzog Ernst zu stürzen ins Gefecht?
Soll ich unrühmlich auf der Warte stehn?
Mein Sohn, der du im Kampfe mich vertrittst,
Du bist ein Lehrling in der Waffenkunst;   1750
Jetzt tummle dich! Es ist dein erster Strauß,
Es kann der letzte sein: an einem Tag
Mußt du erringen deine Meisterschaft.
Schwing hoch dein Schwert, wirf sicher deinen Speer,
Triff unsre Feinde, triff den Herzog nicht!   1755

Warin.

Zur Heilung, meine Kranken, führ' ich euch!
Man wird euch zapfen euer giftig Blut,
Man wird euch schneiden euer bös Geschwür,
Man wird euch kühlen euern Fieberbrand.

Der Fahne reiß' ich ab den Trauerflor;   1760
Jetzt ist die Witwe wieder eine Braut,
Jetzt geht's hinab zum lust'gen Hochzeitreihn.

Ernst.

Ein Held, der in das Schlachtgewühl sich wirft,
Soll an die Frau gedenken, der er dient:
O Edelgard, geliebte Gottesbraut,   1765
Aus deinen Schleiern blick' auf mich herab,
Dein ernstes Bild begeistre mich zum Tod!

Werner.

Allmächt'ger, Gott des Friedens und des Zorns,
Der du den Bach anschwellen kannst zum Meer,
Die stille Luft erregen zum Orkan,   1770
Laß jetzt auch unsre, dieser Männer, Kraft
So riesenhaft anwachsen und erschwellen,
Daß uns das Ungeheure möglich sei!
Hinein! für Herzog Ernst!

Die Andern.

Für Herzog Ernst!

(Alle ab, außer Adalbert mit einigen Kriegsleuten.)

Adalbert.

Hin braust der Sturm, die Wolke fährt dahin. 1775
Wenn aber so der Menschheit Kraft und Gluth
Dahinfährt ohne Wiederkehr, dann bebt
Ein menschlich Herz. Da stürmen sie hinab,
Und drunten schon die Lanzen vorgestreckt,
Daran verbluten soll der Helden Brust.   1780
Von Raubgevögel wimmelt schon die Luft.
Und durch die Wälder hallet Wolfsgeheul.

8—2

Ein Kriegsmann.

Jetzt, jetzt sind sie zusammen.

Andrer.

Welch ein Stoß!

Dritter.

Sie brechen durch.

Abalbert.

Ha! sind das Männer? Sind
Das Wellen, die des Schwimmers Arm zerwirft? 1785
Durchbrochen ist das erste Glied.

Kriegsmann.

Schon tritt
Das zweite vor.

Andrer.

Seht mir den Werner, seht!

Abalbert.

Ein Todesengel, uns zum Hort gesandt,
Ragt er aus allen vor; sein blitzend Schwert
Fährt aus den Wolken, nicht den einzeln Mann   1790
Schlägt er, er schlägt die ganze Schaar.

Kriegsmann.

Wer liegt
Am Boden dort, zerspellt den blanken Schild?

Abalbert.

Der Mangold ist's.

Kriegsmann.

Er rafft sich wieder auf;
Er führt die dritte Reih' heran.

Andrer.

O schaut!
Die Unsern rasten.   1795

Dritter.

Traun, kein Wunder ist's,
Wenn sie ermüdet sind.

Erster.

Sie sammeln sich.
O! die sind stark geschmolzen.

Zweiter.

Seht den Wall
Von Leichnamen!

Dritter.

O seht den Strom von Blut!

Adalbert.

Der Werner aber steht vor seinem Trupp,
Wie mit gespreizten Fittigen der Aar   1800
Die Brut umschirmt, wenn über seinem Horst
Ein fremder Vogel kampfandrohend schwebt.
Jetzt lüftet er die Schwingen! jetzt.   Gebt Acht!

Kriegsmann.

Sie holen aus, sie brechen furchtbar los.

Andrer.

Jetzt gilt's.   1805

Dritter.

Jetzt ist's ihr Letztes.

Abalbert.

.   Jetzt wär's Zeit,
Der Bürde los zu werden, die mich drückt.

Kriegsmann.

Sie sind umflügelt.

Andrer.

Sie sind mitten drin.

Abalbert.

Kaum seh' ich noch des Herzogs roth Gewand.
Das Banner schwankt, ein Segelbaum im Sturm.

Kriegsmann.

Dort blickt man durch.   1810

Andrer.

Sie sind auf einen Knaul
Gerollt.

Abalbert.

Der Werner stemmt sich wie ein Mann,
Den eine Riesenschlang' umflochten hält,
Ihn selbst und seine Söhne, dem sie schon
Den Zahn ans Herz gesetzt, der sich aufbäumt
Und mit der letzten Spannung seiner Kraft   1815
Die gräßliche Umkettung von sich drückt.

Kriegsmann.

Der Kampfplatz schließt sich wieder.

Andrer.

Jetzt sind sie
Verschlungen.

Dritter.

Nein, sie reißen sich hervor,
Den Rückzug haben sie sich frei gekämpft.

Adalbert.

Wo ist der Werner?   1820

Kriegsmann.

Wo? Ich seh' ihn nicht.

Andrer.

Dort ist er.

Dritter.

Weh! sie führen ihn herauf;
Er ist getroffen.

Adalbert.

Ernst hat ihn im Arm,
Auf seiner Schulter hängt des Recken Haupt.
Die Feinde stürmen nach; vergeblich wehrt
Der kleine Rest so großer Übermacht.   1825

Ernst, ten verwundeten Werner führend, tritt auf.

Ernst.

Nicht weiter bring' ich ihn; auf diesen Stein
Muß ich ihn niederlassen. Adalbert,
Hast du kein Kraut, das diese Wunden stillt?
O spar' es nicht für deinen Sohn! Der ist
Schon längst erschlagen. Rette meinen Freund! 1830
Du giebst den Vater mir, den du mir nahmst.

92   Ernst, Herzog von Schwaben.   [ACT V.

Abalbert.

Reiß mir die grauen Locken aus! Versuch's,
Ob sie ihm stopfen seines Blutes Qualm!

Werner.

Ist's Leben noch nicht gar und blutet doch
Aus so viel Wunden? Soll mich dieses Volk   1835
Lebendig fangen? Brüder, stecht mich todt!
Kann ich noch leben und bin so zerhaun?
Bin ich ein Wurm, lebt jedes Stück von mir?
Hört ihr? sie kommen. Ernst, du bist mein Freund,
Schlag mir den Schädel ein!   1840
Jetzt reißt's. Gelobt sei Gott, ich sterbe frei!
Ernst, rette dich . . .

(Stirbt.)

Ernst.

                Er stirbt, der Werner stirbt!
Die Lüfte wehen noch, die Sonne scheint,
Die Ströme rauschen, und der Werner todt!

Abalbert.

Er ist geborgen. Herzog, laß ihn los!   1845
Schon schwirret das Gefecht um unser Ohr;
Auch dort im Rücken bringt der Feind herauf.
Komm, folg' mir schnell! Ich weiß noch einen Pfad,
Durch Felsenklüfte schleicht er sich hinan.
Laß mich dich retten, komm!   1850

Ernst.

                Ich wurzle hier.

120

Abalbert.

Komm, zaudre nicht! Die Rettung ist gewiß.
Ein Felsstück, das wir rollen in die Schlucht,
Sperrt die Verfolger aus.

Ernst.

          Du drängst umsonst.

Abalbert.

Sie ziehn sich rings herum: jetzt ist's zu spät.
*(Der Rest von Ernsts Kriegsleuten erscheint, mit den Verfolgenden
kämpfend.)*

Hieher, ihr Brüder! Weichet fürder nicht!   1855
Hier um den Herzog! Wehrt euch auf den Tod!
In manchem ist noch eine Neige Bluts,
Noch mancher hält sich aufrecht wie ein Mann.
Rührt diesen Todten an! Das kräftigt euch.
Brecht ihm die Zähn' aus, sät sie in den Grund,   1860
So wachsen uns Geharnischte hervor!
    Graf Mangold tritt auf mit Kriegsvolk.

Mangold.

Dort steht er. O wie klein sein Häuflein ist!
Einst war er Herzog, es erbarmt mich sein,
Und seine Mutter hielt mein Schwert umfaßt.
Ergieb dich! Widerstand ist Raserei: 1865
Sie bluten alle, die dir übrig sind.
Todt ist der Werner, todt ist Kunrads Feind,
Die Fackel und das Heerhorn alles Streits;
Jetzt kann der Kaiser dir verzeihn.

Ernst.

             Meinst du?
Nein, wenn der Letzte fällt, ich fechte fort.   1870

War ich sonst träge, jetzt bin ich ein Held.
Hier muß ich sterben, bei dem Todten hier,
Hier hast' ich, hier ist meines Lebens Ziel,
Hier ist der Markstein meiner Tage, hier
Ist meine Heimat, hier mein Haus und Hof,   1875
Mein Erbgut, meine Blutsverwandtschaft, hier
Mein Wappenschild und hier mein Herzogthum.

(Er wirft Schild und Fürstenmantel auf den todten Werner.)

Mit diesem Mann hab' ich mein Leben lang
Geeifert und gewettet in der Treu',
Der Tod nur hat dem Wettkampf noch gefehlt: 1880
Jetzt stürzt er in die Schlacht und stirbt für mich.
Nicht laß' ich ihm den Preis; sterb ich für ihn,
Dann greifen beide nach dem Siegeskranz.
Halt vor!

(Er dringt auf Mangold ein.   Gefecht.)

Mangold.

Verzweifelter!

(Sinkt getroffen zurück.)

Gott steh mir bei!

(Stirbt.)

(Mangold wird weggetragen, seine Krieger dringen auf Ernst ein.   Gefecht.
Ernst fällt.   Der Kampf hört auf.)

Adalbert.

Der Herzog sinkt.   1885

Ernst.

Die Welt hat uns verworfen;
Der Himmel nimmt uns auf. Mein Werner!

(Stirbt.)

Adalbert.

Geächtet ward die Treue von der Welt;
Zum Himmel, ihrer Heimat, schwebt sie auf.
So grauenvoll hat dieser Kampf geendet,
So blutig. Ich allein, der sich den Tod   1890
So heiß ersehnt, muß ohne Wunde sein,
Als jene, die des Sohnes Tod mir schlug.
Tragt, Männer, diese Leichen weg! Der Tod
Versöhnet Feinde. Laßt sie nicht dem Wolf
Zur Beute, legt sie unter dies Gezelt!   1895
Ihr zögert? Ha! weil sie geächtet sind.
O thut es doch! Der Priester spricht euch los,
Gott wird's verzeihen.

(Die Leichen werden in das Zelt getragen.)

Werft den Vorhang zu!

Warin tritt fechtend auf, das Banner im Arme.

Kriegsleute.

Das Banner her!

Warin.

So lang ich athme, nicht.
Ich hab' es durchgehaun durch euer Heer,   1900
Vom Fels bin ich gesprungen, durch den Strom
Hab' ich's gerissen. Lebt der Herzog Ernst?

Adalbert.

In diesem Zelte liegt er todt.

Warin.

Hier sei
Das Banner aufgepflanzt! Hieher gehört's,

Die Herzogsfahne vor das Herzogszelt.   1905
Was ist's? Das Schwert entsinket meiner Hand,
Die Kniee brechen ...

(Er sinkt an der aufgepflanzten Fahne todt nieder.)

Adalbert.

Treuer Fähnrich du!

Ein Ritter mit einigen Kriegsleuten tritt auf.

Ritter.

Der Kaiser naht. Es ruhe jeder Kampf!

Adalbert.

Hier ist schon Friede, hier ist tiefe Ruh'.

Der Kaiser, Gisela, Heinrich, Warmann, mit Gefolge, treten auf.

Kunrad.

Was ist geschehn? Wo ist mein Hauptmann? 1910

Adalbert.

Dort
Trägt man ihn todt hinab.

Warmann.

O Hoffnungen!

Gisela.

Wo ist mein Sohn?

Adalbert (das Zelt aufdeckend).

Er schläft in Freundesarm.

(Wirft es wieder zu.)

Giſela.

Das war mein Ernſt, er war's, ich hab's geſehn.
Der Hermann tobt und nun auch dieſer tobt,
Auch dieſer, dieſer, der mein Liebling war!   1915
Weil er die meiſten Schmerzen mir gemacht,
Darum hab' ich am meiſten ihn geliebt.

Kunrad.

Herr Biſchof, unbedenklich werdet ihr
Die Todten von dem Kirchenbann befrein,
Damit wir chriſtlich ſie beerdigen.   1920

Warmann.

Es ſoll geſchehn.

Giſela.

Die Kerzen mögt ihr neu
Anzünden, das erloſchne Leben nicht.

(Zu Adalbert.)

Du, der du Wächter dieſer Todten biſt,
Ich kenne dich, ſag' mir, wie ſtarb mein Ernſt?

Adalbert.

Er ſtarb den Heldentod, den Freundestod: 1925
Der Werner ſtarb für ihn, für Wernern er;
Er wich von ſeines Freundes Leiche nicht,
Bis er als Leiche ſelbſt darniederſank.

Giſela.

O dieſen Werner, dem ich oft gezürnt,
Weil er den Sohn mir ins Verderben riß,   1930
Ich muß ihn lieben, weil er meinen Sohn
Geliebt hat und für ihn erſchlagen iſt.

Abalbert.

Für ihn erwürgt ist auch mein einzig Kind
Und, leb' ich selbst noch, ist's nicht meine Schuld.
Geschehen ist, zu was du mich erweckt: 1935
Drum wenn der Kaiser mir die Freiheit läßt,
So gönne du mir, daß ich meinen Sohn
Bestatte, daß ich bei des Jünglings Grab
Jetzt dürfe rasten und das meine baun!

Graf Hugo von Egisheim mit Gefolge tritt auf.

Hugo.

Erhabner Kaiser, eures Weges Spur   1940
Bin ich in großer Eile nachgereist,
Um mich der Botschaft zu entledigen,
Die mir so wichtig und so ernst bedünkt,
Daß ich es wag', auf dieser blut'gen Statt
Noch länger festzuhalten euren Schritt.   1945
Die Urne hier, die dieser Kriegsmann trägt,
Schickt euch zum Gruße Herzog Gozelo
Von Lothringen, ein grauenvoll Geschenk:
Sie birgt das Haupt des Odo von Champagne!
Der Herzog schlug's ihm ab in wilder Schlacht,   1950
Dem Unglücksel'gen, den ich Freund genannt
Und dessen Kühnheit ich umsonst gewarnt.
Ein zweites Angebinde sendet euch
Der König Rudolf, der in Gott entschlief;
Hinscheidend übergab er's meiner Hand: 1955
Es sind die Reichskleinode von Burgund,
Die Krone sammt dem Scepter und dem Speer
Des heil'gen Moriz. Nehmt sie huldreich an!

Kunrad.

Nicht mich, den König Heinrich ſchmückt damit!

(Es geſchieht.)

O Knabe, wüßteſt du, wie ſauer mir　　　1960
Die Frucht geworden, die du ſpielend pflückſt!

Heinrich.

Mich ſchauert's, Vater, unter dieſem Schmuck.

Giſela.

Das alſo, dieſer Reif und dieſer Stab,
Das ſind die hohen Dinge, derenthalb
So edles Leben hingeblutet iſt!　　　　　1965
O Kaiſer, ſtaunen wird die Folgezeit,
Wenn ſie vernimmt vom Aufſchwung deiner Macht,
Von deines Herrſcherarmes Feſtigkeit;
Doch rühren wird es ſpät noch manches Herz,
Wenn man die Kunde ſinget oder ſagt　　　1970
Vom Herzog Ernſt und Werner, ſeinem Freund,
Von ihrer Treue, die der Tod bewährt.
Ihr Männer, die ihr hier im Kreiſe ſteht
Und ſo mit tiefem Mitleid blickt auf mich,
Meint ihr, daß alles mir erſtorben ſei?　　1975
Hat ſo viel Wärme nicht ein Mutterherz,
Daß es beleben kann den todten Sohn?
Soll der mir todt ſein, deſſen Leben eins
Mit meinem iſt, den meine Bruſt geſäugt?
Nein, leben, leben ſoll mein treuer Ernſt;　1980
Fortleben wird er in dem Mund des Volks,
Er lebt in jedem fühlenden Gemüth,
Er lebet dort, wo reines Leben iſt.

Nicht wieder deckt mir dieſen Vorhang auf,
Darunter Leiche neben Leiche liegt!   1985
Dort oben öffnet ſich ein himmliſch Zelt,
Wo Freund in Freundes Arm erwacht und wo
Der Frühgealterte verjüngt erſcheint.

NOTES.

BOOKS REFERRED TO IN THE NOTES.

Eve's School German Grammar (uniform with the Wellington College French Grammar), *David Nutt*, 1880. The references are chiefly to the Syntax.

Aue's German Grammar. *W. and R. Chambers.*

Whitney's Compendious German and English Dictionary, with Notation of Correspondences and Brief Etymologies. *Macmillan & Co.*

NOTES.

Introductory Note. Poetic Diction. Before a poetical work is studied, the rules that determine the order of words (Eve's Germ. Gr., Syntax, 194 ff.; Aue's Germ. Gr., p. 15 ff.) should be so mastered, that the deviations from them in metrical composition, which are too frequent and varied to be pointed out in detail in a commentary, may be recognised by the student as giving to the style a distinctively poetic character, and may not lead him into errors in his own prose composition.—Not only should the archaic or poetic expressions or constructions, the chief of which are remarked upon in the notes, be carefully kept distinct from what is current in modern prose, but it should further be noticed that it is characteristic of poetry (i.e. of the higher style of diction generally), to make a freer and more frequent use of some modes of expression and construction which are not in themselves poetical, but would sound forced and affected if they recurred frequently in ordinary prose. A few such may here be pointed out:—The omission of the article, cf. Prol. 22, 35; 12, 72, 96, &c.: in 14, 60, 137, 295, 1242, 1305, &c., it would hardly be appropriate in plain prose.—The placing of the genitive before the noun it limits, Prol. 3, 20, 26, 28; 23, 47, &c.: as occurring in cases like Prol. 39; 130, 296, 590, 1018, &c., it would be out of place in any but a higher or poetical style. Least common of all is this construction with the objective genitive (i.e. one which marks the object of the action indicated by the governing substantive, cf. Eve, 78, 80), cf. Prol. 16; 134, 535, 1096, 1159, &c.—The use of the uninflected adj. before a neut. subst., 272, 763, 766, 923, &c.— The omission on the one hand (Prol. 1, 5, 15, 26, &c.), and the retention on the other (Prol. 27, wirfet; 132, 139, &c.), of the vowel *e*, chiefly to suit the metre, contrary to the usual practice in modern prose.—The similar omission of i (Prol. 11; 9, 74, &c.) is indicated by an apostrophe, and is often really more for the eye than the ear, the difference in pronunciation being hardly appreciable.—Other peculiarities and licences

9—2

more or less characteristic of poetic diction are remarked upon in the notes; cf. among others the position of the adj., Prol. 4, n.; the use of the conjunctive as imperative, Prol. 40, n.; the use of the imperf. indic. for the perf., 277, n., &c.

Prolog.

As regards the circumstances under which the Prologue was written, see the Introduction, p. xi.

Line 1. Spiel: here concrete, = Schauspiel, play, spectacle. Further on, in l. 39, it is abstract, =the subst. inf. Spielen.—euch vorübergehn: verbs compounded with vorüber or vorbei are in common prose constructed with a prep., as an, vor, and the dat., Er ging an mir vorbei, cf. 246.

3. Die längst hinab ist.... The ellipse of a verb of motion is common, where the idea of motion is conveyed by an adv. or adverbial expression, cf. 906, 1592; further 1899. It is especially frequent with the 'verbs of mood,' cf. 634, after which also other verbs than verbs of motion are often omitted, cf. 1499. In many cases however, of which the present and l. 701 may be regarded as examples, the ellipse (if we assume one at all) is rather logical than real, i.e. it lies in the thought rather than in the expression: there is no actual omission of a word or words necessary to complete the construction, an adv. of motion being simply used predicatively (as advs. of rest are commonly used, Er ist eben, &c.), generally in order to indicate the condition after the motion has taken place, as in Er ist fort, es ist vorbei, &c.—Strom is here of course acc., after the prep. in, indicating motion, cf. Prol. 26; 692.

4. Kämpfe, längst schon ausgekämpfte (sc. Kämpfe), lit., struggles, long ago fought-out ones, cf. 274, Des Augenblicks, des ewig wechselnden, of the ever changing moment, 892, andere Zeiten, strengere, 294, 451, &c. A construction peculiar to poetry, to be distinguished from the less exclusively poetical construction of the appositive uninflected adj., or participle used as adj. (Ein Gebirge, wüst und unbewohnt), and from that of the contracted rel. sentence,—e.g. here, Kämpfe, [welche][1] längst schon ausgekämpft [(worden) sind].

---

[1] Square brackets [ ] indicate a double reading, according as the letters or words enclosed in the brackets are read or omitted. Thus the above gives with the words in the square brackets the full, without them the contracted relative sentence.

6. 3ween Männer: zween (monosyll.), m., zwo, f., zwei, n., is the old declension, uniformly used by Uhland, but now surviving only in the dialects, of the nom. and acc. of the numeral zwei.—The word bieber (originally, useful, helpful) has generally, since its revival by Lessing, a slightly quaint or archaic character; it indicates frank and hearty, sometimes bluff, integrity, cf. 953.—fromm also meant originally, useful, helpful (hence still, frommen, 997, to be of use, profit), then generally, excellent, worthy, honest, &c. = wacker, brav (so Luke xix. 17, Ei tu frommer Knecht, 'Well thou good servant'; Luke xxiii. 50, ein guter frommer Mann, 'a good man and a just'); finally, in its present sense, pious, god-fearing; also innocent, harmless, cf. 285.

8. Preiswerthe Namen...: Preis means both *praise*, 870, *price*, and *prize*, 1882 (all four words coming through Fr. *prix*—O.Fr. *pris*, *preis*—fr. Lat. *pretium; prize*, reward of merit, however blending with, if its form be not taken from, *prize*, booty, fr. Fr. *prise*, fr. *prendre*, Lat. *prehendere*); preiswerth means both worthy of praise or honour, and also, worth the price, reasonable in price.

12. barniederliegt: the singular verb is explained by regarding Freiheit and Gesetz as closely connected ideas, forming a kind of unity in thought. There is also in German a tendency to make the verb agree with the nearest subject, especially when the verb precedes. Cf. 1045, 1514, and Eve's Germ. Gr., Syntax, 9, Obs. 1 and 2.

15. Daß, die fürs Vaterland...glühn. The demonstr. antecedent der, die, das is usually dispensed with, when it would be in the same case as the following rel. pron. (cf. below, Prol. 17; 1455, 1602), or when, though not in the same case, it would still be of the same form with it (i.e. when in the fem. or neut. sing., or in the plur., one stood in the nom. and the other in the acc., cf. 392, 914). The rel. pron. then used is always der, never welcher. For the neut. however was is used, not das.

17—18. Uhland probably had in mind the recent case of Joseph von Görres, who in 1819 published a work, *Deutschland und die Revolution*, and was in consequence compelled to fly to Switzerland. His after career however was such as Uhland would have been the last to regard as patriotic.—heißen is both tr., to call, and intr., to be called, to bear a name or character, cf. 6; here Retter hießen = für Retter erklärt or gehalten wurden, cf. 127.

20. Erblühen (blühen, to 'bloom'), 'spring up.' The prefix er has here its root meaning, 'out of, up,' indicating an emerging, or rising into being or activity, cf. erstehen, to arise, Prol. 47; erschließen, to open up, 199; ergehen, to go forth, 162. It thus often denotes the action

especially in its beginning, so erſchaffen, to begin to sound, to sound forth, 871, cf. 1409; erglänzen, to shine forth, 887; cf. also 67, 1772. Thus also in verbs formed from adjs. it indicates *becoming* or *causing to become*, cf. ergrauen, to grow gray, 188; erhellen, to make light, to light up, 702; erblaſſen, 1358; erſtarren, 191, &c.—wuchernb in ter Hölle Segen : wuchern, to grow luxuriantly, flourish. in marks the element in and through which the growth takes place.

21. Schergentienſt. Scherge, a lower officer of the law, bailiff, catch-poll; the executor of the will of a despot, satellite, myrmidon; hence now used chiefly in a bad sense. Schergentienſt thus means the service rendered by the servile tools of tyranny.

24. feſtgepflanzt (sc. haben). At the end of dependent sentences the auxiliaries haben and ſein are often omitted, both in poetry and prose, cf. 17, 70, 86, 231, &c. Less usual is the omission of a part of ſein used as copula, 677. Aue's Germ. Gr. § 285; Eve, 177.

25. ſo was formerly used for the rel. pron. in all genders and both numbers. It is common in Luther's Bible and in older poetry, Bittet für tie, ſo euch beleitigen unb verfolgen.

28. für is to be taken with wirfet; belebenb and fürternb are pres. participles used adverbially. förtern (fr. the obsol. förter, or fürter, 836) to further, promote, help on, cf. 1710; fürternt, helpfully, helping.

32. An allusion to the custom of the ancient Romans, still kept up in parts of Italy, of training vines up the elms, wreathed from tree to tree.

33. Heiligthum means both a sanctuary or holy place, and a sacred thing, the object of veneration, as in 763. Here it seems to mean *arae et foci*, 'hearths and homes,' all that is dear and sacred to a free people.

34. mit Gut unb Blut : with life and goods. For other examples of these alliterative combinations, in which German abounds, and in which the two words generally express nearly related, often identical ideas, cf. 506, n., 534, 1875, 1970.

35—36. The flight out of gloomy reality into the serene ideal sphere of art, was a favourite theme of Schiller; see e.g. Das Ideal unb tas Leben.

39—42. If the feelings of any present should be painfully touched by the dramatic presentation of this tragic story of a bygone time, let them find comfort in the glad occasion to-day celebrated, the re-establishment of a constitution based upon those great principles of liberty for which heroes have died.

39. wen..., ter getente. It is not strictly correct, in point of gram-

mar, to treat the pron. wer as 'a rel. pron. the antecedent of which is omitted or follows' (as Eve, 141, and others). The pron. wer,—classed with others as 'relative,' for want of a more distinctive term,—has never taken, and cannot take, under any circumstances, a grammatical antecedent; it does not 'relate' to an already defined or conceived sub-stantive notion, but rather contains in itself or points out a general or indefinite one. The original meaning of wer as a rel. (M.H.G. *swêr*, from *sô wêr*=wenn jemant) is: if any one, any one who, 'whoever.' ('Who' in this meaning is common in Shakspeare and in the Bible; 'Who steals my purse steals trash.') The case of ter that often follows in the main sentence is in no sense the 'antecedent' of wer, but an independent demonstrative, taking up the part of wer which has pre-ceded, and representing it in its further syntactical relations. It is not essential, though present usage generally requires it in ordinary prose, as contributing to clearness, when the case of wer in the dependent sen-tence requires to be represented in the following main sentence in a different case, as in the present passage and in 877. (Cf. '*Who* seems most sure, *him* soonest whirls she down.') In 689—91, the form of the sentence does not easily admit the insertion of the demonstr.; in 792, 1128, 1369, it is not necessary, ter in 1369 serving simply to give em-phasis. The pron. was, besides retaining its functions as the neut. of wer, has so far become an ordinary rel. pron. that it takes as a gram-matical antecedent certain words expressive of indefinite notions, as alles, nichts, viel, &c. In many cases where was (or one of the compound forms woraus = aus was, &c.) stands alone, we may understand either a following demonstrative, taking it up, or a real antecedent, cf. 757—9. Often however only the latter mode of filling up the construction is possible, as in 1550, 1935. Was as an ordinary relative comes under the rule explained in Prol. 15, n.

40. ter getente: the free use (see Introd. Note) of the 3rd pers. (still more that of the 1st pers. plur., cf. 198) of the pres. conjunctive as im-perative is characteristic of a poetical or elevated style. Cf. below, 51, and 178, 225, 1025, &c. In common prose and in the language of conver-sation it is less frequent (of course excepting the 3rd pers. plur. used for the 2nd pers., gehen Sie, &c.). Its place is often supplied by the employment of a verb of mood with the infinitive, as in 729, 1174, 1550, &c.—sich (dat.) zum Troste, as a consolation to himself, = zu seinem Troste, for his consolation, cf. 181, n.

42. Da mag er sehn: mögen here in its original but now almost obso-lete sense, =vermögen, to be able. So in 1591, 1921.—für was: cf. 1935,

ju was. More usual, and for careful composition as a rule preferable, are the compounded forms wofür (1550), wozu, &c. Sometimes however the uncompounded forms are used in order to throw more emphasis upon the pronoun.

44—5. treten...in bas Leben ein: find entrance into, and become realised in, the actual life of men.

45. In prose : als or für die höchsten achtet, cf. 1633.

46—49. It was in the time of reaction which followed the peace of 1815 that the constitution of Württemberg was re-established. (See Introduction, p. x.) King William I., under whom the final settlement took place, was for those times a remarkably moderate and liberal prince : in conversation with Uhland himself he had said that he entered with hearty good will into the free compact with his people just concluded.

52. Heil diesem König...! Heil (subst. fr. adj. heil, Eng. *hale* and *whole*), originally wholeness or health; then extended to mean welfare or happiness in general, cf. 991; also 'salvation,' cf. 1204, and Heiland, 'saviour.' As an invocation of blessing, it is less weakened down to a mere salutation or interjection than the Eng. 'hail,' cf. 1336, 1704.

Personen.

Gisela: pron. Gísèla, with the accent on the first syllable.—Söhne der Gisela erster Ehe: G's sons (lit. of, i.e.) by (her) first marriage. erster Ehe (gen. of origin, equiv. to aus erster Ehe) is attributive to Söhne,—as it were, first-marriage sons. It was really her second marriage; see Introduction, p. xix.—im Elsaß: Elsaß, as a neut. (cf. 142; sometimes also masc., which however Grimm condemns) is an exception to the rule that neut. names of countries are used without the article.—Reichsstände, 'estates of the empire,' used with regard to the 11th century, can only mean the nobles and dignitaries, ecclesiastical and secular, who at court and in various assemblies, Hoftage, Reichstage (cf. 257), &c., took an important part, though without any very fixed organization or well-defined rights, in the government of the empire. A Reichstag, or Diet, in the sense of a definite legal or administrative body, and Reichsstände, or members of the empire with a definite qualification to sit and vote in it, did not exist until a much later period.

Erster Aufzug.

Erste Scene.

Line 1. Die Sonne,... | Sie...: this repetition of the subject in the form of a pers. pron. (cf. 182) is poetical. A similar repetition, in the form of a demonstr. pron., der, die, das, may often be heard in animated conversation among the lower classes.

2. folgeschwer: more usually folgenschwer, heavy with consequences, momentous.

4—6. The coronation of the German Kings was celebrated in earlier times at Aachen, latterly at Frankfurt, once or twice at Regensburg. Henry's coronation really took place two years earlier than the date here assumed. See Introduction, p. xxiii.

7. vor allen to be taken with herrlich, glorious before or above all, i.e. as the most glorious of all. Cf. 833, 1223.

8. sich stellen (stellen factitive of stehen), to put or place oneself, take up a position,...'my great hope gains firm ground, becomes confirmed.' Cf. 181, n.

9. der fal'sche Frankenstamm, the race of the Salian Franks; see Introduction, p. xvii, note 2.

10. Begründet, established, placed on a firm foundation or Grund.— sei: 'is' as an accomplished fact and consequent state or condition, cf. 205, n.

14. Denn reiche Zukunft...: see note above on poetic diction.—ob = über, obsol., except in poetry, chiefly of the graver style. So 841, 881, &c., and the compound darob or drob, 42, 84.

15. Wohl glaub' ich.... Wohl is not here to be taken as qualifying adv. (cf. 1490) to verstehen. The particle wohl is very commonly used (generally without emphasis, and unaccented), to express qualified or deferential assertion, an assertion that assumes or tacitly asks the assent of the person addressed, cf. 566, 928, n. Here the assertion is made in response to expressed doubts, giving confirmation (cf. 187, n.) of what has been called in question, and wohl thus becomes mildly emphatic, hence its position at the head of the sentence. It is almost equivalent in its ultimate force to doch—Ich glaube doch—'I think I do [indeed]

understand....'—glaub' ich...ju verstehn: cf. 990, Seib ihr überzeugt, sein Heil ju förbern, 'You are convinced that you are promoting...,' and note that in this construction (infin. with ju as obj. of verbs of thinking, hoping, &c.) the—logical, but unexpressed—subj. of the infin. must be the same as that of the main sentence (cf. Eve, 218—19); and that the *acc. and infin.* construction, 'I believe him to be,' &c., must be rendered in modern German by a dependent sentence, Ich glaube, baß er...ist. But we still say, Ich glaubte ihn in Paris, Er wähnt sich recht klug, &c., cf. 278, though modern usage confines this construction also to somewhat narrow limits. Cf. 1239, n.

16. lehren is to teach, communicate knowledge, erziehen to 'bring up' (cf. Prol. 20, n.), train, educate. A home tutor, to whom the general care of his pupils is confided, is called Erzieher.

22. Dahinjugehn... | Zum hohen Dome... Her means *hither*, in the direction towards (19, 176, &c.), hin, *hence*, in some direction away from, the speaker or person in question (214, 549, &c.). Used indefinitely, i.e. without further indication, express or given by the context, of a particular direction, hin='away, off, &c.' often expressing swiftness of motion or entire disappearance (1151, 1775); hence also extinction and loss, Meine Ruh' ist hin, my peace is gone, Sie siechten hin, they pined away (to death). In this application bahin is often used (ba being quite indefinite, without reference to any particular point), for the simple hin, cf. 1177, 1430, 1775. Like the latter, it often serves merely to give a fuller expression to the idea of motion in some direction 'away' from the present scene to one not further defined, so bahinwandeln, to wander along, &c., and may thus add an appropriate picturesqueness to the description. It is however not often used in prose when, as here, a nearer definition of the direction is given; we should say, Hinjugehen ...jum....

23. Dom (Lat. *domus dei* or *domini*), a cathedral; less frequently like the Fr. *dôme* for a 'dome' or cupola.—ber Krönung Fest, cf. Intr. Note.

25. Der Armen viel' unb ber Unglücklichen: in plain prose, viele Arme unb Unglückliche. Cf. 1063. But we say quite commonly, Es waren beren viele, unser fünf, &c.

26. Hilfflehenb, contracted from hilfeflehenb, the usual form.

29. Laß mich bie erste fassen...: in ordinary prose als bie erste would be required. So in 1346, Als ein Warner....

30. Ist boch mein Leiben.... This strengthening use of boch (cf. 122, n.) with the inversion of subj. and finite verb, is common both in prose and poetry. Sometimes boch may in this construction be rendered by

'truly, surely, indeed,' but its force can frequently be given in English only by position and tone. It sometimes serves to put forward a statement or reminder that is regarded as needing no proof, but as proper to be brought into special notice and recognition. It has then a force similar to that of the Eng. 'why,' often becoming, like this, a mere expletive, simply adding force and liveliness to the style. Cf. 791; Eve, 197, Obs. 2.—baß letzte, the last, i.e. the least.

33. Nichts je gebeten hat mich Gisela: the regular construction is Einen um etw. bitten. Sometimes however bitten is used with such words as nichts, etwas, was, &c. as simple acc. of the object, cf. 660.

35. alles Welt: the art. is not usually required after all=Eng. 'all the,' except when it has more or less of real demonstrative force (as in 937, all die Treue, see note). When it simply means 'the...in question,' as indicated by the context, it is more usually omitted, cf. 687, allen Reichthum, 1868, n., alles Streits. But the art. is sometimes used when its demonstrative force is only slight, e.g. in 687 all ten Reichthum would but alter the expression by a shade.

37. Ob ich...solle,... Sollen—Eng. *shall*—to owe, be under obligation to (do or be), expresses moral constraint, or determining influence, proceeding from the will of some third person or personified agent, more or less definitely conceived and indicated by the context. Cf. 99, n., 1764. Sollen often='to be to' (i.e. according to the will or arrangement of some competent authority, or to mutual agreement, or even, cf. 1499, n., only to some one's conception), cf. 4, 32, 108, 1251, &c. Here Ob ich solle='Whether to...,' solle expressing the dictate of circumstances, which make a certain course appropriate; cf. above, 36, Soll ich...? 'Must I...?' i.e. is it a sad necessity of the circumstances?; also 321, Soll ich...? 'Shall I...?'

39. Darin=worin; so 709, tafür=wofür, 1696, &c. This use of the properly demonstrative compounds with ta (cf. 42, where trob=tarüber is demonstr.) instead of the relatives with wo, is now unusual in prose.

40. Inteß (fuller form inteſſen) is here conj.='while' (cf. 77), the verb going to the end of the clause; in 43 inteß is adv.='meanwhile,' at this same time (cf. 736), and standing at the head of a principal sentence, causes the inversion of the subj. and finite verb. We have the same construction in 1028—30 and 1478—82. Instead of inteß in the former sense we now more commonly use intem or während.

43. verzehrt: zehren, to consume; ver='away' (cf. 252, n.), 'up.' So in verbrauchen, &c.

45. ber Schwaben Herzogsfahne, the ducal banner of the Swabians, see 347, n.

48. Drei Jahre sitzt er...: 'for three years he has been (and still is) a prisoner.' For this idiomatic use of the pres. in Germ., as in Fr., cf. 421, 717, and Eve, 150. sitzen is the standing expression for to suffer imprisonment, cf. 1049.—Gibchenstein, see Introduction, p. xxi.

50. rauscht. While in Eng. 'rush' the chief idea is that of strong and swift *motion*, that of accompanying sound being merely subordinate, in the Germ. rauschen the original conception of rushing or rustling *sound* has remained the prominent one, the motion, rapid or gentle, being of consequence only so far as it produces the sound.

53. Du habest...: oblique oration, used in reporting the words or ideas of another (cf. 436), or one's own given as a message, i.e. thought of as spoken by another, cf. 405—7, 436, 1734, &c. See Eve, 221, ff.— Ernsten, cf. 1036, Wernern. This inflection of proper names in the dat. and acc. is in general obsol., though not seldom heard still in familiar conversation.

55. Damit ich...werten soll=werte, 'may become,' soll however retaining something of its own force (cf. 37, n.), indicating the act or condition in question as having its source in the will of some person other than the subject, and thus serving to strengthen the expression of purpose already indicated by damit.

57. Ward Herzog Ernst...= Wenn H. E....ward, cf. 78, 81, &c.; Eve, 267. Line 58 contains the apodosis or consequent clause, which according to the rule for the inverted construction (Eve, 205, 196; Aue, § 48) would be (cf. 79, 82, 653, &c.), so sitt er nicht.... But deviation from the rule for the sake of emphasis is not at all uncommon (cf. 317, 1264, 1268, 1870—71).

59. Spruch, judgment, verdict. Cf. Recht sprechen, to administer justice, ein Urtheil sprechen, to pronounce judgment.

61. Begnadigt (Gnade, grace, favour; hence, 63, mercy, clemency), 'pardoned.'—|frevelhaft, wantonly wicked. Frevel usually denotes a wanton, purposed mischief or ill-deed. Cf. freventlich, 1330.

63. selbst belongs to the subject of the verb, er (not to Gnade).

64 ff. See Introduction, p. xix ff. Giesebrecht calls Rudolf ter weibische und wetterwendische König.

67. meisterlos (not a current expression), having or owning no master, submitting to no control, hence=unbändig, ungovernable, intractable.

68. Vasall, pron. with initial *v*, not *f*.—wanrt' er sich: the subj. is removed, by the three appositions, so far from the verb, that it is repeated

in the form of a pronoun. The break in the construction takes place at Mann; the adverbial clause Erzitternt, &c. standing at the head of the sentence as thus begun afresh, the inversion, wantte er, takes place.

69. In prose: an ten mächtigsten seiner Blutsverwantten.

71. Damit er tiesen sich verpflichtete: Imd. [sich] verpflichten, to put one under obligation, attach him to oneself by rendering him a service. But, 'I should like to oblige him'=show courtesy to him, Ich möchte ihm gern gefällig sein.

72. Ernannt' er ihn... | Zum Erben...: cf. zum König wählen (909), to elect king, zum Nachfolger ernennen, to nominate as successor, and 218.—turch bündigen Vertrag: bündig, in this sense,=rechtsgiltig bintent, 'binding,' is obs. or rare. It is currently used only in the sense: binding in point of reasoning, convincing, and in the expression turz und bündig reten, to speak plainly, to the point, without mincing matters.

74. Königthum=Königschaft (itself a rare word), king*ship*, king*hood* (cf. Witmenthum, 1175); the royal dignity or office (Königswürte), but not properly (though occasionally used in this sense) Königreich, king*dom*, and thus not analogous with Kaiserthum, Herzogthum (109), &c.

75. Rathschluß, a conclusion or determination (Schluß, cf. 374, n., from schließen, to close, conclude), as the result of holding counsel (Rath), hence a decree or ordinance.—fügt' es: fügen, to fit or join, adapt, hence to arrange or order events, to dispose or ordain, cf. 1646.

76. zu ten Vätern: the biblical and more usual form of expression is zu seinen Vätern.

78. War Heinrich... (or, Wenn H....war, cf. 57, n.), so tratest tu.... A common construction, conditional or concessive in form, but simply antithetic in signification,=Während H...., tratest tu.... So in 81—2.

79. tratest tu...in ten Anspruch ein, lit. stepped or entered into, i.e. succeeded to, the claim.

82. Etw. blüht Einem (or erblüht, cf. 215, where the original figure is clear), is a poetical expression for etw. wirt Em. (1218, 1349), something falls (lit. becomes) to or is given to one, one receives something. —Anwartschaft (warten, to wait), expectancy; as a law term, 'reversion.'

83. Schwesterenkel: Enkel, a grandchild; for the compound, cf. Techtermann, the husband of one's daughter, Schwesterkind, a sister's child, &c.

86. Sich auszusprechen, wie...: sich aussprechen and other refl. verbs of similar meaning, although they are themselves composed of a transitive verb with sich as its object, are so felt as one expression, conveying a single idea, that they can take an object clause, as if they were

ordinary transitive verbs; 'to speak out and say how...,' or simply, 'to declare how....'

88. turch schlimmer Freunde Rath, 'by the advice of evil companions.' schlecht is simply bad in quality or character, opposed to good (schlechter Wein; ein schlechter Freund); schlimm is bad chiefly as bringing or threatening harm and annoyance. So we say, eine schlimme Wunde, ein schlimmer Vorfall, &c., where schlecht could not be used. Ein schlechter Mensch is a bad man, morally, ein schlimmer Mensch, one whose bad qualities are dangerous or hurtful to those around him. Hence, 'my worst foe' (cf. 129) would always be rendered, mein schlimmster Feind.

90. überschauen or übersehen (1743), to have or take a full view of, to survey, cf. 681, 1581.

91. At the time when Ernest was imprisoned, after his second revolt, Rudolf of Burgundy had not yet transferred the right of succession to the Emperor Konrad. See Introduction, pp. xxi—ii.

97. beschwor die Pflicht, cf. 387, n., swore to, i.e. swore to fulfil.

98. Der zugebrachten Söhne: zubringen is the legal term used with regard to whatever a wife 'brings to' her husband in marriage, whether fortune, or children by a former marriage. Say, 'to care for the sons she brought me.'

99. pflegen is here used in the same (now in ordinary prose unusual) wider sense as in the compound Pflegevater, foster-father, guardian. In its current meaning, to tend, nurse, cherish, pflegen more usually takes the acc.—wie ein rechter Vater soll, as a true father is bound to (according to the dictate of the recognised moral authority, cf. 37, n.), as is the duty of a true father.

102. Da steck' ich mir...Grenzen...aus: ausstecken, more commonly, abstecken, to mark out or off—lit. with Stecken, stakes—to lay down lines or boundaries.—wohlermeßnem: ß is here used instead of ss, though following a short vowel, because the double ss, in consequence of the dropping out of the e after it, comes at the end of a syllable. Cf. beßre, 220, 1237, &c. But in older and some modern authors ß is found, where ss is now generally accepted as more correct; see Eve, p. 3.

104. Burgund gehört..., Schwaben bleibt...: pres. tense (with pres. and fut. meaning, cf. 202, n.), both as considered from the standpoint of the past time to which handelt' refers, and to which the speaker mentally goes back; and also as representing what still is and will be the principle of his action.

105. darnach, cf. 151, n.; da=diesem, i.e. this principle laid down, this fixed arrangement.

106. von etwas (or Imb., 544, 1209) laſſen, to leave one's hold of, let go, abandon, = aufgeben, verlaſſen.

107. Vogt (Low Lat. *vocatus*, Lat. *advocatus*) is here used in its most general sense, overseer, governor. Cf. 407, Schirmvogt, protecting overseer, guardian; 1375, Burgvogt, and 1221, bevogten, to administer as overseer.

108. ſoll, 'is to,' i.e. according to the disposition or arrangement already made, cf. 37, n.—Ließ ich...bis jetzt..., cf. 277, n.

111. belehnen, to invest with a Leh[e]n (Eng. *loan;* from leihen, to 'lend'), or fief (265), to enfeoff. Cf. 941, Lehnsmann, a vassal, 235, Lehnsbrief, &c.

113. Verleitete: the force of the prefix ('astray,' cf. 92, 252, n., &c.) can hardly be expressed in translating.—Thun, subst. inf. = Handeln or Handlung[en], action[s], cf. 525, 776, &c.

115. unterweilen, obsol., = mittlerweile, unterdeſſen.

117. erlauchteſter Gemahl: erlaucht, 'illustrious,' august (cf. 947), an old form of the perf. part. erleuchtet from erleuchten, to light up, cf. Lat. *illustris.* Used at first simply as a general epithet for distinguished personages (cf. 328), it was afterwards also applied in a subst. form as a specific title, interchangeable with Durchlaucht, from which however it subsequently became distinguished, denoting the lowest degrees of princely rank. Erlaucht is now the title chiefly of mediatised counts.

118. Herrſchergang: Gang (fr. gehen) is the gait, or bearing in onward movement. Hence Herrſchergang = course and bearing as a ruler. Compounds of Gang with words signifying persons are not common (Goethe has Heltengang); on the other hand cf. Rechtsgang, course of justice, Lebensgang, &c.

121. der Fehl, pl. die Fehle, obsol. and poetical, = Fehler.

122. War doch von je.... Most of the numerous usages of doch may be explained under the form of an antithesis, 'Though..., *yet still, for all that, in spite of that, on the other hand...*,' in which the first member of the antithesis is often but vaguely indicated, or not distinctly present to the mind, cf. 457, 818, 1141, 1264, &c. (It may be noted that doch is etymologically the same word with the Eng. 'though'; cf. the still current colloquial use of the latter, 'Surely he did not say so. He did though.') It often differs little from aber, and may be rendered by a simple 'but,' cf. 19, 20, 120, 248, 294, 488, 924, 1114, &c. It is very commonly used (unaccented) in a similar way to wohl (cf. 187, n.), with the chief difference that wohl, though reserved and modest in statement, rather assumes agreement as probable, while doch, like 'surely, really,'

adds emphasis to the affirmation, and conveys a tacit challenge to the statement of any disagreement, or of proof to the contrary; it expresses reserved or modest statement just so far as such disagreement or proof is regarded as probable. In the present passage its force may be paraphrased 'as will surely be granted.'—von je. Je has its ultimate origin in the same root as Eng. 'ever,' with the same two chief meanings, 'at all times, always,' and 'at any time' (1349). In the former it is now hardly used except in the expression von je [her] (cf. 297 with 1130; and for her, 22, n.), from indefinite time past up to the present, 'ever, always.'

124. an Würden die erhabenste. Würden, 'dignities,' outward distinctions of rank and position, i.e. as daughter, wife and mother of illustrious princes.

126. Vermittlerin | Von Zwiespalt. vermitteln, to 'mediate in' a matter, to effect by mediation, as einen Frieden verm.; also, to compose or remove by mediation, as eine Differenz verm. 'and often didst thou allay dissension.'

127. welcher unversöhnlich hieß, cf. Prol. 17, n.

131. herbeiführen, to bring up to where we are (cf. 22, n.), as of place, so of time, hence, to 'bring on,' cause.

133. den ital'schen Zug, 'my march—or progress—to Italy,' made by Konrad, as by most of the German Kings up to Frederick III., to receive the crowns of Italy and of the Empire. The usual term is Römerzug or Romfahrt. italisch, Italic, of ancient and mediæval times, italienisch, Italian, of modern times.

134. meiner Schaaren Führung, objective genitive, cf. Introd. Note.

135—7. The 'resentment of the offended clergy' is indicated in Wipo's words, 'licet contra fas et jus esset liberam rem nisi liberaliter servire.'

139. im fernsten Apulien : in that most distant region (of the empire), Apulia; 'in far-off Apulia.' For this poetic superlative, cf. Milton, *Vac. Ex.*, '...whether thou be the son | Of utmost Tweed,...'

140. die Normannen, the Northmen, who early in the eleventh century effected considerable settlements in Italy, and founded the duchy of Apulia, which finally comprised nearly the whole of the southern half of the peninsula.—nehm' in Lehenspflicht. Lehens- (cf. 111, n.)='feudal.' Pflicht was used both for the condition of service or allegiance into which a vassal entered, and the oath or vow by which he did so. En. in [Eid und] Pflicht nehmen, to exact or receive the oath of allegiance from.

144. irгgeführt: the usual form is irreführen. Cf. verführen, 92.

145. Verließ, common but less correct form for Verlies, a subterranean dungeon; originally, according to Weigand, ein sich (unter die Erde, dem Auge) verlierender (M.H.G. and in dialects, verliesen) Raum.

146. jebo, obsolete form of jebt.

149—50. Prose order: und er sich gleichwohl ungebeffert, unbeschämt, wieder gegen mich aufsehnte.

151. nach deinem weisen Sinn. nach, after, according to, in accordance with. weiser Sinn, wisdom. 'Couldst thou, wise woman as thou art...?'

161. des Gerichts, | Das furchtbar über ihn ergehen muß: say, 'of the terrible judgment that must be passed upon (lit. go forth over, cf. Prol. 20, n.) him.' Note that Gericht, 'judgment' (from richten, to judge), is not simply synonymous with Urtheil, sentence, but comprehends the whole judicial process, even where one part of it may be chiefly thought of.

164. einem theuren Eid, a solemn oath, one held in the greatest reverence as sworn by whatever is dearest and most sacred. So, hoch und theuer, or hoch und heilig schwören, versprechen, &c.

165. ihm nicht zur Hülfe sein, poetic, = ihm Hülfe leisten. Hilfe (fr. helfen, cf. hilfst, imperat. hilf) is etymologically the correcter form.

166. was ihm geschieht, what is done to him. geschehen is not merely to 'happen' (228, &c.), but also serves as a passive to thun, like *fieri* to *facere*, cf. 1705, 1921.

168. bei dem wahrhaft'gen Gott, 'by the God of truth.' wahrhaftig (usually and properly with the chief accent on the first syllable; cf. 310, n.), as adj., = wahrhaft, truthful, truth-loving, is now little used; wahrhaftig, as adv., really, in very truth, is common.

175. diese Nacht, signifying the night *which lies nearest*, may mean according to context either the present night, that which is just past, or that which is to come.

181. die den Purpur mir (= meinen Purpur) benebt. For this frequent construction, in which a dat. of the person (subst. or pron.), combined with the def. art., is used in place of a genit. or a poss. pron., cf. 1086, 1116, 1306; 8, 188, 236, 623, 1363, &c. The two constructions are however not exactly equivalent in force; in the former the dat. of the subst. or pron. is usually more or less distinctly recognisable as a 'dat. of interest' (see 237, n., and cf. 1756—8), serving to make more prominent than the poss. pron. or gen. would do, the person affected by the act or condition in question. The substitution of the poss. pron. or gen.

U.   10

would often weaken the expression, e.g. here,—very decidedly in 1306,—and in most of the above quoted passages. The def. art. is in German also often used alone instead of the poss. pron., when the possessive relation is clear from the context, cf. 31, 242, 696, &c.

186. ħat iħn rerſtört (ver—cf. 261, n.—here serving to intensify) has confused, perturbed him, shaken the firmness of his mind.

187. Woħl war eð...: woħl (cf. 15, n.) emphatically confirmatory, 'It was indeed...,' 'Verily was it....' Ernest gives a significant turn to Hermann's words, applying them to the long night of his imprisonment. Cf. 1075 for an exact parallel. In 698 woħl has similar force, but is perhaps somewhat less emphatic.

190. Mutterliebe, tir...: tir comprehends here a twofold force,— under thy melting and warming influence (cf. 1316, n.), and,—towards thee; 'maternal love, thou hast melted towards thee this frozen heart.'

194. aufleben, used absolutely (cf. 786), is to revive, as it were to rise up or open out (auf) into new life.

198. öffnen wir, pres. conj. as imperat.=laßt und...öffnen, cf. 'Prol. 40, n.

201. ħarren is here used as a more poetic word for erwarten; it generally indicates patient expectancy, cf. 843. Its poetical complexion is heightened by the construction with the gen.; it is now more usual with auf and the accusative.

202. Ħernach...wird...belehnet.... The pres. with fut. meaning is much commoner in Germ. than in English, both in poetry and in prose. It is often used as terser and more vivid, especially when the certainty or nearness of the future event is assumed or indicated, cf. 166-7, 314, 317-18, 320, 381, 1622, 1732, 1897, &c. In Gothic and O. H. G. the pres. regularly stood for the fut., for which there existed no special form.

204. teine Ħuld an mir: in prose, gegen mich. We say an Em. ſo oter ſo ħanteln, to deal by, an Em. etw. tħun (1322), begeħen (848), üben (1553), &c., to do to, commit against, show or exercise towards, &c. Ħuld (grace, favour) has here the force of a substantive infinitive, =ħuldvolles Ħanteln; we might render, 'thy generous dealings towards me.'

205. Soll tir...vergelten ſein. ſein is often used to form the passive infin. where, following the distinction observed in forming the finite tenses of the passive (viz. that werten expresses the taking place of the action, cf. 4, ſein the condition consequent upon its completion, cf. 10, n.), werten might seem more correct. The use of ſein however often indi- cates that the mind, springing over the act, dwells upon the state of

completion, and perhaps most of the cases of the pass. inf. with ſein (cf.
197, 513–14, 1331, 1476, 1612, &c.) may be so explained; though it
may still be a question, why in this particular form this point of view, of
condition consequent on a completed action, should be so often preferred to that which logically might seem more natural, in which the
action is considered in its course.   The inf. with ſein often serves to put
the matter as more certain and decided, it being contemplated as
already accomplished; so in the present passage and in 514, 539, 1612,
&c.   Something may be due to euphony, the dissyllabic werten often
sounding heavy and awkward, in comparison with the quick and light
monosyllable ſein.   The imperat. pass. is also, in the 2nd pers. always,
in the other persons often, formed with ſein, cf. 521, 957, 1329, 1903;
on the other hand with werten, 1477 (where ſei would express a deci-
siveness that might appear too brusque to the person addressed), and
1628.

211. O nehmt an mir ein Beiſpiel: generally ſich ein Beiſpiel an Em.
nehmen, to take example by one, which may mean either ſich En. zum
Beiſpiel (=Vorbild) nehmen, to take as a model, or as here, as a warning
example.

213. zu tem (=teinem) erſten Kampf: cf. Act IV., 1409 ff.   The real
date of the Italian campaign in which Hermann took part, dying on the
return home, is 1038;—see Introduction, p. xxvi.

217. tu,...ter tu...wirſt....   This repetition, after the relative ter, of
a pers. pron. in the 1st or 2nd pers. which stands as antecedent to it, is
always necessary if the verb is to agree with the pers. pron., cf. 1279,
1391.   The same construction is required when the antecedent is a
noun in the vocative, cf. 1749, 1769.   When the relative is not followed
by the pers. pron., the verb stands in the 3rd person, in agreement
with the relative, cf. 1523.   Hence in 702 and 1890 hat, not haſt, is the
auxiliary to be supplied.

218. Zum Erben...geweiht: cf. 72, n.—eines hohen Thrones: hoch figu-
rative=erhaben, exalted, august; often so used of royal personages, cf.
972.

221. Dank teinem Wunſche: in prose, für teinen Wunſch.   Dank with
a dat.='thanks to...' (Dem Himmel ſei Dank, &c.), especially in the
sense of the Fr. *grâce à*.

10—2

Zweite Scene.

232. zur Gespensterschau (schauen = sehen, Schau, inspection, cf. Truppen-schau, review), 'for ghost-seeing.' The mode of expression, a compound being formed for the purpose, conveys contempt.

234. Kanzler, probably Wipo himself; see Introduction, p. xvi.

235. Lehensbrief. Brief (L. Lat. *breve*, fr. Lat. *brevis*; Eng. *brief* through the Fr. *brief, bref*), originally a *short* writing, then any document, a letter, &c. So Lehensbrief (cf. 111, n.), a bill of enfeoffment, title deed; cf. 323, Gnadenbrief.

237. Sprich mir deutlicher! mir is not here for zu mir, 'to me,' but is an example of the so called *dativus commodi* [*vel incommodi*], or ' dat. of interest,' its force being, 'in my interest, *for* me'; cf. 731, Die Eiche breitet uns..., spreads for us..., 496, Er führe...mir das Heer, Let him lead me the army, &c. For other exx. of this dat., which is often used in German where we should in English express its force otherwise or not at all, cf. 658, 1001, 1163, 1189, 1861, &c., also most of the passages quoted in 181, n. It is frequent in Shakspeare : 'the sack that thou hast drunk me would have bought me lights as good cheap...,' 1 *Hen. IV.,* III. 3, 51, 'Inquire me first what Danskers are in Paris,' *Ham.* II. 1, 7. It is sometimes hardly to be distinguished from the ethical dative (cf. 1787, n.), e.g., in the present passage, where we might render, ' Pray speak more clearly.'

242. an der Hand den jungen Sohn: absolute accusative, cf. 1153, in der Seite meinen Speer, with my spear in his side; so 838, 1792.

248. Ein Blick, nicht strafend...: strafen, orig., to show keen displeasure, in the first place and chiefly, by words, to rebuke, reprove; then to chastise, punish, fine. The more original meaning still survives in the expressions, mit Worten strafen ; En. Lügen strafen, to reproach with lying, give the lie to ; Gm. etw. strafend bemerken ; En. strafend ansehen, &c., and in the adj. strafbar (429), which means not only punishable, but also culpable, censurable. So, ein strafender Blick, a look of rebuke. Cf. 1279.

251. hinabgewallt. wallen, a poetical word, = wandern, ziehen, to walk, wander, travel, more especially (1186) = wallfahrten, to go on a pilgrimage, or in solemn or festive procession, cf. 874. It is to be distinguished from wallen (cf. Welle, a wave), to·undulate, wave (1419), surge, boil. The two verbs, distinct words, but allied in derivation

and also in some of their applications, are not seldom confused, and are classed by most dictionaries (not by Whitney) under one head.

252. verhallet war. The prefix ver has here its root meaning, 'away'; verhallen, of sound (cf. Hall, 1293, n.), to 'die away': cf. 278, 289, 349, 1333, &c. It often means 'astray,' in a wrong or undesirable direction, cf. 113, n., 261, n., 347, n., &c.

257. Hab' ich gefolgt. In the meaning obey, comply with, conform to, folgen is often (in that of obedience to a person, and when used absolutely, always) used with the auxiliary haben, as it formerly was in all senses.—auf dem Tag zu Ulm, see Introduction, p. xxi, and note on Reichsstände, p. 108. Tag, in a legal sense, the day appointed for a transaction or session; then also the session itself, and the sitting body, the 'diet' (Low Lat. *dieta, diaeta,* Lat. *dies*).

258. von dem Herzog wich. weichen, to give way (1727), to retire, yield (312).—von einer Stelle, von Amts. Seite weichen, to quit, yielding to some pressure, actual or apprehended,—most common with a negative, cf. 1927. In the sense of abandonment without this accompanying idea of pressure or compulsion, as apparently in the present passage, it is unusual. It must be taken in its literal local sense, like the similar expression in 383, von dir getreten.

261. Verwöhnter Sohn des Glückes. The prefix ver (cf. 252, n.) here denotes the wrong or mischievous direction of the action, as in verführen (92), verzärteln, &c.: gewöhnen, to accustom, verwöhnen, to lead by custom into degeneracy, to spoil, pamper.

262. jüngst, lately; cf. in jüngster = neuester Zeit, recently; das jüngste Gericht, the last judgment.—Kärnthen, Carinthia. See 918–19, n., and Introd., p. xxii, and note 2.

265. dich mit...begnadigte. Cf. 148, n. Here begnadigen means, to treat with favour, bestow favour[s] upon; En. mit etw. begn., to bestow something on one as a sovereign favour. Cf. Gnadenbrief (323), a patent conveying a royal favour.

269. glücklich, happily, i.e., it is a happy thought that you remind me...

271. Heerfahrt, and Heereszug (1089), are poetic or archaic words, = the modern Feldzug, campaign.

272. die entehrte Stirne. The prefix ent is identical with ant in Antwort, *an*swer, and emp in empfangen, &c. Its original meaning seems to have been 'against, towards.' It indicates a change of condition, either with reference to the new condition, thus indicating the action in its beginning, as in entschlafen (chiefly fig., cf. 786, 1954) = einschlafen, and

entblühen (1274)=erblühen (cf. Prol. 20, n.); or with reference to the old condition, out of or away from which the change takes place, so that ent often denotes reversal of the action of the simple verb, or becomes directly privative, as here, entehren, to *dis*honour, cf. entfühnen, 1327, n., entfünbigen, 1396, n., entfärben, 1694. Cf. also entftellen, 1081, n., entfetzen, 57, &c. For the general meaning, 'away, off, out,' cf. entfliehen, 321; 690, 1066, 1536, 1906.

276. Da warft bu freubig in bes Kaifers Dienft: freubig is best taken as adj., standing in antithesis to verftoßen and entehrt in 278.

277. Nun is often used as a conjunction, being really a contraction for nun bu (or for nun baß, which is found in M. H. G.), as in Eng. 'now' is used for 'now that.'—Nun Herzog Ernft...kam=gekommen ift. The correct distinction between the imperf. and the perf. tenses, neglected by many prose writers, is still more frequently set aside in poetry. The use of the imperf. is to narrate past events in their connection with other events either mentioned or thought of, to express facts mentally viewed as existing at a past point or period of time regarded in itself, without reference to the present. The perf. is used to state facts or events viewed singly and independently, and especially to express action but just completed, or regarded as extending in its effects and significance up to the present. Cf. 570, ff., Jhr habt...euch überzeugt, of a fact viewed in its present significance, followed by faßt, &c., when the speaker, going back in imagination to the past scene, proceeds to connected narration: 723, Gott verließ mich nicht, where (if the imperf. is intended by the poet in its strictly correct application), the speaker mentally reverts to some past time when he had been tempted to believe that he was forsaken: 1564, Du erfchienft, 'You appeared' (viz. just now); Du bift erfchienen would have the same force as the Eng. perfect. In 1647, the imperf. empfieng shows that the time of receiving is regarded, from the standpoint of the fut. time of restoring, as past and gone. But in 109, the imperf. ließ (with the qualifying words bis jetzt, indicating extension of the action up to the present) is at least a deviation from the strict rule; in the present passage, and 390, 642, 1531, &c., only poetic licence would justify it. Cf. further 689, 736, 750, 1039, 1282, n., &c. In general it may be said that where in Eng. the perf. *must* be used, there also in German it would be required in a correct prose style. (The perf. is of course also required where in Eng. it would not be used; but the inaccurate use of the perf. instead of the imperf. is much less common than the converse deviation from rule here mentioned.)

278. wähnft bu bich verftoßen...: cf. 15, n. wähnen (fr. Wahn, ground-

less fancy, illusion, delusion, cf. Wahnsinn, Wahnwitz (607), madness,
&c.), to believe erroneously, to be under a delusion, cf. 1334.—verstoßen
(cf. 252, n.), thrust away, rejected.

279. wie eine Reiterschaar sich schwenkt. schwenken is factitive of schwingen, *swing* (cf. 1425); like fällen (1287), to fell, fr. fallen, to fall; tränken
(1403) fr. trinken; säugen (1979) fr. saugen (300), &c.   Sich schwenken, as
military term, to wheel.

281. (Sc. Es ist) Wohl wahr… : wohl is used, like 'indeed,' not only
as emphatic and confirmatory (cf. 187, n.), but also as concessive (like
freilich, 'to be sure'), some qualification or counterbalancing statement
being either expressed (often introduced by doch, as here in l. 294, cf.
488), or understood, cf. 892.

282. mit einem Schlag (the spaced type represents our italics), at a
single stroke, i.e. suddenly.

283. Zum seligen Paradies. The def. art. in the compound forms
zum, zur, &c. often appears in its representative and generalising sense,
where in Eng. the indef. art. or none at all would be required.   So,
Ein. zum Freunde wählen, to choose as *a* friend, im Zorn, in a rage, in
wrath, &c.; cf. Prol. 40; 613, 699, &c.

284. sich zum Lamme hingestreckt: cf. sich zu Em. setzen, which means
to sit down by some one on neighbourly terms (cf. 863), while sich
neben Em. setzen may mean merely to take possession of a vacant place
beside some one.

285. mit der frommen Taube: fromm (see Prol. 6, n.), harmless,
gentle.

289. Note that versteckt (cf. 252, n.) is perf. not pres.; cf. Prol.
24, n.

290. walten, rule, hold sway, prevail, generally used of a benefi-
cently ordering activity.

292. verdächtig (fr. Verdacht, suspicion) is 'suspicious' = calculated
to awaken suspicion. Das sieht verdächtig aus, that looks suspicious.
Er ist mir verd., I suspect him. Einer Sache verd. sein, to be suspected
of a thing. 'Suspicious' = entertaining suspicion, is argwöhnisch, miß-
trauisch.

293. uns belongs as dat. to geziemt.—zurückstehen, to stand back,
withdraw into the background, cf. 854.

294. am Abend noch…: noch, 'still, yet,' of time past, pres., or fut.
(77, 152, 317, 390, &c.); 'further, in addition,' cf. 1156. It is frequently used to indicate that something 'still' continues, or 'yet'
occurs, within certain limits that might perhaps be thought to terminate

or exclude it: often, though not to be translated, it may be paraphrased by 'as late as,' 'so far on as,' 'still, though so late,' cf. 691, n., 1448, 1595, n. Sometimes it may be rendered by 'very,' or 'even,' noφ tieſe Πaφt, cf. 774, 1437. With a designation of past time it is often equivalent to Eng. 'only, but,' noφ geſtern, cf. 440, n.

295. ſteigt Gewitter auf. Gewitter, though in origin a collective from Wetter (cf. 287 baϐ Gezweige, 1450 baϐ Felᴐgeklüſt &c.), is rarely used in the singular without article.

299. Dem Herzog wurmt eϐ: wurmen is now more commonly used as a transitive verb, though the older construction with the dat. is more suitable to the meaning. Etw. wurmt [in] Em., lit., causes one a feeling compared with the griping pains of worm disease, annoys, galls, torments. 'The loss of Burgundy never ceases to rankle in the mind of the duke.'

301. Herrſchſuφt. Suφt (formerly = Krankφeit, cf. ſieφen, to be sickly, to pine, Sφwintſuφt, consumption, &c.) always denotes a *morbid* or *inordinate* desire or propensity, cf. Habſuφt, avarice, Gefallſuφt, &c.—ter Stänte Troζ: see note on Reiφϐſtänte, p. 108, and Introduction, pp. xvi and xxvii.

302. ein uralter...Zwiſt. The prefix ur (identical with the insep. prefix er, cf. Prol. 20, n., and Urlaub, 972, fr. erlauben) has now in many words the sense of primitiveness, remote origin; thus Uranfang, the very beginning of all, Urwalt, the primæval forest (cf. 765), &c. · Hence uralt, so old that the origin is almost lost, very old, ancient.

303. feſt | Μuβt tu tiφ ſtellen: ſiφ ſo oter ſo ſtellen (cf. 8, n.) genly. means, to pretend to be...; here of course the meaning is: You must take up a secure position, one in which you will not be liable to be taken at a disadvantage, or to miss an opportunity, whatever turn things may take.

309—10. fremte Regung and neue Reigung are to be taken in a generalising and collective sense;—impulses (emotions, springs of motive, currents of will), or some impulse;—new inclinations (affections, likings), or, some new inclination. fremt here = hitherto strange to him, unfelt by him.—einmal, at some time or other, once, either in the future, as here, in the present, or in the past, as in 661. As thus used, einmal commonly has the chief accent on the second syllable (cf. 661); here the metre demands at least an equal accent upon the first; cf. 168, 691, and notes.

314. Du wirſt hervergerufen, pres. passive with fut. force, cf. 202, n., and below, 317-18.—bewäφrt...in teiner Unentbeφrliφkeit. bewäφren (root

maþr) to give active proof or confirmation of anything, 441, of its reality or genuineness, 332, 1972. ſich bewähren, to approve oneself. bewährt, 'tried and approved.' '...proved to be indispensable.'

316. iſt auch...=wenn auch...iſt, cf. 57, n. wenn auch is concessive, 'even if,' 'though.' Eve, 273.

318. begehren in prose now usually with the accusative (435).

322. Pergamēn (Low Lat. *pergamenum*, Gr. Lat. *pergamena*—sc. *charta*—, adj. subst., fr. Pergamum in Mysia, where the use of parchment was first introduced by King Eumenes, B.C. 197—159), is the older form of the now current Pergamént.

323. Gnadenbrief : see 265, n., and 235, n.

328. eurer Gegenwart, poetic gen.=für eure G.

329. ſeib bedankt : bedanken is now used only reflectively, ſich bedanken, to tender one's thanks.

331. verhoffen=hoffen is now rare. The word is usual only in, gegen alles Verhoffen, contrary to all expectation, and in the adj. unverhofft, unexpected.

336. Auf öfteres Erſuchen (subst. inf.; erſuchen, to request)...; at the frequent or repeated request of.... öfter (or with redundant adverbial s, öfters), compar. of the adv. oft, is often used in an absol., not compar. sense,=oft, manchmal, then as an adj.=häufig. It usually however indicates a less degree of frequency than oft and häufig; cf. längere Zeit= 'some length of time,' &c.

339. Rath or Raths pflegen, to take counsel, deliberate. In this and a few other still current phrases pflegen is strong (pflog, gepflogen); in its commonest uses, to take care of, and to be accustomed (667), it is weak.

343. ſich befrieden mit..., obs., to come to terms of peace with, to become reconciled to.—ihn durchaus in...herzuſtellen : etw. [wieder] herſtellen, lit., to place it here (hither) again, i.e. where it was before, to 'restore' it to its former place or condition. The use of the word here, and again in 576, =wieder einſetzen, to 'reinstate,' is not a current one.— durchaus, adv. (992), thoroughly, entirely, 'to re-establish him in all his dignities and honours.'

346. auserkieſt, weak form of the perf. part. instead of the more usual auserkoren (949), fr. auserkieſen. (kieſen, afterwards superseded by the form küren, 847,=wählen, is with most of its compounds obsol. or archaic. The same root is seen in Kurfürſt, elector, and in Willkür, caprice, i.e. choice determined only by the arbitrary will.

347. das verwirkte Fahnenlehn. verwirken (cf. 252, n.) indicates a

'working' or action in a wrong direction, wrong-doing, cf. verbrechen, 494, n. In its present current use it means to 'forfeit' by such action (ver as in verscherzen, to trifle away, forfeit by heedless levity). Its use as in 931, for to 'incur, bring on' by such action, is now almost obsolete.—Fahnenlehn, a secular fief of the first rank, held directly from the king or emperor, the investiture with which was effected by transferring to the new lord the distinctive banner of the race or clan placed under his feudal supremacy, cf. 368, ff.

348. neuertings=von neuem, anew, now obsolete in this sense. Its current meaning is, lately, recently.

349. verleihen, here in its primitive meaning, =leihen (ver = away, cf. 252, n.), i.e. als Lehen (111, n.) geben. Hence its current signification, to confer, bestow.

350. Mißhelligkeit, misunderstanding, disagreement, is etymologically the exact counterpart of *dissonance*, the adj. hellig (only prov.) being from the same root with Hall, sound. Cf. einhellig, 578.

353—5. ten alten Erbvertrag..., | Auf Unsere Person bestätigt hat: (Erbvertrag, treaty of inheritance or succession. bestätigen, to make stät or steady, to confirm), a pregnant construction, =has confirmed the treaty, transferring its application to me. See Introd., p. xxii.

356. tie Abkommniß, obs.=tas Abkommen, tie Uebereinkunft, ter Vertrag.—sich bei etw. beruhigen, to be satisfied with. bei has here its usual local sense (cf. 1108, n.), the literal meaning being, to rest satisfied *at* a certain point reached or defined.

360. ausstellen, of documents, to draw up, frame, compose.

361. wenn es euch geliebt (obs.=beliebt), if it please you.—etw. vornehmen, to take up or in hand, begin upon.

364. nach Gebühr=wie es sich gebührt, as is right, becoming.

367. Machtvollkommenheit, sovereign power.

368—70. The right of leading the van in battle, in the imperial army, appears to have been from early times a privilege of the Swabians.

370. tas Vortertreffen. Treffen, subst. inf. fr. treffen, to hit, fall upon (cf. Zusammentreffen, meeting, encounter), means both an engagement with the enemy, and a line of battle. Hence Vortertreffen, the 'van.'

373. Zugehörte (i.e. was zu etwas gehört), 'appurtenance.' Of the forms Zugehör[te], Zubehör[te], Zubehör is now alone current.

374. In prose: sämmtlicher or ter gesammten (408) Fürsten.—Schluß, determination, resolution, decree (of a deliberative body); more usually Beschluß (823). Cf. Rathschluß, 75, n.

376. 3u = in addition to.

377. ein Gedoppeltes (gedoppelt instead of the usual deppelt), adj. used
as subst.   In translating such expressions a subst. must usually be
supplied according to context; here, 'a double oath,' or 'two things.'

381. rächest, cf. 460, n.—zu Cm. halten, to side with, be an adherent
of, cleave to.

382. Mann (924) = vassal, Lehnsmann (941, cf. the collective Lehnsmannschaft, 401), has plur. Mannen.

383. Von dir getreten: the meaning is the same as in 258. The
unusual expression is to be taken literally, and is meant to give to the
style more of the concrete or realistic character that belonged to the
earlier forms of the language.

384. Rache dürstend: in ordinary prose nach etw. dürsten.—kehr' ich:
kehren for the more usual zurückkehren (966).

387. beschwören, | Daß...: usually, schwören, daß... (379). The regular
use of beschwören is with an accusative object (cf. 97, 485, 579), which
obj. however may be the neut. pron. es, with a dependent sentence in
apposition: Ich will es beschwören, daß.... With an acc. of the person,
beschwören means to 'adjure.'

388. den landesflücht'gen Grafen Werner: see Introd., p. xxi, note 1.
More usually landflüchtig (546), fugitive (flüchtig fr. fliehen) from one's
native country, exiled.

390. zur Stunde = bis zur Stunde, up to the present hour, time.—sich
unterwarf, cf. 277, n.

392. tiefen, him.—die mit ihm sind, cf. Prol. 15, n.

393. Grenze, for the usual Grenzen (103), must be understood as one
encircling boundary.

394. sich betreffen (treffen, cf. 370, n.) or betreten (treten, to tread, step;
betr., to come upon, surprise) lassen, to be—lit. to let oneself be—caught,
discovered, &c.

395. Ihn greifen: in prose, ergreifen, cf. 596, n.—zu des Reiches Haft:
zu expresses the purpose or end of the seizure, viz. delivery into the
custody of the imperial authority.

396. Cm. etw. erlassen, to let one off a thing; to remit, spare;
cf. 435, 585.

397. We say, es geht mir ein Licht auf, i.e. a light rises or breaks
forth (cf. die Sonne geht auf), in which the matter in hand becomes clear,
'now I begin to see....' Then simply, es geht mir auf, es geht mir hell
auf, used either absolutely or with a dependent sentence. In the analogous phrase, Jetzt gehen mir die Augen auf, aufgehen = sich öffnen.

398. auf ben Tag, to the diet, cf. 257, n., and Introd., p. xxi.

399. Usually wegen einer Sache or über etwas unterhanbeln.

402. Treu' and Kraft are dat., they represent the firm ground, as it were, upon which he securely trod.

406. Entgegen ihrem Herrn, in opposition to, contrary to the will of, their lord. entgegen is genly. used only together with fein (976), or in close or loose composition with some other verb, cf. 157, 1700.

407. Schirmvogt, cf. 107, n.

416. Auf Kiburg warf er fich, He threw himself into, withdrew to. Auf Kiburg, as we still say: Ich ging auf fein Zimmer (in an upper story); Er ift auf bem Schloß (the position being thought of as an elevation); auf bie Burg fahren, &c.—fein feftes Schloß: feft (cf. 419, n., Befte) = befeftigt, fortified; so 658.

418. Mond as poetical for Monat (1721) takes the pl. Monden.

419. Befte, archaic form of Fefte, itself now only biblical and poetic, = Feftung.—brach, destroyed.

420. mit genauer (or fnapper) Noth, scarcely, 'narrowly.'

421. Und irrt feitbem: cf. 48, n.—bie Lanbe, a chiefly poetical plural, with the general and collective meaning: tracts of country, expanses of territory, lands or provinces taken together as an indefinite whole; while Länber means a number of separate and individual countries.

423. ber fo feft | An mir gehalten: generally (381, 659) zu Em. halten.

428. Mit großen Dingen trägt fich biefer Mann. fich mit etwas (einem Gebanken, Plan, &c.) tragen or herumtragen, = bamit umgehen, lit. to go about carrying it with one everywhere; to have habitually in one's thoughts, to ponder over, entertain, &c. We also say, einen Gebanten mit fich herumtragen. 'This man cherishes great designs.'

433. ber Meuterer. Meuterei is etymologically the same with Eng. 'mutiny' (Meuterei for the—in this sense—obs. Meute, from Fr. *meute*, L. Lat. *movita*, Lat. *mota*, fr. *movere*, which in O.Fr. = *émeute*, a revolt; hence *meutin*, now *mutin*, fr. which 'mutiny'), but is less confined in meaning, being applied to any active insubordination or rebellion, not on a grand scale, against the powers that be.

438. Troß allem, was ich Bitteres erfuhr. Cf. 1071, Was je ein Pilger Seltfames erzählt. The neut. adj. used substantively after such words as was, etwas, nichts, viel, &c., and now generally regarded as standing in apposition to them, is originally a partitive genitive, cf. Lat. *quid novi? quidquid boni*, &c. When used after the interrog. or rel. pron. was, this partit. gen. is separated from the latter by the subject of the sentence, and often also by other words: Was habe ich benn Böfes gethan?

Sieh nur, was ich hier Schönes habe. When was has an expressed antecedent, as in the present passage, the partit. gen. might be transferred
to the main sentence, standing in apposition to the antecedent, or
when the antecedent through the transference becomes an adj., itself
becoming the antecedent,—Troß allem Bitteren, was ich erfuhr. On the
way to render such adj. substantives, cf. 377, n.

440. um Treue rühmet: in prose wegen der Treue.—noch (cf. 294, n.)
jüngst (262, n.), but lately.

441. so schön bewährt, cf. 314, n.—schön, nobly, worthily.

442. Als Misiko.... The incident here related is historical, but
really occurred in 1032. The proper name of the Polish prince was
Mieczislaw; Wipo writes Misico.

445. Zorn, den ihr ihm tragt: in prose usually, den ihr gegen ihn hegt
or tragt; cf. 929.

446. sühnen is to expiate, make atonement for; den Zorn sühnen is
a pregnant expression for den Zorn durch Sühnung der Schuld besänftigen,
to appease the wrath by expiation of the guilt.—anerbet: anerbieten = an-
bieten (1698) is usual only in the inf. as subst., das Anerbieten, offer.

448. verschmäht is here of course perfect, not present; cf. Prol. 24, n.

454. hegen, lit. to fence round, 'hedge' in (surround with a Hag,
Hege, Hecke), to 'preserve' from injury or unauthorised use (so, gehegtes
Holz, Wild hegen, cf. 1385), to tend (Jmd. hegen und pflegen), entertain or
cherish plans, feelings, &c., cf. 853, 929. As used here and in 518,
= 'harbour,' give shelter and protection to, it is no longer in current
use.

460. Schwörest du den Eid? The pres. w. fut. meaning (202, n.) is
often in German, as sometimes in English, the expression of *will*, Den
Eid schwöre ich nicht, 'I will not...'; and in many cases where in German
this is not, or not necessarily, the case, 'will' must be used in translating, even when it will be felt as conveying the idea not only of
futurity, but of volition, cf. 381, 632, 1852.

461. bedingen, to stipulate for (cf. Bedingung, a condition, 485);
now more usually ausbedingen.

463. Es handelt sich um etw., the matter treated of, in hand, in question, is.... ''Tis not a matter touching merely the duchy....'

465. Des Kerkers bist du ledig: ledig, = frei von, is generally used only
with regard to something that binds or oppresses, that may be shaken
off, not simply escaped from; here we might say in prose, der Fesseln
bist du ledig.

469. Acht (meaning originally, hostile persecution,—a distinct word

from Acht, attention, though probably from the same root) is the 'ban' of the civil authority, proscription, outlawry. The power to 'put to the ban' belonged only to the king òr emperor, and to him only after a judicial process and with the assent of the princes, cf. 161, 499—500. Bann denoted originally, the legal power and jurisdiction of a civil or ecclesiastical judge or ruler; then the district over which his jurisdiction extended; an edict or prohibition issued by him; finally, the punishment denounced against offenders. In the middle ages Bann was used only for the punishment decreed by the church, excommunication; this was often united with or followed upon the secular ban.

471. erinnern, to remind, is used w. an and acc., w. gen. only in poetry. sich erinnern, to remember, takes the gen., or an and acc.

476. nicht qualifies verschont, and would according to the more usual order immediately precede it.

477—8. Der heil'ge Gallus, St Gall; see Introd., p. xxi. —das Stift, pious or charitable foundation or institution, monastery, &c. (der Stift, peg, sprig).—erseufzten eurem Drang, poetical for unter eurem Drang. Drang = Druck, Unterdrückung, oppression.

479. Bannstrahl: the ban is compared to a thunderbolt ready to be hurled. Strahl, now 'ray (1053), jet,' &c., originally meant an arrow, = Pfeil; afterwards a flash or bolt of lightning, = Wetterstrahl, 1341, Blitz.—zücken, to draw a weapon, is the same word with zucken (or zücken) to 'flash' of lightning, the root meaning being, to make a brief, quick movement, or a succession of such movements.

480. Fürsprache = the common Fürbitte (cf. 1277), mediation, intercession.

482. Deß (=dessen, cf. 779) warnet euch... We say, En. vor etwas (a danger, person, course of conduct, &c.) warnen, to warn one of or against something, = admonish him to caution with regard thereto; but the construction of warnen with the gen., and its use in the sense of giving warning information or reminder of a fact or event, are obsolete or poetical. Cf. 1252, n.

484. mit Bedacht = bedächtig, with reflection, deliberately. Cf. bedenken, to think upon, take into deliberation; hence sich bedenken, to hesitate; bedacht (1473), perf. part. as adj., thoughtful, reflective; unbedenklich (1918), without hesitation.

486. hauchen, here used poet. for [ein]athmen, to inhale, breathe.

488. worten for geworten; the omission of the prefix ge in the perf. part. of werten as an independent verb, and of certain other verbs which according to the modern rule require it, is not uncommon in

poetry and in the dialects, cf. 607, &c. Goethe wrote in familiar letters as perf. part. gangen, blieben, triegt, &c.

490. zernichten (1608) is an intensified vernichten, the more usual word. zer denotes the breaking· or resolving into parts, generally in the way of destruction, cf. zerknicken, 1001, zersetzen, 1137, &c.—daß ich ten verriethe, that I should betray, i.e. 'as to betray,...' Cf. Eve, 239.

491. mir...Treue hielt = bewahrte (cf. Wort halten, Farbe halten), preserved his loyalty to me.

494. Entgelten. The prefix (cf. 272, n.) has here but slight force; gelten (cf. 1805, n.) formerly meant to restore, to give an equivalent or compensation for : hence entgelten, to pay, atone or suffer for; so 1027. —was der ältere verbrach. verbrechen (ver indicating the wrong direction of the action, cf. 252, n.), to transgress, do amiss (hence Verbrechen, a crime), was formerly used with substs., as, einen Bund, einen Eid verbrechen, = brechen (also = verwirken, cf. 347, n.), but is now used only with was nichts, etwas, &c. as obj.; Was hab' ich verbrochen? What wrong have I done?

499. nach dem Schluß | Der Fürsten, cf. 374, n.

502. als offenbaren Ächter: offenbar here = 'declared,' made conspicuous to the public eye. Ächter, originally the person who ächtet, puts to the ban, very soon took the meaning of ein Geächteter (541), one put to the ban, an outlaw.

503. Friede in its old technical sense (dating from the days of the Faustrecht, when powerful individuals asserted the right of settling quarrels and avenging injuries by private warfare, without reference to a superior civil authority), denoted the condition of security to person and property guaranteed within the limits of a certain territory, or to the members of a certain organized society, by the powers in authority (whether within the territory or society, or exercising superior lordship over it), being thus almost equivalent to Geleit as used below, 511. Hence the old expressions Burgfriede, Kirchenfriede, Jmd. in feinen Frieden (= Schutz) nehmen. So Sch., Euch schützt des Königs Frieden, 'the King's peace.' Here the guarantee of protection is that of the empire, which was regarded in spite of the Faustrecht as the supreme civil power; so that Unfriede, the condition of one from whom this guarantee has been withdrawn, is equivalent to Vogelfreiheit, outlawry, exclusion from the protection and benefits of civil society generally.

504. theil' ich hin, an old expression occurring in the formulas of the ban, = ertheile ich dahin,.... 'I apportion, or assign, to whence it came.'

505. Dein eigen Gut, = Allot, allodial possession, the estate pos-

sessed in his own right, not as a conferred fief.—geſtatten and erlauben, in an application no longer usual, and the language generally of the ban and excommunication, are taken from the old formulas.

506. männiglich (fr. an old gen. pl. of Mann, and gelich or glich as seen in jeglich, each or every) is an old word belonging chiefly to the language of law and public affairs, now used only as an archaic term, =jedermann, here as a dative.—Leib und Leben: Leib, M. H. G. *lip*, meant not only 'body,' but also 'life,' in which sense it formed with its synonym Leben the above alliterative combination; cf. Prol. 34, n.

507. geb' ich tem Thier...preis: Preis (cf. Prol. 8, n.) is here the Fr. *prise* (orig. perf. part. of *prendre*, to take), a prize or booty, and Preis or preis geben (often preisgeben) is thus to give up as a defenceless prey or booty, to abandon [to the mercy of], &c., cf. 1894.

509. in die vier Straßen..., into the four roads, i.e. the four quarters, of the world.

511. Geleit (cf. leiten, to 'lead'; begleiten, das Geleit geben, to accompany), escort, safe-conduct, i.e. either an actual, armed convoy, or a documentary warrant of security. Here it is used in the wider sense in which it is almost equivalent to Frieden as used above, 503, (with which it is here coupled, in one of those combinations of synonymous words noticed in Prol. 34, n.), the guarantee of safety and protection afforded by the ruling powers in the state, *fides* [*publica*]. Cf. 1498, ſicheres Geleit (*salvus conductus*, strictly speaking, the safe-conduct given to an accused person called upon to appear before a court of trial, as to Luther at Worms), for the guarantee of safety implicitly granted to an enemy and outlaw during the fulfilment of a mission; so again, 1562.

512—14. The glove had in very early times a symbolical use among the Germans. In some tribes, among which were the Franks and the Alamannians, estates were transferred by the presentation or throwing down of a glove, apparently in token that the owner divested himself of his property and put it from him. The king or emperor, when pronouncing the ban, threw down a glove in token of the outlaw's changed relations to the society from membership in which he was thrust out. This is probably the origin of the custom of the middle ages, of challenging to combat by throwing down a glove, as a symbolic announcement that the previous relations of peace and amity were at an end. Gloves were also used as symbols in the investiture of knights, and generally in the conferring of powers and honours by a superior lord upon his vassal. When the emperor bestowed upon a town special privileges, he sent a glove in token of their conveyance, &c., &c.

516. ſämmtlicher tes Reichs Biſchöfe : an unusual order of words, formerly used in the legal style, = ſämmtlicher Biſchöfe tes Reichs.

519. Aus unſrer heil'gen Kirche Mutterſchooß. Schooß, lap (1337), is used figuratively like Eng. 'bosom,' e.g., im Schooß ſeiner Familie, &c. Say, '...from the bosom—or pale—of our holy mother church.'

521. Verflucht ſeiſt tu...: conj. as imperat., 'Mayest thou be...,' or, 'Be thou....' Cf. 205, n.

522. Heerweg, in prose more usually Heerſtraße (which is accordingly used in the stage direction, p. 31), a military road, then generally, a public highway. The first good roads were as a rule constructed for military purposes.

525. thun unb laſſen, do and leave undone, Thun unb Laſſen, 'omission and commission,' are standing combinations.

527. was tu macheſt,...: poetic for tein Wachen, &c.

529. Wirbel (Eng. 'whirl,' circular motion) is the top or crown of the head as the spot round which the hair is circularly disposed. It thus differs from Scheitel, which marks the top of the head as the place where the hair parts (ſich ſcheitet).

532. Orem, poetical for Athem, breath.

534. Mark, marrow, in German the symbol of strength and vigour, cf. 810, 1313.—Schritt unb Tritt, cf. Prol. 34, n.

535. ter Kniee Beugung, cf. Introd. Note, p. 103.

541. Hin fahr' ich. fahren as a synonym of gehen now genly. means to travel by some artificial mode of conveyance, zu Wagen, zu Schiff, mit ter Eiſenbahn fahren. It was formerly used almost like ziehen, implying travelling motion in its most general sense, usually with the idea of greater speed and energy than gehen or ziehen ; hence its still current use = to sweep, start, dart, &c., cf. 1067, 1775, 1790, often in a fig. sense, cf. 784. hinfahren (cf. 22, n.) conveys here the idea of a rushing away into destruction, cf. abfahren, hinfahren, von hinnen fahren as expressions for ſterben ; zur Hölle fahren, in tie Grube fahren, &c.

543. ter Hals is the neck, ter Nacken only the back arched part of it, the nape, extending downward into the space between the shoulder blades; bas Genick is strictly the joint between the first and second cervical vertebræ, but often in a more general sense = Nacken. But we say only tas Genick (or ten Hals, not Nacken) brechen.

U.   II

Zweiter Aufzug.

546. Nicht darf ich's wagen, I may not, must not, venture. dürfen never means to 'dare,' with the now obsol. Germ. form of which verb (türren, pres. ich tar, imperf. ich torste or turste) it has no etymological connection, though it was at one time often confused with it: dürfen (formerly to need, in which sense now bedürfen) has always in its current use the meaning, to be at liberty, be authorised or have permission to,—ich darf, I 'may,' there being nothing to restrain or forbid, cf. 51, 434, 550, 997, &c.

549. ziehet sich (lit. draws itself), runs, stretches upward.

550. gebahnte Straßen. bahnen (fr. Bahn, 563, a path or made way), to open up or clear a way, is generally used only with a cognate acc., einen Weg, &c. b., to open up or construct a path or road. gebahnte Straßen are therefore the regularly made, and thus open and public roads, as distinguished from mere trodden paths.

551. Wild and the Eng. 'game' are both used, as still collective in force, even when they happen to comprise but a single individual (cf. 746, 1148); the Germ. Wild is however also used with the indef. art., for a single head of game, though it does not take a plural.

555. Schattensitz, only poet., = schattigen Sitz.

564. für immerdar, poet., = für or auf immer. immerdar is a strengthened immer, dar or dare being an old form = hin, dahin, cf. Prol. 22, n.

566. in vor'gen Zeiten. vorig is now usual only = next preceding, as voriges Jahr, vorige Woche, &c., being obsolete = früher, 'former,' past.—wohl, see 15, n.

567. um Rath befragt. We usually say, En. um Rath fragen (where fragen, to put a question, must not be confused with bitten, to prefer a request, which might also be used), to ask a person's advice, consult him. befragen here but slightly modifies the meaning; it is often used to express inquiry of a somewhat general or detailed character, = to question, make inquiries of, *ply* with questions, &c.

571. Großen, magnates, nobles.

573. Nun? corresponds exactly to the Eng. 'Well?'

574. The neut. pron. es, representing and announcing a subject-clause to follow, is in German necessary only in a direct principal sen-

tence, i.e. where it stands directly before the finite verb at the head of the sentence; e.g. Es wurde gemurmelt, daß.... Cf. 1665, 1711.

576. hergestellt in...: cf. 344, n.

577. all = alles, adj., ...it was all forgotten, namely that, &c.

578—9. See Introduction, p. xxii.—einhellig, cf. 350, n.—beigestimmt (sc. hatte, cf. Prol. 24, n.).

580. den gleich | Betheiligten. sich an etw. betheiligen, to take part in; ein Betheiligter, a participator.—Gedränge is here abstract = das Drängen, the 'thronging,' crowding; in rendering, it may be more convenient to say, the 'crowd.'

582. Die Losung: Ernst.... The watchword [being]: Ernest.... Losung is nom., and must be taken either as elliptical, or as an absolute case, cf. 1779, n.

584. verlauten, = laut (i.e. öffentlich, kund) werden, to become known, transpire.

586. gehabt euch wohl (gehaben = haben, cf. Lat. *se habere*), = lebt wohl. Except in this greeting, still sometimes used, though quaint, gehaben is obsolete.

587. Das eben macht..., 'That is just what makes me anxious.'

588. mit verbißnem Groll: verbeißen, used with regard to pain, laughter, anger, &c., to keep 'away' or down the expression of them, by clenching the teeth (cf. to 'gulp down'); to suppress, smother.

590. alterschwach: the more usual form is altersschwach, feeble with age.

596. Könnt ihr's...erzwingen. The prefix er (cf. Prol. 20, n.) often conveys the idea of acquisition or attainment of what is desired, through the action indicated by the simple verb; thus greifen, (Eng. *gripe*), to grasp = make a grasp, ergreifen (31, &c.), to grasp = actually get hold of; zwingen, to force, erzwingen, to attain or effect by force; similarly langen (1714, n.) and erlangen (1070); so erfechten (1426), to win by fight, erringen (1753), &c.

602. darauf, upon it, in solemn assurance of it.

603. Emphasis on Ein, and in the next line on du.

604. Was bettelst du? The regular construction of betteln is the same as that of bitten, cf. 33, n.

606. Geist, der...spukt. Spuk (fr. the Low Germ.), spectre, ghost, &c.; spuken, to wander about as a ghost, often used impersonally, es spukt hier, this place is haunted. Cross-roads were regarded by the superstitious as the gathering places of evil spirits.

607. Wahnwitziger!...wahnsinnig, cf. 278, n.—werden, cf. 488, n.

608. Wen dürft' es wundern? Es wundert mich or mich wundert, I

11—2

wonder. 'Who could wonder at it?' Lit. (cf. 546, n), who would be
at liberty to..., who 'might,' with reason or propriety,...?

610. Miterbe: cf. Mitbürger, fellow-citizen, Mitmenjch, &c.

611. Einem auflauern, to lie in wait for.

613. Zur (283, n.) böjen Stunte: böje=inauspicious, unfavourable,
'in an evil hour.'

614. The subject of the verbs focht and brennt is the subst. clause in
the following line, indicated beforehand by the es in mir's, cf. 574, n.
'When your having so shamefully deceived me (lit.) seethes in my
bosom....' Or, perhaps better, es may be taken as impersonal, '...my
bosom seethes, my brain is on fire,' the following line being epexegetical (i.e. following by way of explanation), beim Getanken taran, or
something similar, being mentally supplied with it,—'when I think
how, &c.'

616. an Heeresſpitze=an der Spitze eines Heeres.—Kampfgenoß in the next
line being nom., Herzog must also be nom., and to complete the construction a verb was required to which the nom. tu implied in them
should stand as subject (e.g., jo hätteſt tu erſcheinen ſollen). Instead of
this we have in l. 618 a changed construction, which if foreseen from
the beginning would have required Herzog and Kampfgenoß in the acc.

619. Für einen Lantsverwiejnen. (Fn. tes Lantes verweijen (cf. 917), to
banish from the country, hence lantesverwiejen, banished, ein Lantesver-
wiejener, an exile.

620. läufft nun jelbſt daher. daher (cf. 22, n.) means strictly (1),
from a specified point hither. But (2), the point of departure may be
indefinite (cf. tahin=hin, 22, n.), and taher then=her, heran, herbei,
'hither,' up to the speaker or person in question. Further (3), both
beginning and end being alike indefinite, taher is used, like einher (cf.
1013), to denote simple motion 'along,' so taherfahren, to drive along.
Here it may be taken in the second meaning, '...and now you come
running to me....'

622. tie nackten Lenten tir mit Purpur | Bekleben. In composition with
verbs already transitive, the prefix be generally changes the direction of
the action expressed by the verb. In many cases a subst. which with
a prep. may be used as an adverbial extension of the simple verb, becomes the direct object of the compound verb, while the direct object
of the simple verb becomes a dat. with the prep. mit; e.g. Weizen [auf
ten Acker] jäen, to sow wheat..., ten Acker [mit Weizen] bejäen, to sow the
field. Cf. Eng. 'sprinkle' and 'besprinkle.' So kleben, to stick or
paste, bekleben, to cover with something by sticking or pasting, as, Die

Wände waren mit Anzeigen belebt. The word beleben is here used to express contempt, like ftoßen, to thrust, and ſchleppen, to drag. Cf. Eve, p. 82, Aue, p. 236.

625. Thronan, cf. bergan, up-hill, himmelan (1333), up to heaven, &c.

629. Der weiß für alles Rath. der is the demonstr. pron., which regularly stands in place of the 3rd personal pron., where the latter, as having demonstrative force, becomes accented. Thus ' I know *him*,' is Den—not Ihn—kenne ich. Cf. 1568, 1588, 1797, 1829, &c.—Rath, counsel, advice (977), retains in certain idiomatic expressions its old meaning, means, expedient, way out of a difficulty; dafür ist Rath, that can be managed, or remedied; für etw. Rath ſchaffen, &c. ' He knows a way to every end.'

630. rachelos is here as much a poetic licence as ' revengeless,' = not to be avenged, would be in English.

631. Auch du bist ehrlos, i.e. involved in the dishonour of its master through the ban.

634. foll ich nicht von hier (sc. gehen, cf. Prol. 3, n.): foll ich... (cf. 37, n.), ' I am not to...,' i.e. it is not your will to let me....

637. hörſt: hören here for anhören, to listen to.

638. Em. fern ſtehen is generally used only in a fig. sense, to have but a distant connection, not be on near terms with him. Contagion with persons under the ban was avoided as with the plague-stricken.— daß...berührt...ſtreift. The use of the indicat. in a final sentence generally marks the result as practically certain, not, like the subj., as a mere conception which may or may not be realised (1184, 1773); it is therefore here more vivid than the subjunctive. But daß... might also be taken as a consecutive sentence, = so that my breath will not....

644—45. werben um or ſich bewerben um, to make suit for, to woo. Hence Werbung or Bewerbung, suit.

646. Bräutigam and Braut are here 'bridegroom' and 'bride,' but their use is wider than that of the English words, extending over the whole period between engagement and marriage.

649. kreuzte ſich das Volk (in prose usually bekreuzte ſich), would make the sign of the cross in order to ward off from themselves all harm from his baneful presence.

651. des Thurmes Kranz, the crown or battlement of the tower.

654. träuen, archaic and poetic for drohen, to threaten. So berräut, 1027.

655. Und ſpräche Fluch ſtatt Segen.... ſtatt (or anſtatt, originally an Statt), used as a preposition with a subst., takes the gen. case (1285,

1584). ſtatt followed by an acc. (or a dat.) is really an elliptical conſtruction, the acc. being the obj. of a verb in a suppressed subst. clause; so here ſtatt Segen = ſtatt daß er Segen ſpräche, or ſtatt Segen zu ſprechen.

657. Etw. um Gn. verdienen, to deserve something, good or evil, of a person.

661. wenn einmal (cf. 310, n.) von mir...die Rede ward, 'when I chanced to be spoken of.' Note the force of ward, when I *became* the subject of conversation.

664. ob das Aug' ihr flüchtig überlief: change from the direct to the indirect question, ich möchte wiſſen, das frage ich, or something similar, being mentally supplied.—flüchtig (fr. fliehen), lit., fleetingly, for a moment.—überlaufen (sep.), to run over, overflow, be suffused.

671. Armuth, abstract for concrete, = den Armen.—hin, 'away,' 'up,' (cf. 22, n.) marks the completeness of the self-devotion.

672. ſpenden (Eng. *spend*), to bestow as a gift, dispense as alms, cf. 1273.

677. mit Acht belegt (cf. Prol. 24, n.), 'laid under the ban,'.... belegen formed like betleben (623, n.); cf. Gn. mit Ketten belegen, to load (by laying on) with chains, &c.

679. The Ottilienberg, or more correctly Otilienberg, the site of a nunnery founded by St Odilie, lies south-west of Strassburg, in Lower Alsatia. Not far from the nunnery is the Otilienbrunnen, the waters of which are still resorted to, as possessing peculiar virtues, by persons suffering from weak eyes.

681. weithin, far away (from where we are to an indefinite point in the distance, cf. 22, n.), 'far and wide.'—überſchaut (cf. 90, n.), 'commands.'

682. Zelter, a horse that goes at an ambling pace (im Zelt), an ambler; formerly used of a horse suited to a lady's use, a palfrey.

689. erſtarb: cf. on the prefix er (here = 'out,' 'away') Prol. 20, n.; on the use of the imperfect, 277, n.; on wem, without a corresponding demonstrative der to represent it in a different case (as nom. to muß), Prol. 39, n.; and on the prefix ent in entwurzelt, 272, n.

691. noch (cf. 294, n.), still, so late, even after having gone so far. —Note that umkehren is a sep. verb, with the accent on the prefix, and cf. 310, n.

692. Mit dieſem instead of the more usual damit.—Kreis is acc.

695. der Blindheit nächt'ge Binde löſt. nächtig fr. Nacht, night-like, dark as night. Binde, bandage. löſen, to 'loosen,' untie. 'Lifts the dark veil of blindness.'

697. hub (now less usual than hob, 964) fie an: anheben, to begin, but only in this limited application, = begin to speak (die Stimme anheben.

698. wohl, with a certain degree of emphasis (cf. 187, n.), 'truly.'

699. Zur ew'gen Klarheit mir den Blick erschließt. Klarheit here = Verklärung; zur Klarheit erschließt = verklärt (verklären, to suffuse with light, to transfigure, raise from the dim and finite into the serene light of the eternal); '..., to open my eyes, and purify my vision with eternal light.'

702. Der...erhellt (sc. hat, cf. 217, n., and schien in next line), 'who hast (or didst) shed sweet light on....' It seems uncertain whether Uhland wrote erhellt (hat) for erhellte, coordinate with schien in the next line, or whether he intended a difference by the use first of the perf. and then of the imperf., cf. 277, n.

707. Wenn fie mir blieb: imperf. indic. for pluperf. subj., geblieben wäre.—Noch kannt' ich: either the imperf. is used for the perf. (cf. 277, n.); or it indicates that Ernest goes back in thought to a past time (probably that of his outlawry and excommunication) when his hopelessly forlorn condition began, and noch means, up to that time.

710. erquickte is indicative (as appears from the following Gefangenen), she refreshed me when I was a prisoner, not subj. as conditional, co-ordinate with the following line.

714. herberglos (Herberge, Eng. *harbour*, shelter, fr. bergen, cf. 1386—7, and 723, n.), houseless and homeless.—will abgehen, 'is about to....'—Kriegsknecht, archaic term for a common soldier, especially a foot soldier.

716. mich zu merken (so 1409): in the literal sense, and with an obj. expressed, ermerken (so 1208) is more usual.

717. Heb dich hinweg: cf. Luther, Matt. iv. 10, Hebe dich weg von mir, Satan, 'Get thee hence, Satan.'

718. Noch wehr' ich um mein elend Leben mich. wehren with the dat. (1824) is to resist, ward off, &c.; sich wehren (1856, cf. sich zur Wehr— 1410, n.—setzen), to defend oneself. sich um (or für) etwas wehren = sich desselben wehren, to act on the defensive with regard to it, to defend it. sich seines Lebens, seiner Haut wehren, kaum wehren können, are very common expressions. The prepositional construction (Wehr' dich doch um deine Sachen!) seems to be current only in parts of Germany; though both Goethe and Schiller used it.

719. kampfgerecht (cf. bühnengerecht, kunstgerecht, &c., in accordance with the laws and requirements of the stage, of art, &c.; or jagdgerecht, gewehrgerecht, &c., expert in hunting, in the use of the gun, &c.; and

the phrase Em. or einer Sache gerecht werden, to do justice to, satisfy the requirements of) generally=kampffähig, fit or able to do battle. A comparison with 632—3 however suggests that Uhland here intends kampf= gerecht in the unusual sense, zum Kampfe berechtigt, having the right to do battle.—Stch zu! zu is used with verbs='away, on,'—Fahren Sie zu! Er läutete zu wie toll, &c.

723. Jetzt bin ich geborgen (cf. above, 714). bergen is primarily, to bring into safety, afford safety or shelter to, to harbour (1386); hence also to hold or contain (something concealed from view), 1949; so, to hide, now generally verbergen. geborgen, perf. part. as adj.=safe, in harbour, beyond the reach of harm, cf. 1845.—Gott verließ......: cf. 277, n.

727. Nie vergelt' ich dir's. The pres. with fut. meaning (cf. 202, n.) is often almost equivalent to können with the inf., and may or must be so rendered, 'Never can I...;' cf. 718, 1597, esp. 1826.

729. der einzig Treue. The context seems to indicate that einzig here=allein (cf. 414); it also means, singularly, in a unique or unexampled degree.

732. Mir ist, als ob ich...sei, | Als wären.... Meseems—I feel—as though I were...,—I could fancy that...; cf. 1179. According to strictly correct usage, sei should here be wäre (cf. the following wären, hätten, and krampfte in 1179), as expressing a merely supposed case, the unreality of which is conceded. Possibly sei is used as conveying more of the idea of actual presence and reality, and thus rendering the picture more vivid.

735. zu Mittag=zum Mittagsmahl, to or for the mid-day meal.

737—8. sah ich zu, wie...: zusehen, to look on, observe, watch.—der König, Robert (997—1031), the successor of Hugo Capet.

740. der nach Solde gieng: cf. the common phrase nach einem Dienst gehen, to look out for a situation, and 1127. Sold (Fr. *solde*, Lat. *solidus*), pay, in the first instance military pay, hence Söldner (1549), a mercenary soldier; cf. Soldat, taken direct fr. the French.

742. gebannt is here of course not 'outlawed' (geächtet), nor 'banished' (verbannt), but=mit dem Bann (in the special meaning explained in 469, n.) belegt, 'excommunicated.'

743. Und zwar, 'and that....'—Augenblicks, a genit. adv. form=augen= blicklich or im Augenblick, preferred by Grimm to the latter, but not in common use.

746. lief nach deinen Fährten, followed your trail. Fährte (fr. fahren, used, cf. 541, n., of the swift movement of wild animals) is the

Fußſpur of game, the *spoor*, track, trail. Werner compares himself to a hound on the scent.

749. Wie haſt bu es gemacht, daß du...? How have you managed, been able to...?—bliebeſt, cf. 277, n.

752. Es heißt (cf. Prol. 17, n.), =es wird geſagt, man ſagt, they say.—Saat means both seed (219), especially seed that is already in the ground and has begun to germinate (1193); the young green plant (1314); and the standing corn.—Wetterſchein is occasionally used for the common Wetterleuchten, the harmless 'summer lightning'; here Uhland employs it for Bliß, Gewitter.

757. Woraus..., was..., [das] iſt...(or [das], Woraus...): cf. Prol. 39, n.

763. Heiligthum, cf. Prol. 33, n.

764, ff. A reference to the custom in the middle ages of affixing crucifixes or images of the Virgin on trees in the forest, where no chapel was near, for the benefit of lonely wanderers.—Bild means anything formed or fashioned (gebildet) by art, picture, image, &c.; here, picture drawn by words, of the 'great day' of the imperial election; see Introduction, p. xvii.

768. Erhebend ſich beweiſe...: ſich beweiſen was formerly used =ſich zeigen, ſich ſehen laſſen; now we say only ſich ſo oder ſo—e.g. ehrlich, tapfer—beweiſen, or ſich als etwas—e.g. einen ehrlichen Mann—beweiſen, to prove or show oneself to be.... Here the current usage gives a sufficient meaning, but possibly ſich beweiſen is intended at the same time to contain the original meaning of ſich zeigen; 'that just in the very depths of our distress it may present itself to our view, and prove to us its power to raise and support the soul.'

771. Nicht bloß, daß..., Not only (sc. is it the case) that.... Cf. the common construction, Kaum daß er Einen anſieht, = Kaum ſieht er Cn. an, and the similar commencement of a sentence with Vielleicht, daß..., Nicht einmal, daß....

772. Der Sterne Wechſelſtand, an unusual expression, = der gegenſeitige Stand..., 'the mutual, i.e. relative, position,'—the position of the planets towards each other.

773. vorbeſtimmt: more usually vorherbeſtimmen, to determine beforehand.

774. Noch (cf. 294, n.) mitten ins Leben, lit., into the middle. 'Even in the middle of life there often comes a day....'

775. Weſen (old inf. of verb to be, fr. which come war—orig. was—, wäre, geweſen, cf. Eng. *was, were*), mode of being, essential character.—der Gehalt (halten, to contain), contents. Das Gehalt, salary.

778. ergriff (cf. 596, n.), lit., seized, took possession of (cf. 1528), made a deep impression on; so 1444.

783. tie Botſchaft, the message or announcement of the emperor's death, which was accompanied by the summons to the election of a successor.—ergieng, cf. Prol. 20, n.

784. fuhr...in, cf. 541, n., sprang up in (lit. into), came over, inspired.—alles Bolt, cf. 35, n.

785. heraufzuziehn, to rise as it were on the horizon. 'A new era seemed to dawn.'

789. Dem ſonſt ſo Hohes (cf. 377, n.) nie zu Hirne ſtieg, whose brain had never yet conceived such high designs. zu Hirne ſteigen, not a current expression, is here used for (Einem) in ten Sinn kommen, to enter one's mind, come into one's head (cf. ſich etwas in ten Kopf ſetzen, to take into one's head), with the added colouring derived from the current phrase, etwas ſteigt Em. zu Kopf, lit. and fig., gets into his head, makes him overweening, &c.

791. Kann's tech, cf. 30, n.—Recht, law.—wohl, 'well,'=leicht, easily. We may here mark the transition from wohl with full adverbial force to the usually unaccented particle wohl, cf. 566, and 187, n.

792. wer..., cf. Prol. 39, n.—"The old writers...decide that two things, and no more, are required of the candidate for Empire: he must be free-born, and he must be orthodox." Bryce's *Holy Roman Empire*, p. 252. In practice however only Germans and nobles of some standing were elected. In theory every free man had a vote; in practice the lower vassals, when present at the election at all, only followed with acclamation the choice of their lords.

795. Hubgericht (Hube, H.G. but now obsol. or prov. form of Hufe, L.G. form which has superseded it, = a hide or portion of land), landcourt, court composed of Huber, or persons possessing a Hube, and deciding disputes as to the land.—Haingericht, fr. Hagengericht (Hain now =grove, 686; Hagen meant a hedge or fence, = Haz, cf. 454, n., then a place that was umhegt or fenced in with a Hag, and thus a village with a defined boundary), village-court.—Martgeting, the court (Ding or Geting) for deciding matters concerned with the gemeine Mart (1028, n.), or land belonging to the community, comprising wood, water, and meadowland.

796. Eſch (fr. an old derivative fr. eſſen, = Saat), an expression still found in parts of Germany, = Saatfelt, cornland, with various special applications. The Eſch seems never to have been strictly speaking common land, but its cultivation and all measures with regard to its

management were more or less a matter of common agreement among
the owners within the bounds of a village community.   This is still the
case in parts of South Germany and of Westphalia, where Gſch denotes
that part of the arable land within a community or an estate which at
any time is either under cultivation or left fallow (so Sommereſch,
Wintereſch, Bracheſch).—Holztheil, share in the wood belonging to the
community.—Sprache halten, archaic legal expression, = verhanteln, 'do
business.'

799. Maienfeld, usually Maifeld, before the time of Charles the
Great Märzfeld (*campus martius*), was originally the place of assembly
of the whole Frankish army for review, the discussion of affairs of
war, and the offering of the customary yearly presents. After its ex-
tinction in the Gallic part of the Frankish empire it continued to exist
in a modified form on German ground; here it was at first more or less
combined with and finally gave place to those assemblies of the
magnates and dignitaries of the empire which finally developed into
the Reichstag of the completed German constitution. See note on
Reichsſtände, p. 108.

801. unabſehbar: abſehen, to reach with the eye, see to the end of;
unabſehbar, extending so far that the eye cannot reach to the end of it,
hence almost = unermeßlich, measureless, boundless.

803. Der Andrang: Andrang is here concrete, the crowd; more
frequently it is abstract, as in 1100, = das Andrängen, onward pressure,
thronging.

805. ſpannten = ſpannten...aus. Uhland here uses Gezelt collectively;
it is generally equivalent to the simple Zelt, 'spread their tents.'

806—9. See Introduction, p. xvii, n. 2, and p. xxi, n. 2.

810. das Mark von Deutſchland (cf. 534, n.), 'the flower of Germany.'

811. jeden Volks, usually jedes Volks; cf. 842. The euphonic use of
the weak for the strong inflection in the gen. sing. masc. and neut. of
adjectives not preceded by an article or pronoun, as guten Muthes, &c.,
is only exceptionally extended to the pronominal adjectives.

813. ein Händeſchlag (altered by Uhland from the ordinary Hand-
ſchlag, now chiefly used for the giving of the hand in token of a solemn
protestation or contract) = Händeſchlagen, usually Händerdrücken, a shaking
of hands.

816. Wuchs (wachſen), stature, figure.—Haltung (ſich halten), bearing.
—Mundart (Mund, mouth, Art, kind, peculiar way or manner), dialect.
—Sitte, here collective, manners, customs.—Tracht (tragen, to carry,
wear), garb.

817. Waffenfertigkeit, skill in arms, thereby differing from Waffenfähigkeit (cf. 719, n.), ability to bear arms.

818. doch = yet, in spite of all that.—Brüdervolf, a people of brothers; ein Brüdervolf, a brother people, a people of the same race, an allied nation.

820. jeder im Besondern, each one in particular, i.e. privately, with his nearest friends.

822. mählig, often written mälig, but most correctly mählich (root same as in gemächlich), chiefly poetical, = allmählich.

825. erkor, cf. 347, n.—zween, cf. Prol. 6, n.

826. Allbeide, prov., = alle beide, a common pleonasm for the simple beide.

827. Namensbruder = Namensvetter, namesake.

835. selbst is pron., 'themselves,' i.e. when separated from the rest, as the worthiest, and compared now only with each other.—Würde (cf. 124, and 1423) in its abstract and most general sense, personal worth and dignity of position.—fürder, cf. Prol. 28, n.

844. sich legen, of a storm or commotion, to subside.—so, in so far, in such measure, so completely.—Zug, march, 'flow.'

846. diesen oder den · den demonstr., jenen might be used instead; this one or that one, the one or the other.

847. Zu küren, cf. 346, n. In German, the word for 'to elect' (now wählen) is also used with regard to the electors singly, = 'to vote for.'

848. Um nicht am Andern Unrecht zu begehn, cf. 204, n.

850. die beiden Herrn. The form Herrn is now generally reserved to mark the sing., the plur. being written Herren (553). The title Herr belonged in older times to noblemen who without possessing sovereign power were lords of subjects, and thus stood between the Fürsten and Grafen above them, and the plain Edelleute below them. In common usage however it was applied to all the higher and ultimately also the lower nobility (with the addition of the name of their estates,—der Herr von Trosberg, &c.), finally becoming the ordinary prefix to a man's name, = Mr. Here and in 895, 1217 the word is used quite generally for noblemen of some distinction.

854. Und jeder stand dem Andern (= hinter dem Andern) gern zurück (cf. 293), willingly gave the other the precedence, was ready to withdraw in favour of the other.

856. Weil doch.... The force of doch (122, n.)—'though one might wish or think otherwise, yet...,' 'anyhow'—will be best rendered by emphasising the verb ' must.'

858. Gefammte for fämmtliche or tie gefammten, cf. 374, n.

867. Reichskleinote. The more usual plur. of Kleinot, jewel, is Kleinotien, which, formed from the Low Lat. form of the Germ. word, *clenodium*, has displaced the true Germ. plural.

870—73. An almost literal reproduction of Wipo's words: tantas laudes Deum accepisse ab hominibus una die in uno loco, nondum comperiebam.

Si Carolus magnus cum sceptro vivus adesset,
non alacrius populus fuisset... Wipo's naive poetic warmth leads him not seldom to break forth into a line or couplet of hexameter verse in the middle of his prose.

872. Kaifer Karl, Charlemagne, in German always called Karl ter Große (18). It is often forgotten that Charles the Great was a German, not a Frenchman.

875. Wofelbft (so tafelbft, hierfelbft), in which same place, a more precise and formal expression for wo.

877. Wen... (Cf. Prol. 39, n.). Though the speaker has a definite person in his mind, he expresses his sentiment in a general form,—wen = 'any man whom.' Den might have been used, but would have meant 'this man, whom.' Cf. 1055, n.

884. faßt...auf, lit., takes up, viz. by mental perception, 'apprehends,' that is, instinctively selects from what is offered to view and experience that which is congenial to itself.—Bilter, pictures, 'scenes.'

885. Dazumal, a more familiar and colloq. tamals, at that time, then.

887. Erglänzte mir, cf. Prol. 20, n.—ter erften Liebe Huld, 'first love's kind favours were beaming forth upon me.'

888. minniglichem Blick: minniglich fr. Minne, O. and M. H. G. word for Liebe, common in mediæval literature, and revived in the last century as a poetical and archaic expression.

889. ftand in Vormuntfchaft | Von meinem Ohm = unter ter Vormuntfchaft meines Oheims. (This was not really the case, see Introd., p. xix.) The foreign Onkel has almost superseded the German Oheim.

894. O nicht vergeff' ich's. In prose we usually say Ich habe es vergeffen, for 'I forget,' in the sense, do not remember, = have forgotten. The pres. is however often used for the fut., Das vergeffe ich nie!

898. Da kameft tu...herabgefchifft. In German a past part. is regularly used with verbs of motion like kommen, ziehen, &c., where we use the pres. part., cf. 1661, 'the Count came trotting,' &c.

899. Jacht, taken like the Eng. 'yacht' from the Dutch; connected with jagen, which is Dutch as well as German.

911. iħn verlangt | Nach... When the object of an impers. verb is placed first, the impers. subj. es is omitted; es verlangt mich or mich verlangt nach... (cf. 1587), I desire, feel a 'longing' for. For verlangen as tr., 'desire'=require, demand, cf. 423.

913. nach ter Erblichkeit, i.e. of the imperial crown, which he wished to make erblich, hereditary, in his own family.

914. Die iħn erwählten, tritt er..., cf. Prol. 15, n.

917—19. Des Reichs verwiesen, cf. 619, n. On Welf and Adalbert (cf. 262), see Introduction, pp. xxi—ii and notes to p. xxii.

921. Vom Anbeginn (more commonly von Anbeginn): Anbeginn is really the union into one word of two M.H.G. words, *anegin* and *begin*, but is in usage a somewhat strengthened form for Beginn or Anfang, 'from the very beginning.'

922. Ich bin tir zugethan turch Lehenseid. zugethan=verpflichtet, 'bound to,' is quite exceptional. Cm. zugethan sein=to be 'attached' to, well-affected towards.

926. Damit ich iħn bekämpfe, tem auch ich.... A pers. pron. is occasionally used in poetry, instead of the demonstr. ter, tie, tas, as antecedent to a rel. pron. heading a clause of nearer definition. Usually however the pers. pron. has its regular force, viz. that of a simple substitute for a subst. representing an object already spoken of, or present to the thoughts. The relative sentence is then one not merely of nearer definition, but of added statement. Here it may be somewhat doubtful in which way the pron. iħn should be taken, i.e. whether it should be rendered by an unemphatic 'him' (referring to er in 920, i.e. to Mann in 909), or by 'him' accented, =ten, cf. 629, n. For a further illustration, cf. 1866, n.

928. Wohl wittert...: wohl accented, but not specially emphatic; it combines confirmatory force (187, n.) with that of modified assertion (15, n.). It might be paraphrased, 'It is indeed true (as all will probably agree) that...,' and approximately rendered by commencing the sentence with 'Every,' with something of deliberate stress upon it.

929. ħegt auch tir...wiltern Haß...: in prose gegen tich; cf. 445. The dat. may be taken as a *dat. commodi* (cf. 237, n.), = 'for thee.'

931. Haß, ten ich...verwirkt, cf. 347, n.

934. in mich gesaugt: saugen is genly. and more correctly conjugated as a strong verb (so in 300), but is sometimes found weak even in good authors.

937. all (or alle) tie Treue: cf. 35, n. alle Treue would here convey a more general sense, all the fidelity you may have shown me;

while all die Treue means, all that fidelity which you have actually shown me.

939. Auf dich hinblicke, wie du...: might perhaps be taken as a pregnant construction similar to that noted in 86, n., '...look down upon thee, and see....' More probably however wie = 'as', wie du nun...being equivalent to, 'now that thou...' (as in 949).

945. For the common use of was = warum (i.e. um was) cf. Lat. *quid?*

959. alles, neuter collective = alle.

961. Koller is etym. the same with Eng. 'collar' (Fr. *collier*, L. Lat. *collare*), and originally meant the neck-piece of a coat of mail or other garment, but afterwards took the wider meaning, doublet, jerkin, in which it is here used.

Dritter Aufzug.

970. unausgesetzt: aussetzen, to set out or aside (something looked upon as a link in a regular sequence), to make a pause in, suspend; e.g. Der Professor hat seine Vorlesungen auf einige Tage ausgesetzt. Hence unausgesetzt, uninterrupted, unbroken.

971. Einer Sache (dat.) vorbeugen or vorbauen, to *pre*vent or *anti*cipate by taking precautionary measures (orig. stooping to avoid, building up a defence, &c.).

972. Noch fehlt mir euer Urlaub. Urlaub (now = furlough, leave of absence) originally meant Erlaubniß (cf. 302, n.), especially Erlaubniß zu gehen. Adelung (*Deutsches Lexicon*, 1801) gives this meaning as already obsolete, but the expressions um Urlaub bitten, von Em. Urlaub nehmen, as phrases of courtly politeness, may still be heard and read. Much commoner however is sich beurlauben = Abschied nehmen.

975. Der dem, was... | Entgegen wäre, cf. 406, n.

977. Ansehen. ansehen, to look at, to regard; whence perf. part. as adj. angesehen, held in regard, respected, and the subst. inf. Ansehen, esteem or respect enjoyed, influence, authority, Lat. *auctoritas*.

978. Allwärts: usually allerwärts.—Söhnung for Versöhnung (131).

981. Daß er nicht...wanke dem Vertrag: in prose in dem Vertrag.

983. am andern Theil = anderntheils, auf der anderen Seite, andererseits.

984. gährenden: gähren (1093), to ferment; 'excited.'—dämpft den Muth...: dämpfen, to 'damp' sound, soften down light, &c.; to moderate, calm down. Muth is the 'mood,' frame of mind, temper; often with epithets implying boldness and high spirit, cf. 1416, 1502; hence

without further qualification = courage, bravery, 1736. Here we may render, 'the fiery mood.'

985. ber Berwegne8 finnt. verwegen (again in 1501) is an old part., used as an adj., from the now obsol. verb fich verwågen (M. H. G. *sich verwëgen*, = fich auf bie Glück8wage legen, to throw oneself boldly on the chances of fortune; cf. wagen, to venture, from Wage, balance, chance), to be bold enough to, to dare, in which the prefix acquired something of the same force as in fich vermeffen (cf. 1237, n.). verwegen, bold, daring, venturesome from an underestimate or contempt of the danger, differs however from vermeffen, overweeningly and presumptuously bold, in not necessarily implying moral censure, and not seldom even conveying more admiration than blame.

986. Unb hütet..., baß nicht..., usually in prose verhüten, baß....

987. Verbinbung knüpft: in prose, Verbinbungen [an]knüpft. Eine Verbinbung anknüpfen, to form (lit. to tie or knot on) a connection.

988. ahnen, to have an instinctive or intuitive feeling of, forebode, suspect; 'I divine the motive—the reason—of your words.'

990. feib ihr überzeugt, | Sein Heil (cf. Prol. 52, n.) zu förbern (Prol. 28, n.): cf. 15, n.

997. eurem Sohne frommen: see Prol. 6, n. frommen is however rarely used with a subject denoting a person.

1002—4. The King of France is here (cf. 737—8 and note) Henry I., who succeeded Robert in 1031. See Introduction, p. xxvi. An elder daughter of Gisela had died earlier.

1005. Nicht follt' ich...: 'I was not to...,' i.e. according to the will of the power that disposes over events, cf. 37, n.—Traualtar, marriage-altar. trauen, Trauung indicate the actual celebration of the marriage ceremony, and are thus never interchangeable with heirathen, Heirath.

1013. Einhertritt: see 620, n., (3).—ber...Braut, | Der liebenben, cf. Prol. 4, n.

1015. aufgethan | So feligem Empfang: in prose, zu fo f. E.

1018. anberen Berufes Eile, the haste required by other avocations.

1019. Auf En. hören, to give ear to, is more than En. anhören (637, n.), to listen to one; it implies the giving respectful heed to, listening with deference or obedience.—gehet jebem vor: usually geht allem [anbern] vor.

1022. verfchonte is imperf. subj., = verfchonen würbe. En. mit etw. verfchonen (476), to spare one something; Verfchonen Sie mich bamit!— wenn fie anber8 bir: anber8, lit. 'otherwise, in other respects', as to the rest,' almost = fonft or übrigen8, is used in conditional or hypothetical sentences with a weakened and generalised force, = Lat. *modo*. The condition is generally assumed as at least presumptively true, while at the same time the possibility of some slight doubt is suggested; hence wenn anters, *si modo*, may sometimes be rendered, 'if indeed,' 'if really.' anters is however frequently merely expletive, like nämlich, and to be left untranslated.

1026. laßt es ten Boten nicht | Entgelten, cf. 494, n.

1028—9. In 1030 Konrad made war upon King Stephen of Hungary, because he had made incursions into the territory of the Bavarians, in retaliation of wrongs they had done to him. In 1031 the young king Henry concluded peace with him without the knowledge of his father, "iuste et sapienter agens, qui regem iniuste iniuratum, ultro petentem gratiam, recepit in amicitiam." (So Wipo; but Bresslau thinks that a correcter account is given by the *Annales Altahenses,* which say, "rediit autem de Ungaria sine militia et in nullo proficiens, ideo quod exercitus fame periclitabatur, et Vienni ab Ungris capiebatur.")

1028. Intes...Intes..., cf. 40, n. —(sc. tie) teutsche Mark. Mark, Eng. 'march,' is the original word for the modern Grenze, boundary, border; hence border-land; also portion of land, larger or smaller, with definite boundaries, territory or domain generally. It still survives in the names of certain provinces, as the Mark Brantenburg, and in some parts for the boundaries of a district, especially the lands belonging to a village community (cf. 795, n.).—betraut, cf. 654, n.

1029. Aufgebot (aufbieten, to 'bid' or call 'up'), general summons to arms.—ergeht, cf. Prol. 20, n.

1031. Durch...streift | Unheimlich...: heimlich, lit., 'home-like,' homely, familiar, producing the feeling of trustful ease; unheimlich, inspiring uneasiness and distrust, uncanny, sinister, weird. The full force of these words can seldom be given in English; here we might say, 'are haunting, infesting.'

1034. Zehrung (fr. zehren in the sense, to eat and drink, live,— von etw., bei einem Wirthe, &c., zehren—; to spend in living), here simply food and drink, the necessaries of life. The word is now comparatively little used, and generally only for the *cost* of living, while away from home, 'score' at an inn, travelling expenses, &c.

1038. unberitten: beritten, mounted, furnished with a horse.—bewehrt (not fr. wehren, 718, n., but fr. Wehr, obs., = Waffe, weapon), = bewaffnet, armed.

1039. Noch öffnete sich...: in prose noch hat sich...geöffnet would be

U. 12

more correct, cf. 277, n. The statement extends up to and includes the present moment.

1041. ᜑumpf (connected with ᜑampf and ᜑämpfen, cf. 984, n., Eng. 'damp,'—cf. Addison, ' A secret damp of grief'; to 'damp the spirits,' &c.), heavily moist, musty, oppressive; of sound (1483), hollow, muffled; gloomy, dull and depressed.

1044. Erwartet, was..., waits to see what....—will, is going to, about to, will, cf. 714, n.

1047. Uhland represents the popular legend of Duke Ernest (see Introd., p. xxv) as springing up during the lifetime of its hero. In the following narrative, ll. 1062—74, he closely follows the Volksbuch.

1050. In...wandeln fie: in prose verwandeln in..., change into, transform.

. 1052—3. Em. etw. ſchuld geben (ſchuld orig. subst.,=guilt, fault, blame; for the construction, cf. preis geben, 507, n.), to lay the guilt or blame of something on some one, to accuse of, attribute to.

1055. Wie, der ſo jung ſei... (cf. note on 877, Wen...). Though the observation or reasoning of the speaker is in a manner general,—' How one so young...'; yet her mind dwells on the definite person of her son, so that 'one' (or whatever other antecedent we may supply to the relative der) is not really indefinite, and der, not wer, is the appropriate pronoun.

1058. Denn='than' is now seldom used except to avoid an awkward repetition of als.

1067. Magnetberg, a magnetic rock, situated in the Lebermeer, a fabulous sea mentioned in many mediæval legends, the waters of which were curdled and thick, so that ships were held fast in it.

1071. Was je ein Pilger Seltſames erzählt, cf. 438, n.

1074. Leichtgläubige Gemüther, credulous minds, dispositions.

1075. Wohl, cf. 187, n. Gisela gives a figurative application to the mythical stories of Ernest's adventures, making them symbolise his actual adverse fortunes, and especially the treachery and inhumanity of those (Mangold himself being chief among them) whose faithlessness and selfish ambition had caused his ruin.

1078—9. ſcheitern, to be wrecked, fr. Scheiter, pl. of Scheit, a hewn piece of wood, billet; here 'spars,' or wreck.—treibt: the Germ. treiben, unites in itself the uses of its two Eng. cognates 'drive' and 'drift.'

1080—81. Weh ihm...: Weh with the dat. may mean either 'Woe to...,' as imprecation, or 'Alas for...,' as an expression of deep commiseration. Here of course the latter; cf. 1154, n.—entſtellen (ſtellen,

303, n., ent, 272, n.), to change the position of a thing, out of the old one into a worse, to *dis*place, distort.—ihm in 1081 is dat. commodi (cf. 237, n.), =for him, in his personal experience. The meaning is: Alas for him, when the noble human image, in those with whom he has to do, transforms itself into savage and distorted shapes (cf. above, 1066, 1069).

1086. Nicht um tarauf zu ruhen. Note that the subject of the inf. is not that of the main sentence (cf. Eve, 246); it is however easily deduced from the context, which shows the meaning to be: nicht tamit tu tarauf ruhest.—ten Totten nue...: cf. 181, n.

1090. so war tie Abſicht tie: tie demonstr., =tieſe.

1092. Bewahrte is subjunctive, 'that I might....'

1093. Der Augenblick iſt ta, is here, has come. In this common usage ta loses its strictly demonstrative force—'there' as opposed to 'here'—, and means simply vorhanten, existent, present, on the spot, to hand.

1094. in ter Brut: Brut is here abstract, 'during incubation.'

1098. Die Kriegsmacht, concrete (cf. 1467), =tie Truppen, tas Heer, the 'forces.'

1101. nüßen, as trans. oftener nußen (or benußen), to turn to use, 'take advantage of.'

1102. Mit nächſtem, presently, shortly.

1104—6. Geblentet..., | Berſagt mir jeter Austruck...: while we are expecting a nom. case, viz. that of the subject implied in the part., we are met instead by a dat. of the same, and a new subject. The construction is not uncommon, but at least in prose is better avoided. In translation, either the attributive clause must be remodelled, or the proper subject restored in the main sentence, 'I fail to find words....'

1108. Die Vollmacht, i.e. the document conveying the Vollmacht, or powers of a plenipotentiary.—ablangen, prov. = abholen.— bei tem Kanzler: note that bei (cf. 356, n.) means 'at' the chancellor's, though whether we so render into Eng. will depend upon the word used to translate abholen, to fetch, call for, &c.

1109. Usually, Gn. an etw. gemahnen (in common prose mahnen), 269; cf. 471, n.

1114. rühren (cf. 154), touch to pity, move the hearts of.

1116. O gnatenreiche Mutter... The *mater dolorosa*, represented by religious art with her heart transpierced by a sword, according to Luke ii. 35.—ter ein Schwert | Durchs Herz gegangen, cf. 181, n.

1122. Pilger or Pilgrim (1395), pilgrim (Ital. *pellegrino*, Lat. *pere-*

grinus), denoted in the middle ages especially those who performed journeys on foot to Rome, Palestine, or other holy places.—Säulengang, passage supported by pillars, colonnade, cloister.

1135. Luſt means both desire for (1154), and pleasure in (1302); often the two ideas run into one another.

1136. ħeżen means both to hunt, pursue game, and also to set on (the dogs, &c.), let loose on, incite to pursuit.

1138. Wethränten Auges, adv. gen., with tearful eye.

1139. The legend of St Hubert relates how he was hunting one Good Friday in the forest of Ardennes, when he was met by a stag with a flaming crucifix between its horns, and was induced by its warning words to give up his wild hunting life. The story forms the subject of a well-known engraving of Albrecht Dürer.

1141. tođ (122, n.) emphatic, = tennođ (924—5), nevertheless, still.

1144. ein Zwanżigenter, a stag with twenty Enten, ends or points to its horns, 'a twenty-tined stag.'—ſtreiđen, hunting term for fliegen, laufen, &c.

1145. Kurżweil, what makes the time (Weile, 'while') short, 'pastime,' amusement. Cf. the not precisely analogous Langeweile, ennui.—ħätt' iđ iħm (= für iħn) gewußt, lit., should I have known, i.e., could I have devised for him.

1147. ſđweißbeträuft is used for ſđweißtriefend, dripping with sweat. beträufen or beträufeln is to ' bedrip,' to drip something on, the thing signified by the object of the verb.

1149. Siđ...vorgelegt, bent forward to take aim.

1150. gönnen, to bestow of free good will, grant, vouchsafe (1724, 1746); often simply to see with pleasure that something falls to some one's lot, e.g., Iđ gönne iħm von Herżen ſein Glüđ. Hence niđt gönnen is precisely to 'grudge.'

1152. baš leb'ge Pferb: lebig (cf. 465, n.), without a rider, riderless.

1153. in ter Seite meinen Speer, cf. 242, n.

1154. Weħ bir! cf. 1080, n. Weħ seems here also to express chiefly commiseration, but not without a certain approach to or intermingling of its force as an imprecation. We might here render, 'Unhappy man!'—ſeine Luſt büßen (the only surviving use of büßen in this sense), to satisfy or indulge one's desire or passion.

1162. wenn irgenb Noth...: irgenb may be connected either with wenn, = ' if at all'; or (perhaps better), with Noth, = irgenb welđe, 'any...,' 'some...or other.'

1163. ter...mir | Die...Vergangenħeit bebedt, cf. 237, n.; 1189.

1166. tie ift verziehen: verzeihen, like all verbs governing the dat., can be used in the passive only impersonally (Eve, 179, Aue, 297). The impers. subject es is required only when it directly precedes the finite verb at the head of the sentence (cf. 574, n.).

1168. einen Kreis schließen, to 'close,' hence simply to form, a circle.

1174. Sagt meiner Frau,...fie soll (cf. 37, n.)... In 1734 the subj. is used, as simply giving a message to be delivered ; the use of the indic., in the *oratio directa*, conveys at the same time more or less of direct assertion or command. It therefore sometimes serves to express energy of will or desire.

1175. Witwenthum, cf. 74, n. Witwenstand (1227) is the word in most general use for widowhood.—mein vergessen: the gens. mein, dein, fein (1863) are chiefly poetical, cf. Vergißmeinnicht. vergessen usually takes the acc. in prose.

1176. Ward's euch ausgerichtet? Was (it, i.e.) the message delivered to you? etw. ausrichten (Aufträge, Grüße, Befehle), to 'execute,' or 'deliver.'

1177. Mein Friede war...dahin, cf. 22, n.

1179. War mir's, als krampfte sich...: cf. 732, n. sich krampfen an... (Krampf, cramp, spasm), to cling convulsively to....

1183. Nach St. Georgen (sc. Kloster). Georgen is an old genitive.

1186. Zum heil'gen Grabe, to the Holy Sepulchre.—wallte, cf. 251, n.

1197. Distinguish between the sep. durchdringen, which is always intrans., and the insep. durchdringen, which is trans., = to penetrate, i.e., permeate and fill.

1198. Klausnerhaus = Klause (through L. Lat. fr. Lat. *claudere*), a hermitage. Klausner, a hermit, 'recluse.'

1199. tie Straße, acc. of space or direction, 'as I wandered along the road.' Most frequent with advs. and compd. verbs, ten Weg hinauf [ziehen], &c.

1200. Siedelei (ultimately fr. Lat. *sedere*), a settlement, here = Einsiedelei (ein adj. = allein, cf. Einöte), a hermitage.

1205. tes Weges, adverbial gen., = along the road, as in the phrases tes Weges gehen or kommen, and seines Weges or seiner Wege (also seinen Weg or feine Wege, cf. 1199, n.) gehen, to go one's way.

1207. Prunkgemach, not 'state-room,' as most of the dictionaries render, but simply a sumptuous apartment.

1208—11. In reference to the popular belief that the dead cannot find rest, so long as their last wish remains unfulfilled.

1217. Die Herren (cf. 850, n.) des Landes, the chief nobles of the country, i.e. of Swabia.

1218. Daß meinem Sohne,... | Ein zweiter Vater werde, cf. 82, n.—Note that der zum Schutz...sei, and der bevogte (107, n.) are adjective final sentences=damit or daß er...sei und...bevogte. Eve, 248.

1227. Witwenstand, (Stand, rank, class or condition), cf. 1175, n.

1233. Landesherr is now used only=Landesfürst, for the sovereign prince of a country. It was formerly applied to the chief noble in a certain district, in distinction from the sovereign ruler. Here it seems to be used simply as a variation for die Herren des Landes, as above, 1217.

1234. sollten, *debebant*, i.e., 'whose duty it then was...,' used instead of hätten vertheidigen sollen, 'who ought to have...,' cf. 1340. This use of the imperf. ind. in place of the pluperf. subj. (perf. cond., Aue) is not unusual in the 'verbs of mood' können, müssen and dürfen, (Das mußtest du thun=hättest du thun müssen), but it seldom occurs with sollen or mögen, on account of the ambiguity that would often be caused.—jubelten der...Entführung zu, greeted with cries of delight.

1237. Vermeßner Sinn. vermessen (again in 1545) is a part. used as adj., from sich vermessen (cf. sich verwägen, 985, n.), to measure one's forces and make a bold resolve, to dare; then (ver having the same force as in sich verrechnen, to calculate falsely, to *mis*calculate, &c.), to be presumptuously bold through taking a false estimate of one's own powers. Hence vermessen as adj., presumptuous, arrogantly audacious; cf. verwegen, 985, n.

1239. Den du den Hort...geglaubt: a rare construction in German, and admissible only in poetry, though it differs from that noticed at the end of the note on l. 15 only in that here the complement of the omitted verb *to be* is a subst., and there an adverb or adverbial expression.—Hort (Eng. *hoard*), orig., treasure; used by Luther for the object of confidence and trust, 'rock' of refuge, salvation, &c. After becoming obsolete, it was revived as a general and poetical expression for that which affords sheltering protection, applied chiefly to persons, but also to things and places; cf. 1788.

1242. Inmitten doppelseitigen Verbands, placed between a twofold tie, i.e., bound and drawn in one direction by the conjugal, in the other by the maternal bond.

1244. stiefmütterlich, adv., (cf. 482, 1301), in stepmotherly wise, as if you were his stepmother.

1246. Ein Warner komm' ich dir: in prose Als ein Warner (cf. 29, n.).

1248. In prose jürnen usually takes a dat. only of a person or of something more or less personified.

1249. tes Kunrats: it is unusual to inflect proper names when used with the def. art.

1254. um ju warnen..., | Daß tu entfageft... This construction of warnen, and its use in the sense of ermahnen, to admonish to do something, are only archaic and poetical. The usual meaning of warnen is to put one on one's guard *against* something, to warn him *not* to do something. Cf. 482, n. Possibly warnen is here used absolutely, baß tu, &c. being a final or consecutive sentence.—mit tem letzten Hauch tes Sterbenten, &c.: a somewhat bold figure, 'with the last breath of the dying man (Duke Ernest), which I drew in—inhaled.'

1260. Em. etw. vorwerfen, to cast before, in anger or reproach; to reproach or upbraid with. The object of vorwerfen is always the offence, or ground of reproach; in the present passage it is only apparently otherwise, the construction being a pregnant one, = 'You reproach me with what no woman ever endured (sc. to be reproached with).'

1263—4. War meine..., | Die Liebe tock..., cf. 57, n.— Einficht, lit., 'insight,' discernment. 'If my judgment was short-sighted....'

1266. So hab' ich...trum gebüßt; in prose, ihn or tafür gebüßt.

1270. teutfche Junge..., poetic or higher style for, tie teutfche Sprache.

1272. Pflegehäufer, -houses where the sick may be gepflegt (99, n.), =Krankenhäufer, hospitals.

1273. Der Armuth (671) fpent' (672) ich meiner Kammern Schatz, 'the treasures of my store-rooms,' i.e. food and clothing.

1277. Vermittlerin (in prose, eine Verm., cf. Intr. Note) bin ich: cf. 126, n.

1279. Du..., ter tu...trittft: cf. 217, n.—ftrafent: cf. 248, n.

1282. Was thateft tu, imperf. for perf. (cf. 277, n.); berechtigte, imperf. subj. as conditional, 'which would, or could, give you a right' (viz., if brought to the test), tas tich berechtigte forming an adj. clause containing a qualification that is implicitly negatived, cf. 975. 'What have you done that gives you—or, to give you—a right... ?'

1293. Hall usually denotes a more or less reverberating sound; it might here be rendered by 'echo.'

1303. Ritterpflicht unt That: Ritter must be understood with That. This might be indicated in prose by writing Ritterpflicht unt -that.

1309. The oath is compared to a lock, closing the lips.

1310. verfchüttet mein lebent'ger Quell. fchütten, to pour or throw down.

ver has in many compounds the force of closing up, shutting out, as in verschließen, verbauen (1594), vernageln, &c.; hence verschütten, to block up, choke. The living spring of maternal love is said to be choked up, because it is prevented by her oath from welling forth towards her son.

1312. Note the use of wollte, not würte, in order to convey distinctly the idea of *will*. On the order of words, cf. 57, n.

1316. Und bersten sollte mir.... The dat. is here not simply a 'dat. of relation,' or a *dativus commodi* (237, n.), but indicates (cf. 190, n.) that the action takes place under the constraining power or influence of the person or thing indicated by it. It serves here to express more fully the force that already lies in sollte, it 'should...,' i.e., I would make it...

1317. Wie ist mir geschehen? Etw. geschieht Em. (cf. 166, n.), something is done to or happens to one; often impersonally, Es ist ihm recht geschehen, it (i.e., his ill-fortune, according to context) has happened to him as was right it should, 'he is rightly served.' So, Ich wußte nicht, wie mir geschah, lit., I did not know how things were going on with regard to me, what was happening to me, 'I scarcely knew where I was,' 'I did not know what to make of it,' &c. Here we might render, 'What has come over me?'

1320. der Oelberg, the Mount of Olives.

1322. An mir gethan (cf. 204, n.), wrought upon me. This example may serve to show the fundamental idea from which the wider uses cited in 204, n. have proceeded.—vermocht: vermögen is very commonly used with ellipse of zu thun, 'to be able to do.'

1324. Der Schuld...bin ich los: los is in prose now generally used with the accusative. The use of the gen. gives to the otherwise somewhat familiar expression the dignity suitable to poetry. So 1806.

1327. entsühnen (ent, cf. 272, n., sühnen, 446), to take away (einen Fluch), but also, as here, to free from the curse, or purify, by expiation. —The subject of entsühnte is the subst. clause in the following line, emphatically pointed out beforehand by the demonstr. das.

1328. wund gerungen (wund adj., cognate to Wunde, a wound), wrung it sore, so as to wound it.

1332. wascht: the more usual and correcter form is wäscht.

Vierter Aufzug.

Erſte Scene.

In Vorgrund, more usually Vortergrund, foreground.

1338. ſich mir angeſchmiegt. ſich ſchmiegen (an, in, turch, &c.), to wind or creep, pressing so as to fit in or adapt oneself to the object, to nestle. ſich anſchmiegen takes the dat., or an with the accusative.

1351. Schmerzenszug: Zug fr. ziehen, to draw, a line, 'trait'; thus the lines of feature expressive of feeling or character, 'expression.'

1358. ter Erblaßte: erblaſſen (cf. Prol. 20, n.), to grow pale, poetical for ſterben. '...his pale and lifeless form.'

1359. Tritt ſacht auf: auftreten, to set down the foot, 'tread.' The force of the prefix is different in auftreten in stage-directions, &c.,—to step up, on to (the stage, &c.), forward, to make one's appearance.

1360. Wacht, now usually Wache, but still Wachtmeiſter, „Die Wacht am Rhein," &c.

1364. Adalbert vom Falkenſtein. Cf. the name of the great Prussian minister, Freiherr vom (not von) Stein.

1371. Das eben ſoll..., 'Just that it is that shall.'—Aechter, cf. 502, n.

1373. Horſt, the nest or eyrie of large birds of prey, cf. 1801.

1384. auf wohnlich Dach. wohnlich is more than wohnbar, habitable; it means, affording a convenient and comfortable habitation. It might here be rendered by 'hospitable.' Dach has in the comparison here made a double sense, meaning literally, 'roof,' on which the vulture alights, and metonymically, house, dwelling, into which the outlaws dare not enter.

1385. behegt : behegen for the more usual hegen (cf. 454, n.). On be in such compds., cf. Eve, p. 83, γ.

1386. Schluft, the original and true H. G. form (fr. ſchliefen, to creep, glide), which has been superseded by the L. G. form Schlucht (1852), gorge, ravine.—birgt,...Herberge, cf. 714, n., and 723, n.

1392. beutſt, old form for bieteſt, fr. bieten, to offer.

1394. Der ſeinen Herzog in tie Seite warf, who struck his duke in the side, viz. with a spear, see 1150; 'who pierced his duke's side.' werfen, to 'throw,' is used metonymically with an acc. of the object struck, Einen mit Steinen werfen, to 'hit' or pelt one with stones.

We also say Einem etw. or mit etw. an ten Kopf werfen (where Einem is
dat. commodi, cf. 181, n.), and perhaps less commonly, Einen mit etw. an
ten Kopf werfen (where Einen is direct obj. of werfen = strike, as above).
When the object thrown is not mentioned, only the acc. can be used
for the person, Ich werfe tich [mit einem Stein] an ten Kopf. Perhaps
however this construction should be characterized as in modern German
chiefly colloquial.

1396. entsüntiget: ent (cf. 272, n.) has privative force, entsüntigen, to
free from sin, absolve.—nach Hause kehrt, 384, n.

1405. Cf. 1209, n. The spirit of the murdered man is supposed to
haunt the place where his blood was shed, until his death is expiated
by the blood of the murderer.

1408. zu...tie Zuflucht nehmen; usually with poss. pron., meine Zuflucht
nehmen. But we say without art. or pron., bei Jmt. Zuflucht suchen.

1409. Der tich gemortet, cf. 716, n.—ertröhnt (for prefix, cf. Prol.
20, n.): tröhnen, fr. the L. G., is the Eng. 'drone,' but has a wider
application, expressing a variety of sounds produced by strong vibration,
to rumble, groan, peal, bray, echo, &c.

1410. Zur Wehr: Wehr (cf. 1038, n.) is here abstract, = Vertheitigung,
defence.—Weicht vom Herzog nicht, cf. 258, n.

1413. Umflort, here in the literal sense, enveloped in Flor (1760),
gauze used like crape for mourning; chiefly used figuratively, veiled,
dimmed, &c.—Panier, in which p has displaced b in the now obs.
Banier, and Benner (1419) are collateral forms fr. Fr. *bannière*.—Schärpe,
a scarf or sash, fr. O. Fr. *écharpe*, and this fr. O. H. G. *scharpe, scherbe,*
first the bag or pocket carried by pilgrims round the neck, then
a soldier's scarf.

1415, ff. On the time and circumstances of Hermann's death, see
Introduction, p. xxvi.

1417. Schlachtgefild: Gefild (ge collective), poetical for Feld or
Felter; cf. Waffenfeld, 214.

1419. Das Banner...wallt' ihm vor, cf. 251, n.; 'waved before
him, to...'

1423. Mal (Eng. *mole*, allied with Lat. *macula*), a mark, stain,
&c.; cf. Branktmal, brand, Muttermal, mole, &c.—tie Würte trug, 'wore'
the (ducal) dignity, bore the office.

1427. gen, archaic, = gegen. hinauf gen Susa, up from the plains of
Lombardy to the higher lying Susa, which was once a margraviate,
situated a little to the south-east of Mont Cenis.

1429. The pestilence is compared to mildew (Thau for Mehlthau, or more correctly, Meltḫau), which was so called because it was believed to come from the air in the form of dew.

1430—31. ſanken...daḫin (cf. 22, n.) is not merely 'sank down,' ſanken nieder, but indicates further their being carried off by death, 'sank down and breathed their last.' ḫin has in ḫingemäḫt the same force.—Schwaden: Schwad or Schwate, 'swath,' line of grass or grain mown by the scythe.

1437. Noch in der Stunde... : cf. 294, n.

1439. ſein Anḫauch, lit., his breathing upon (me), 'his breath.'

1441. The Germ. bringen includes both 'bring' (1451) and 'take,' in the sense of 'convey to,' in which sense 'take' must never be rendered by neḫmen.

1444. Ergriff, cf. 778, n.—beſchämt, ashamed, because they had not recognised his worth, and had served him unwillingly, 1422 ff.

1448. der Steig (also Stieg; fr. ſteigen, to climb, ascend, 872, or with a word indicating downward direction, 241, to descend), a foot-path, more especially a hilly one. Steg, a distinct word, though from the same root, and meaning originally a narrow foot-bridge, which is still its most proper signification, is also used = Steig.

1449. Ḫat...gezeḫntet. zeḫnten is here used to avoid the more usual, but for poetry less suitable decimiren, to 'decimate,' or slay every tenth man. There is also a side-reference to the feudal right of the lord (here death), to the tenth or tithe, der Zeḫ(e)nte (sc. Theil).

1451. dein brüterlich | Vermächtniß, your fraternal bequest, would ordinarily mean, that made by you to a brother, testifying fraternal affection. Here however brüterlich is used analogously with väterlich, mütterlich, in e.g. ſein väterliches Erbe, his paternal inheritance, mein mütter-liches Vermögen, the fortune received from my mother; and dein Verm. means, not that made by you, but that belonging or falling to you, ' ...thy brother's bequest to thee.'—dies trauernde Panier, the banner, draped in black, is personified and represented as sharing in the general mourning.

1454. lichter. eine lichte Stelle or eine Lichtung in a wood is a place where the trees are so cleared away, or so thinly scattered, as freely to admit the light, a clearing. Hence fig. of the ranks of an army, die Reiḫen licht machen or lichten, to 'thin.'

1457. beſſer fällt ein Mann..., 'it is better that a man should fall— for a man to fall'; a common construction.

1459. O ḫerrlich... ! Ernest's words are spoken in mournful irony, and with something of grim humour, in contemplating his singular and tragic fate.

3weite Scene.

1465. Du gehſt kein Schloß vorüber, a very unusual construction (cf. Prol. 1, n.), in which kein Schloß is acc. of space or direction, cf. 1199, n.

1466. unaufhaltſam, not to be aufgehalten, detained or checked; without heeding any restraint or hindrance. The suffix ſam has here the passive meaning usually represented by bar, cf. Eve, p. 255.

1469. ſchmälen (i.e. ſchmal machen, M. H. G. *smeln* fr. *smal*, Eng. 'small,' now used only = narrow, slender, scanty), formerly had the meaning now expressed by the later formation ſchmälern (fr. compar. ſchmäler), to narrow, curtail, abridge; to detract from, disparage. The modern sense of ſchmälen is to chide, rail at, it being usually a less strong expression than ſchelten (1490). It is still sometimes written ſchmählen, but it seems to have no connection, except through the associations of popular etymology, with the word ſchmähen (1561, fr. Schmach, 58, cf. ſchmählich, 410), to use insulting and contemptuous language towards.

1471. heranreiſen, lit., to ripen up, viz. toward maturity. Cf. herankommen, 19, to come up (towards where we are), heranwachſen, to grow up (towards manhood), &c.

1474. meitet: in prose usually vermeiten, to avoid.

1488. Count Burkhard I. of Alamannia or Swabia was the first to assume the ducal dignity, which he held from A. D. 919 to 926. The historical personage who has given his name to the Count Mangold of the play was distantly connected by descent with Duke Burkhard.

1489. Herzogswürbe trug (cf. 1423, n.), archaic and poetic, had ducal rank; 'that our ancestors were dukes in Swabia.' In M. H. G. *kröne tragen* was similarly used absolutely, without article = König ſein, regieren.

1492. zur Unzeit, at a wrong time, unseasonably.—ſich...offen gab, openly manifested itself, when it should indeed have been cherished, but for the time only in secret.

1498. Zutritt, right of approach or entrance, access; here, 'admission to your presence.'—ſicheres Geleit, safe conduct, cf. 511, n.

1499. Was ſoll mir | Der einzle Mann (sc. thun, cf. Prol. 3, n.)? ſoll (cf. 37, n.), 'is to,' i.e. 'according to your conception.'

1500. Der einzle = einzelne. The form einzeln (798) has superseded the earlier form einzel, which is not uncommon in Lessing.

1503. So iſt's doch wahr...! doch, 'really,' 'after all'—i.e., *though* I would not believe it, though it seemed so incredible, cf. 122, n.

1506. As we say, blood 'flows' in the veins, or 'courses' through them, so the German uses both fließen and rollen, the latter word conveying the idea of a more vigorous pulsation.

1510. An old meaning of the word Rede (connected with Lat. *ratio*), = Rechenschaft, 'account' seems to have mingled with its more current uses in the phrases Em. Rede und Antwort geben or stehen, Em. Rede (now less usually zur Rede) stehen, to answer or give an account to one, hold oneself responsible to him, En. zur Rede stellen (cf. 8, n.) or setzen, to call one to account.

1511. des Bluts, i. e., of kinship by blood.

1514. weithin (cf. 681, n.), far away, onward.—sich vererbt (cf. Prol. 12, n.): vererben (fr. Erbe, 604), to transmit—hence sich vererben, to pass —by inheritance. ' ...are the heirloom of a long line of descendants.'

1516. Wett- in compounds denotes competition, rivalry, cf. Wette, a bet, etw. in die Wette thun, to vie with others in doing something. So Wettrennen, a race, Wettrudern, a rowing-match, Wettkampf, a competitive struggle, or in the abstract sense, 'competition.' The abstract and concrete significations so run into each other, that they can often hardly be distinguished, cf. 1880.

1520. von verkehrter Bahn, from a false path. verkehren (cf. 252, n.), to turn out of the right into a false direction or position, to turn upside down; hence verkehrt as adj., = perverted, absurd, foolish, ' false.'

1523. Auswurf, what is ausgeworfen, thrown out, as worthless, the dregs, scum, &c.

1524. sich erkecken, sich erkühnen, and sich erdreisten, differing as the adjs. from which they are formed (keck, kühn, dreist), have all the general meaning, to be bold enough to, to dare, presume.

1525. Dein Blut...hat sich empört. empören (empor, in die Höhe, bringen; erheben) trans. and refl., is now used only fig., to stir up to, or rise in, revolt (cf. 62), or indignant excitement. Formerly it was also used in a literal sense, so Kleist, Ihre Brust empörte sich, heaved. Here the lit. and fig. meanings are blended; Mangold's blood has risen to his cheeks, stirred up by Werner's reproaches to angry shame at his own conduct, not unmixed with resentment against his bold reprover.

1528. ergreifen, cf. 778, n.—der Väter may here mean deiner or unsrer Väter.

1530. verfangen, perf. part. as adj., a law term, applied to property under sequestration or seizure. Uhl. uses it humorously in Der Schenk von Limburg: „Den Spieß muß ich mir pfänden ;...Der Spieß ist mir verfangen." Em. [mit Leib und Seele] verfangen sein is a not very common expression for, entirely given up to the ensnaring influence or power of, wholly devoted to, some one.—blieb: cf. 277, n.

1532. fonter=ohne, chiefly archaic and poetic, excepting in a few standing expressions, as fonter gleichen, without equal.

1533. verpflichten, cf. 71, n.—heim, 'home,' i.e: to him from whom they came. Werner urges Mangold to renounce the fiefs, by accepting which he had incurred obligations incompatible with the loyalty he owed to Ernest, his kinsman and liege lord.

1534. Die eitle Gnadenkette. In eitel (Eng. 'idle'), as in 'vain,' the original idea is emptiness; hence in both the meaning of worthlessness, unreality, futility. Gnadenkeite (cf. 265), a gold chain bestowed by a sovereign as a mark of favour.

1536. fich einer Sache entschlagen, to break loose or free oneself from.

1538. trägt, bears, brings forth, as its fruit.

1543. Er hat mich viel gemühet : En. mühen = Em. Mühe machen, cause one trouble, is now rare; = Em. Kummer, Herzeleid machen, to cause one sorrow, distress, it is still found as a southern provincialism. Probably the first signification is all that is meant here.—etw. reut mich, causes me a feeling of regret, differs, strictly speaking, from the synonymous expression, Ich bereue etwas, I repent of, in that the former represents the person as involuntarily and passively affected, the latter as himself morally active.

1546. ftiften (cf. 477, n.), to found, establish, set on foot, bring into action, hence Gutes, Böses, Schaden, Heil, &c., ftiften, to 'do,' cause, stir up, &c.

1549. Söldner (cf. 740, n.), a mercenary soldier, both in the simply technical sense, and as a term of contempt.

1550. Sie mögen thun (cf. Prol. 40, n.), 'Let them do....'—(sc. das,) wofür...: cf. Prol. 39, n., end, and Prol. 15, n.

1551. Auch hab' ich nichts mit dir = mit dir zu thun. Cf. Goethe, Packe dich, du haft nichts mit uns, wir nichts mit dir (sc. zu schaffen).

1553. An dir nicht üb' ich...: cf. 204, n.

1555. Stammvater, the first founder of a race.

1557. Schranz[e], a parasite, fawning flatterer; now used chiefly in the compound Hoffchranze.

1564. Von hinnen (cf. hin, 22, n.) used chiefly in an elevated style of composition, = fort, 'away.'—Du erfchienft : cf. 277, n.

1565. Mangold compares himself to a stone hurled by destiny, which must crush Ernest and his followers.

1568. ter, cf. 629, n.—Einer Pflicht, &c. genügen, to do sufficient for, satisfy, fulfil.—Wenn tem Aar ter Seinen eines...fällt : a similar construction to that noted in 181, n.—Aar is the original word for eagle, but is now used only in poetry (also of other large birds of prey), having been superseded by Atler, the modern form of the old *adalar* = Edelaar, noble eagle.

1569. aus ten Lüften : the plur. is poetical, 'from its airy height.'

1571. sich vorsehen, lit., to look before one, hence, to be on one's guard, beware. Cf. in colloquial English, to 'look out.'

Dritte Scene.

1573. winken, Eng. 'wink,' is to beckon or make a sign in any way; so, mit tem Kopfe, ter Hand, einem Taschentuch, ten Augen, &c. winken. Here it indicates the nodding of the ripe ears of corn, which seems to invite the reapers.

1575. einheimsen (fr. an old verb heimsen, and this fr. heim, home) = einernten, to get in, house, cf. the Eng. 'harvest home.'

1580. Föhren...Tannenwälber. In Germany as in England the names of the varieties of pine, &c. are much confused in popular and provincial, to some extent even in botanical use. The Föhre (Eng. *fir*) is a pine, *pinus silvestris*, which we call 'Scotch fir.' Its commoner designation is Kiefer; Föhre is chiefly South German. The Tanne, called also Weißtanne, Edeltanne, *abies pectinata*, is our silver-fir ; the Fichte (*pinus*, especially) *pinus abies*, also called Rothtanne, is the spruce-fir.

1585. falb is the same in meaning with fahl, of which it is an altered form, Eng. 'fallow,' tawny, ashy grey; used also, as here, of the autumnal colour of ripe grain, of fading foliage, &c.

1588. Note that gefangen sein (cf. 205, n.) denotes the condition, not the act ; it does not mean 'be captured,' but 'be, or remain, a prisoner.'—ter, cf. 629, n.

1591. mögt ihr = vermögt ihr...zu..., cf. Prol. 42, n.—tiefen, 'him'; tiefer is used like ter (cf. above, 1588) for the accented pers. pron., with the additional function of pointing out the person last spoken of.

1592. Herein! (cf. Prol. 3, n.). The usual German 'Come in.'

1593. Kuntschaft, archaic, news, intelligence, as the result of inquiry ; cf. Kunde, 1970, n., and sich erkuntigen, to inquire.

1594. umȝingeln (ȝingeln fr. M. H. G. *zingel*, an encircling entrenchment, fr. Lat. *cingulus* a girdle), as mil. term, to surround, encompass. —verbaut (cf. 1310, n.), built up, 'closed.'

1595. noch (cf. 294, n.), might here be rendered by 'just,' 'and scarcely have I managed just to...'

1597. Nichts rettet uns, will or can (cf. 727, n.) save us.—Entſcheid, older but now rare form for Entſcheidung, fr. entſcheiten, to decide ; cf. Beſcheid fr. beſcheiten.

1600. Zuwachs, increase to our numbers, 'reinforcements.'

1606. ſich einer Sache getröſten (tröſten, to console, getroſt, of good cheer, confident), to place one's hopes in, rely upon with hope and confidence.

1609. uns erharrt, not now common, =unſer harrt, itself chiefly poetical, 'awaits our coming.' The idea of expectancy, patient waiting, that lies in harren (cf. 843) is strengthened by the prefix er.

1613. Zum Kampf begehren wir. begehren, to desire (1690), or express a desire, demand (612), is sometimes used with an adverbial expression of the direction or aim of the desire, e.g. nach Hauſe, aufs Land (sc. ȝu gehen) begehren. 'To go into battle is our wish and will.'

1616. verdenken (ver denoting the unfavourable—not necessarily *false*, as Whitney, Dict., *sub voce*—direction of the action, cf. 252, n.) formerly meant, to suspect (cf. Verdacht, suspicion), or think ill of a person, to censure; but is now used only in the phrase Em. etw. verdenken, to censure something in a person, find fault with him on account of it.

1620. ſo gut (sc. als) er kann. als after ſo is very often omitted; cf. ſo viel ich weiß, so far as I know, ſo ſchnell er könnte, &c.

1621. Waffenſtück=Waffe, a weapon; cf. Kleidungsſtück, article of clothing, &c.

1624. bloß geben or bloßgeben (bloß, uncovered, exposed), to expose, lay open to attack.

1625. wappnen, in modern Germ. more usually waffnen; both chiefly poetic, =bewaffnen.

1626. Iſt's eine Sturmhaub'...nur. Sturm, 'storm,' onset in battle. Haube, now used only of a woman's cap, formerly also of a man's, then of a soldier's head-piece of metal or leather. In the middle ages Haube or Sturmhaube denoted the helmet of the common soldiers; that of the knights, newer and more elaborate in construction, was called Helm (1636). Uhland seems to have this distinction in mind in the words Iſt's eine Sturmhaub'...nur. The Sturmhaube was also called Pickelhaube (fr.

Beden, a basin), the term still in use for the leathern helm of the common soldiers.

1627. Wetterſeite, the weather side, that on which the storm beats.

1628. Die Brünne, a M. H. G. word, = Bruſtharniſch, breastplate. —werd' um keine Bruſt geſchnallt, cf. 205, n.

1636. teden for bereden, in the literal sense, to 'cover' (cf. 1164), is chiefly poetical, except in a few standing phrases, as den Tiſch teden, &c.

1640. tiefer iſt mein Sohn. The inflected, masculine form, instead of the commoner dies (Aue, § 201, 1), marks from the very beginning that it is a *person*, of the male sex, that is spoken of, and is thus more descriptive, containing in itself a part of the predicate.

1641. Note that der Deine is 'yours' absolutely, not = your son, in which latter case deine would be written with a small d.—Kloſterzwang, the constraint of the monastery-school.

1642. Waffenwerf, the use or trade of arms, warfare, = die Waffenkunſt, 1750. · Cf. Waidwerf (Waid · equiv. to Jagd ·), hunting, sport.

1646. Füg' es Gott...: cf. 75, n.—wie ich ihn empfieng, cf. 277, n.

1648—49. Der ich..., tret' auch ich...: cf. 217, n. The transposition of the two lines will give the usual prose order.—als Kriegsknecht (714, n.) is not to be taken literally, but as expressing his reduced condition, and especially his outward appearance as contrasted with his present knightly accoutrement.

1650—51. wobei = bei welchem, 'in which.' ſolcher (ſolch and welch are exact correlatives, *of such kind, of which kind*) serves here only to give emphasis to the expression, and is omitted in translation.

1655. Laß (sc. mich, cf. 1061, 1850) dir erzählen.—Schwank, a facetious trick, joke, or the story of such, a merry tale, farce, &c. The popular anecdote here told is of uncertain origin. An old topographer says of the little town of Abensberg in Bavaria that it had three gates, eight square and thirty-two round towers, in memory of the first Count of Abensberg, his three wives, eight daughters and thirty-two sons.

1657. Kaiſer Heinrich: Henry II., Konrad's immediate predecessor.

1658. Aufs Jagen ausritt: now usually auf die Jagd gehen, reiten, &c.

1661—62. fam...getrabt, cf. 898, n.—Reiſigen. reiſig, adj. (fr. Reiſe, in the old meaning, Kriegszug, military expedition) = mounted and ready for a war expedition. Ein Reiſiger, a horseman, trooper.

1664. Rößlein is here rather caressing and familiar than really diminutive in force; cf. the similar use of Freundchen, Mütterchen, &c. We might approximately render, 'their good steeds.'

U.   13

1669. befehlen, to commend to the care and keeping of, is almost obsolete, except in a poetical or biblical style. empfehlen, to recommend, does not quite fill its place.

1671. es refers generally to the whole proceeding,—May God let it prosper, 'God give his blessing.'

1674. So, with the full accent, is often used = so wie die Sachen stehen, as things stand, as things really are.

1675. sich lossagen von, to declare one's severance from, to renounce, disown.

1691. Ein Scharlachmantel: note that Scharlach (L. Lat. *scarlatum*), is always a subst., meaning originally scarlet cloth, and later, the colour scarlet. Here and below, 1702, it has the former meaning, in which use alone it could form the above compound. The adj. scarlet is scharlachroth, scharlachen, or scharlachfarben.

1696. Der Schild, shield; das Schild, sign-board, &c.

1698. Er würd' euch angeboten, imperf. subj. as conditional, = würde... werden.—gält' uns nicht | Für schlimmes (cf. 88, n.) Zeichen : für etw. gelten (1805, n.), to pass for, be regarded as....

1702. welt, 'withered' (1582); Scharlach as above. The faded scarlet mantle is compared with a withered flower.

Fünfter Aufzug.

1706. kaum bin ich..., | Schon blickt er... (or in common prose oftener, so blickt er schon...), 'Scarcely..., when....'

1710. Er jedes (= alles, cf. 1019) fördert, cf. Prol. 28, n.—im Schwung, in motion, agoing. Cf. colloq. Eng., 'in full swing.'

1711. Etw. ist Em. angelegen = liegt Em. am Herzen, is an object of interest or care to him. The subject (cf. 574, n.) is here the subst. clause, Daß... &c.

1714. langt: nach etw. langen, to reach, stretch out the hand after.

1717. der Ungar, cf. 1028—9, n.—forthin (cf. 22, n., 681) usually = fortan, 'henceforth,' i.e., *from this time* forward, is here used, = 'further,' of the continuance of something already existing.

1719. kann ich's erzwingen? es, viz. what is demanded of him.

1722. The conditional clause fommen fie ins Felb is to be taken with Sie find verloren, the following ‘Gewiß ift ihr Verderben being an emphasizing repetition of the consequence, the condition being now assumed.— Frift is a space of time, or its termination, within or at the end of which something is to be done, hence often=respite, delay.

1726. The address with Herr without poss. pron. is only archaic, except as used occasionally to express anger or excitement.

1727. Vorwacht, later form (cf. 1360, n.) Vorwache, both now disused, =Vorposten, outpost, outguard.—Handgemenge (mengen, to mingle, cf. handgemein werden, to come to close quarters, to blows), a contest hand to hand, close engagement.—fie weicht, cf. 258, n.—Sie in the next line refers of course to the enemy.

1728. Mähre or Märe, now only archaic, news, report. Its further meaning, story, tradition, legend, is partly preserved in the dimin. Märchen.

1729. Dort unterhalb: the compounds of halb, used as prepositions with the gen., are uncommon as adverbs.

1732. Bald wieder find wir hier: the pres. is here almost commoner than the fut., cf. 202, n.

1733. empfahn: fahen obsol. or archaic form of fangen.

1735. frifch, briskly.—im Saft ftehen is said of trees in full sap, in prime vigour. The metaphor does not seem very happily applied to swords. It is hardly to be supposed that the word Saft can be intended to suggest blood.

1736. Es fämpft fich rafch. Cf. for this impersonal reflexive use of many verbs in German, Hier liegt fich's bequem, it is comfortable lying here, here one can lie comfortably; Da wohnt fich's fchön, &c.

1740. Strom differs from Eng. ‘stream’ in always denoting a strong current (Strömung), and usually considerable volume. So ein Bergftrom, a mountain torrent, der Rheinftrom, &c.

1741. Dem man...: in prose, gegen den man einen fo mächtigen...

1746. das Heil, cf. Prol. 51, n. and 1204, Seelenheil. Adalbert has hoped to find in the sacrifice of his life for Ernest that ‘salvation’ of his soul which he had vainly sought to secure by penance.

1751. Jetzt tummle dich. tummeln (connected with Taumel, Eng. ‘tumble’), to put into vigorous motion to and fro, as ein Pferd tummeln, to exercise, make to prance. fich tummeln, to take active exercise, spring about, wrestle; to bestir oneself, fam., ‘look alive,’ &c.—Strauß, chiefly in poetry, a hard struggle.

1753. Meisterschaft, in allusion to the course of initiation into a trade, in the time of the old guilds. The Lehrling (1750) or apprentice became a Geselle, or journeyman, and finished the course which gave him the right to become himself a master, the Meisterschaft, by producing his Meisterstück, or masterpiece, as the proof of his skill.

1762. Jetzt geht's hinab...: es geht, lit., there is a going, the context telling who it is that goes. Wohin geht's? may thus mean, Where are you going? Where are they going? or, Where shall we go?—Hochzeitreihn: Reihen or Reigen, chiefly poetical, an orderly procession following a leader, especially in dancing, thus 'dance,' especially a circular dance.

1764. In allusion to the custom in mediæval chivalry, according to which every knight devoted himself to the service of some noble lady.— We say an Gn., etw., denken, but more usually Jmds., einer Sache gedenken.

1767. zum Tod, not temporal (=bis zum Tode), but final (=zu sterben); 'inspire me with courage to die.'

1771. dieser Männer, gen. in apposition to the poss. pron. unsre, the subst. Kraft belonging to both.

1772. erschwellen (er—cf. Prol. 20, n.—with similar force to an in anwachsen, indicating the beginning and gradual rise of the action) is a somewhat rare word, in place of the simple schwellen, or of anschwellen, as in 1769.

1779. Und drunten schon die Lanzen vorgestreckt neither is a complete sentence, nor stands in grammatical or logical connection with one. It cannot be strictly called elliptical, since no suitable way of filling up an ellipse offers itself, and the speaker evidently has none even remotely in mind. We have simply the conjunction of a subst. with a perf. part., which expresses the verbal idea in a past but not finite form, the connection of the two being not grammatically indicated and defined, but rendered by the context alone sufficiently clear for practical purposes. Such 'absolute' constructions are not uncommon, especially in animated language, cf. 1153, 1792. Buyck's description of the battle of Gravelines in the opening scene of Goethe's Egmont offers several examples.

1781. Raubgevögel, birds of prey. Gevögel is the old collective of Vogel, which has been superseded by the now current Geflügel.—wimmeln, to be in lively thronging motion, to swarm; Fische wimmeln im See. wimmeln von (der See wimmelt—or, es wimmelt im See—von Fischen), to swarm, or be alive with.

1783. Jetzt sind sie zusammen, cf. Prol. 3, n.

1784. das, 'those,' cf. Eve, p. 34, Aue, § 201, 1. Are they men, or mere passive waves?

1785. zerwirft (cf. 490, n.), dashes aside and into fragments, 'dashes into spray.'

1786. Glied as a mil. term is 'rank,' a number of men abreast. Reihe, when used in contradistinction to this, is 'file,' a number of men one behind the other (so Reih' und Glied, 'rank and file'); but in its more general meaning it denotes a row or line generally. Below, 1794, it is used interchangeably with Glied.

1787. Seht mir den Werner! mir is an example of the 'ethical dative,' which—always a personal pronoun—marks the person as taking or supposed to take an interest in the action or event spoken of, and often serves simply to give liveliness to the expression. It can seldom be rendered in modern English, though not uncommon in Shakspeare: 'Say'st thou me so?' 2 *Hen. VI.*, II. 1, 109; 'leap me over this stool and run away,' ib. 144; 'Whip me such honest knaves,' *Oth.* I. 1, 49. A fixed line can hardly be drawn between it and the 'dat. of interest' (cf. 237, n.), of which it is really but a particular case, cf. the last quoted passage from Shaks., further, 'I will roar you as gently...,' *Mids.* I. 2, 84, &c. Cf. Aue, § 358, Eve, 67.

1790. Fährt, cf. 541, n.—einzeln = einzelnen, cf. 1500, n.

1792. zerspellen, for the modern zerspalten, to split, cleave asunder.

1795. Traun (from in Treuen, old dat. sing. of Treue), 'i' faith,' 'forsooth.'

1797. O! die sind, cf. 629, n.—stark often = very, very much.

1803. lüftet er die Schwingen. lüften (in die Luft, i.e., in die Höhe, heben), to raise into the air, to 'lift,' now generally used for, to raise slightly, as den Hut, Schleier, &c., lüften.—Schwinge and Fittig are both poetical words for Flügel.

1804. Sie holen aus. ausholen, orig. a fencing expression, to stretch out the arm, or throw the body into position, preparatory to striking a blow, hence, to take a deliberate start, to 'make ready.'

1805. Jetzt gilt's. gelten (connected with Geld, and giltig, valid), to be worth, to be valid, of force, to hold good, has numerous idiomatic uses.   The impers. es gilt, used alone, means, it is serious earnest, now's the time, now comes the tug of war.—Jetzt wär's Zeit: the conditional is often used in place of the indicat., to tone down the positiveness of a statement, or to indicate some reserve or diffidence in making it. The same thing is found in English, though less frequently. 'Now, me-thinks, 'twere time...'

1807. umflü'gelt: the usual term for to 'outflank' is überflü'geln.

1809. Segelbaum, archaic for Mast.

1810. Knaul, or Knäuel, more approved form Knäuel (connected with Eng. ' clew'), a ball, of thread or the like. We should usually say in einen or zu einem Knäuel gerollt.

1811. An allusion to the story of Laocoon, Virg. *Aen.* II. 203— 227, represented in the well-known group in the Vatican.

1814. sich [auf]bäumen, to erect oneself (straight, like a tree), to rear.

1822. im Arm, *on* his arm, supporting him, see below, stage-direction.

1823. Recke, mighty warrior, hero, an old word very common in mediæval heroic poetry.

1826. bring' ich ihn=kann ich ihn bringen, cf. 727, n.

1833. stopfen (L. Lat. *stupare*, fr. Lat. *stupa*, tow) is to 'stuff' (Federn in ein Kissen, or ein Kissen mit Federn, &c.), or 'stop,'=fill up, close, obstruct (ein Loch, &c.). Its use for 'stop'=check, arrest, is chiefly Low Germ. (stoppen); it seems not quite certain whether its application as a medical term, die Blutung stopfen (now more usually das Blut stillen), to check bleeding, to stanch, is to be brought under this head, or whether it is to be referred, together with its use=to constipate (verstopfen), to the first quoted meaning.—seines Blutes Qualm=sein qualmendes Blut, his reeking blood.

1834. Ist's Leben noch nicht gar? The original meaning of gar is finished, ready for use. As adj. it is now used only for 'done'= cooked enough. Its use as here=alle, at an end, used up, &c., is a provincialism, found in Swabia, Bavaria, &c. The adv. gar, 'very,' originally meant completely, as is still to be seen in ganz und gar.

1841. Jetzt reißt's, i. e. der Lebensfaden, the thread of life breaks.

1845. Er ist geborgen, cf. 723, n.

1856. auf den Tod is not simply 'till death'; auf with the acc. here marks the *direction* in which the result must lie, as in the expressions auf den Tod siechen,—verwundet sein, 'to be sick unto death,' sich auf Leben und Tod schlagen, to fight so that the issue is life or death, *à outrance.* sich auf den Tod wehren is then to meet death as the inevitable end in self-defence to the last. The Eng. phrase 'to the death' might perhaps be made to convey this meaning.

1857. eine Neige Bluts. Neige (fr. neigen, to incline, descend, go down to the end), the remainder, sediment, lees.

1859. Popular superstition.—kräftigt, cf. 202, n.

1860. In allusion to the story of Cadmus and the dragon's teeth.

1864. Cf. 1110, ff.

1866. Sie bluten..., sie.... (Cf. 926, n.) Sie is not here equivalent to the demonstr. sie, is not the grammatical antecedent to the following rel. sie, but has the regular independent force of a pers. pron., referring to certain persons whom the speaker has in his mind. sie is epexegetical, explaining who these are; it is a rel. with the antecedent unexpressed (cf. Prol. 15, n.). Written in full then, the meaning is, Sie bluten alle, nämlich sie, welche sie übrig sind. The mode of expression is here indicative of excitement.

1868. alles Streits may mean either (cf. 35, n.), of all the strife (viz., in the particular case, just terminated), or by hyperbole, of all strife.—Heerhorn (now little used), war-trumpet.

1869. Meinst du? 'So,' in 'Do you think so?', 'I believe so,' &c., is usually left unexpressed in German.

1870. On the order of words (ich being made emphatic), cf. 57, n.

1874. Markstein, cf. 1028, n.—Haus und Hof, cf. Prol. 34, n.

1876. Blutsverwandtschaft (in 1553, abstract), here concrete and collective (cf. 239, 401), blood relations, kith and kin.

1879. Geeifert und gewettet is a ἓν διὰ δυοῖν for gewetteifert, vied. eifern (mit Imp. in etw., um etw.) is used = wetteifern (cf. 1516, n.), but wetten, to bet, is quite unusual in this meaning.

1884. Halt (sc. den Schild) vor! 'Defend thyself.'

1891. ohne Wunde..., | Als jene: for ohne andere..., als.

1897. O thut es doch! Accent on thut, doch unaccented. doch here strengthens the imperative, adding urgency to the request. Note that if doch were accented, it would be equivalent to dennoch, nevertheless.

1900. Ich hab' es durchgehaun durch euer Heer. We say sich durchhauen, durchschlagen, durcharbeiten durch..., to hew, fight, work one's way through... The above construction is here used somewhat freely for, 'I have hewn a way for it through your army.'

1904. Hieher gehört's, lit., it belongs here (hither), 'here is its place.'

1906. Was ist's? 'What is this?' What ails me?

1907. The Fähnrich (either fr. Fahne, or a corruption of M. H. G. *venre*, = Fahnenträger: the second part of the word is of uncertain origin; Weigand's etymology, followed by Whitney, is at least doubtful) was in the middle ages and later really the bearer of the standard or colours. In modern times Fähnrich became, like 'ensign,' the designation of the officer of lowest standing in the infantry, who is however now more usually called Sekondeleutnant, while the Fähnrich is a non-commissioned officer ranking next to the Feldwebel, or serjeant-major, and serving as a candidate for a commission. He wears the officers' sword-knots (Portépée), and is hence also called Portépéefähnrich.

1921. Die Kerzen mögt (Prol., 42, n.) ihr neu | Anzünden, cf. 536—9.

1933. erwürgen (er, cf. Prol. 20, n.), orig. and properly, to suffocate or strangle, then often used generally for, to kill, slay.

1935. Geschehen ift (cf. Prol. 39, n., end, and Prol. 15, n.), zu was (cf. Prol. 42, n.)…, What you stirred me up to do, is done.

1942. Sich einer Sache entledigen (cf. ledig, 465, n.), to deliver oneself of, discharge, deliver.

1943. Die mir…bedünkt. We say es dünkt mich or mir (754), but the compound with be is properly transitive, taking only an acc. The dat. is not uncommon, but is rightly condemned by Grimm as a groundless deviation from analogy (cf. bedenken, &c.).

1946—58. See Introduction, pp. xxv—vi.

1953. Angebinde, a present, from an old custom of tying presents, as flowers, money, and other gifts, to the neck of the receiver, on birthdays, &c. En. anbinden for Em. ein Geschenk machen, is not yet quite obsolete. Grimm does not sufficiently distinguish Angebinde from Eingebinde, which is only a christening present, originally one tied by the godparents into the child's cradle (einem Pathen etwas einbinden).

1954. in Gott or im Herrn entschlafen (272, n.), to 'die in the Lord.'

1957. The lance of St Maurice was one of the insignia of the kingdom of Burgundy, being regarded as sacred, and bearing a similar symbolical character to that of sword and sceptre. When it passed into the possession of the German kings, and whether there were two sacred lances, one given by Rudolf II. to Henry I. and the other by Rudolf III. to Konrad II., appears somewhat uncertain. (Waitz, *Deutsche Verfassungsgeschichte*, VI. 233—5.)

1960. wie sauer mir | Die Frucht geworden. sauer does not here mean that the fruit has proved 'sour' in the tasting. Etw. wird Em. sauer is a very common expression, meaning, costs one laborious effort, severe toil; Dem Kranken wurde das Gehen sauer. So, Er läßt es sich sauer werden, takes great pains, works hard; Em. das Leben sauer machen, to make one's life a burden, embitter one's life, &c.—spielend, as easily as if it were mere play. '…didst thou know the pain and toil that fruit has cost me, which thou so lightly pluck'st.'

1970. Kunde (knowledge, news, intelligence), is often used by Uhland=Sage, Heldenlied, legend.—The alliterative combination (cf. Prol. 34, n.) singen und sagen expresses the collective functions of the poet or minstrel of the middle ages. In M. H. G. *singen*=to sing, to

read or repeat in a recitative chant, also to compose and recite lyrics;
sagen = to narrate, read or recite poems, or compose them for recitation.
There was thus, in this connection, no sharp distinction between the
two words. (Cf. a similar approach to each other in *sing* and *say*, as
combined in ecclesiastical use, in the Prayer-book.) The phrase is often
used by Uhland and by Goethe to express generally the activity of the
poet. Here we may render, ‘sing or tell.’

1974. Unb ſo mit tiefem Mitleit, for mit ſo tiefem Mitleib, an order of
words at one time common.

1978. Soll ter (cf. 629, n.) mir tott ſein...? Soll... (lit., Is he to
be...? i.e.,—cf. 37, n.—is he according to your conception to be so
regarded), has the force, Do you mean to say that...? Can it be that...?
Cf. the common usage, Er ſoll krank ſein, he is said to be ill (i.e. the
authors of the report will have it that...).

1980. In allusion to the legends preserved in the Volksbuch.

* Excepting the historical notes, and a few others of a character not admitting of being briefly indicated. Parallel and illustrative passages quoted in the notes are not repeated in the index, unless they are also the subject of a separate note.

CAMBRIDGE: PRINTED BY C. J. CLAY, M.A. AT THE UNIVERSITY PRESS.

CAMBRIDGE UNIVERSITY PRESS.

THE PITT PRESS SERIES.

I. GREEK.

Aristophanes. Aves—Plutus—Ranæ. By W. C. GREEN, M.A., late Assistant Master at Rugby School. 3*s.* 6*d.* each.

Aristotle. Outlines of the Philosophy of. Compiled by EDWIN WALLACE, M.A., LL.D. Third Edition, Enlarged. 4*s.* 6*d.*

Euripides. Heracleidæ. With Introduction and Critical Notes. By E. A. BECK, M.A., Fellow of Trinity Hall. 3*s.* 6*d.*

Euripides. Hercules Furens. With Introduction, Notes and Analysis. By A. GRAY, M.A., and J. T. HUTCHINSON, M.A. New Ed. 2*s.*

Herodotus, Book VIII., Chaps. 1—90. Edited with Notes and Introduction. By E. S. SHUCKBURGH, M.A. 3*s.* 6*d.*

———— **Book IX., Chaps. 1—89.** By the same Editor. 3*s.* 6*d.*

Homer. Odyssey, Book IX. With Introduction, Notes and Appendices by G. M. EDWARDS, M.A. 2*s.* 6*d.*

Luciani Somnium Charon Piscator et De Luctu. By W. E. HEITLAND, M.A., Fellow of St John's College, Cambridge. 3*s.* 6*d.*

Platonis Apologia Socratis. With Introduction, Notes and Appendices. By J. ADAM, B.A. 3*s.* 6*d.*

———— **Crito.** With Introduction, Notes and Appendix. By the same Editor. 2*s.* 6*d.*

Plutarch. Lives of the Gracchi. With Introduction, Notes and Lexicon by Rev. H. A. HOLDEN, M.A., LL.D. 6*s.*

———— **Life of Nicias.** With Introduction and Notes by the same Editor. 5*s.*

———— **Life of Sulla.** With Introduction, Notes, and Lexicon. By the same Editor. 6*s.*

Sophocles. Oedipus Tyrannus. School Edition, with Introduction and Commentary by R. C. JEBB, Litt.D., LL.D. 4*s.* 6*d.*

Xenophon. Agesilaus. By H. HAILSTONE, M.A., late Scholar of Peterhouse, Cambridge. 2*s.* 6*d.*

Xenophon. Anabasis. With Introduction, Map and English Notes, by A. PRETOR, M.A. Two vols. 7*s.* 6*d.*

———— **Books I. III. IV. and V.** By the same. 2*s.* each.

———— **Books II. VI. and VII.** By the same. 2*s.* 6*d.* each.

Xenophon. Cyropaedeia. Books I. II. With Introduction and Notes by Rev. H. A. HOLDEN, M.A., LL.D. 2 vols. 6*s.*

———— ———— **Books III. IV. and V.** By the same Editor. 5*s.*

London: Cambridge Warehouse, Ave Maria Lane.

20/7/88

II. LATIN.

Beda's Ecclesiastical History, Books III., IV. Edited with a life, Notes, Glossary, Onomasticon and Index, by J. E. B. MAYOR, M.A., and J. R. LUMBY, D.D. Revised Edition. 7*s.* 6*d.*

———— **Books I. II.** By the same Editors.   [*In the Press.*

Caesar. De Bello Gallico, Comment. I. With Maps and Notes by A. G. PESKETT, M.A., Fellow of Magdalene College, Cambridge. 1*s.* 6*d.*

———— **Comment. I. II. III.** 3*s.*

———— **Comment. IV. V., and Comment. VII.** 2*s.* each.

———— **Comment. VI. and Comment. VIII.** 1*s.* 6*d.* each.

Cicero. De Amicitia. Edited by J. S. REID, Litt.D., Fellow of Gonville and Caius College. Revised Edition. 3*s.* 6*d.*

Cicero. De Senectute. By the same Editor. 3*s.* 6*d.*

Cicero. In Gaium Verrem Actio Prima. With Notes, by H. COWIE, M.A. 1*s.* 6*d.*

Cicero. In Q. Caecilium Divinatio et in C. Verrem Actio. With Notes by W. E. HEITLAND, M.A., and H. COWIE, M.A. 3*s.*

Cicero. Philippica Secunda. With Introduction and Notes by A. G. PESKETT, M.A. 3*s.* 6*d.*

Cicero. Oratio pro Archia Poeta. By J. S. REID, Litt.D. Revised Edition. 2*s.*

Cicero. Pro L. Cornelio Balbo Oratio. By the same. 1*s.* 6*d.*

Cicero. Oratio pro Tito Annio Milone, with English Notes, &c., by JOHN SMYTH PURTON, B.D. 2*s.* 6*d.*

Cicero. Oratio pro L. Murena, with English Introduction and Notes. By W. E. HEITLAND, M.A. 3*s.*

Cicero. Pro Cn. Plancio Oratio, by H. A. HOLDEN, LL.D. Second Edition. 4*s.* 6*d.*

———— **Pro P. Cornelio Sulla Oratio.** By J. S. REID, Litt.D. 3*s.* 6*d.*

Cicero. Somnium Scipionis. With Introduction and Notes. Edited by W. D. PEARMAN, M.A. 2*s.*

Horace. Epistles, Book I. With Notes and Introduction by E. S. SHUCKBURGH, M.A., late Fellow of Emmanuel College. 2*s.* 6*d.*

Livy. Book XXI. With Notes, Introduction and Maps. By M. S. DIMSDALE, M.A., Fellow of King's College. 3*s.* 6*d.*

Lucan. Pharsaliae Liber Primus, with English Introduction and Notes by W. E. HEITLAND, M.A., and C. E. HASKINS, M.A. 1*s.* 6*d.*

Ovidii Nasonis Fastorum Liber VI. With Notes by A. SIDGWICK, M.A., Tutor of Corpus Christi College, Oxford. 1*s.* 6*d.*

Quintus Curtius. A Portion of the History (Alexander in India). By W. E. HEITLAND, M.A., and T. E. RAVEN, B.A. With Two Maps. 3*s.* 6*d.*

London: Cambridge Warehouse, Ave Maria Lane.

Vergili Maronis Aeneidos Libri I.—XII. Edited with Notes by A. SIDGWICK, M.A. 1s. 6d. each.

———— **Bucolica.** With Introduction and Notes by the same Editor. 1s. 6d.

———— **Georgicon Libri I. II.** By the same Editor. 2s.

———— ———— **Libri III. IV.** By the same Editor. 2s.

III. FRENCH.

Corneille. La Suite du Menteur. A Comedy in Five Acts. With Notes Philological and Historical, by G. MASSON, B.A. 2s.

De Bonnechose. Lazare Hoche. With three Maps, Introduction and Commentary, by C. COLBECK, M.A. 2s.

D'Harleville. Le Vieux Célibataire. A Comedy, Grammatical and Historical Notes, by G. MASSON, B.A. 2s.

De Lamartine. Jeanne D'Arc. Edited with a Map and Notes Historical and Philological, and a Vocabulary, by Rev. A. C. CLAPIN, M.A., St John's College, Cambridge. 2s.

De Vigny. La Canne de Jonc. Edited with Notes by Rev H. A. BULL, M.A., late Master at Wellington College. 2s.

Erckmann-Chatrian. La Guerre. With Map, Introduction and Commentary by Rev. A. C. CLAPIN, M.A. 3s.

La Baronne de Staël-Holstein. Le Directoire. (Considérations sur la Révolution Française. Troisième et quatrième parties.) Revised and enlarged. With Notes by G. MASSON, B.A. and G. W. PROTHERO, M.A. 2s.

———— ———— **Dix Années d'Exil. Livre II. Chapitres 1—8.** By the same Editors. New Edition, enlarged. 2s.

Lemercier. Fredegonde et Brunehaut. A Tragedy in Five Acts. By GUSTAVE MASSON, B.A. 2s.

Molière. Le Bourgeois Gentilhomme, Comédie-Ballet en Cinq Actes. (1670.) By Rev. A. C. CLAPIN, M.A. 1s. 6d.

———— **L'Ecole des Femmes.** With Introduction and Notes by G. SAINTSBURY, M.A. 2s. 6d.

Piron. La Métromanie. A Comedy, with Notes, by G. MASSON, B.A. 2s.

Sainte-Beuve. M. Daru (Causeries du Lundi, Vol. IX.) By G. MASSON, B.A. 2s.

Saintine. Picciola. With Introduction, Notes and Map. By Rev. A. C. CLAPIN, M.A. 2s.

Scribe and Legouvé. Bataille de Dames. Edited by Rev. H. A. BULL, M.A. 2s.

Scribe. Le Verre d'Eau. A Comedy; with Memoir, Grammatical and Historical Notes. Edited by C. COLBECK, M.A. 2s.

Sedaine. Le Philosophe sans le savoir. Edited with Notes by Rev. H. A. BULL, M.A., late Master at Wellington College. 2s.

London: Cambridge Warehouse, Ave Maria Lane.

Thierry. Lettres sur l'histoire de France (XIII.—XXIV). By G. MASSON, B.A. and G. W. PROTHERO, M.A. 2s. 6d.

—— **Récits des Temps Mérovingiens I—III.** Edited by GUSTAVE MASSON, B.A. Univ. Gallic., and A. R. ROPES, M.A. With Map. 3s.

Villemain. Lascaris ou Les Grecs du XVe Siècle, Nouvelle Historique. By G. MASSON, B.A. 2s.

Voltaire. Histoire du Siècle de Louis XIV. Chaps. I.— XIII. Edited with Notes by G. MASSON, B.A. and G. W. PROTHERO, M.A. 2s. 6d.

—— **Part II. Chaps. XIV—XXIV.** By the same Editors. With Three Maps. 2s. 6d.

—— **Part III. Chaps. XXV. to end.** By the same Editors. 2s. 6d.

Xavier de Maistre. La Jeune Siberienne. Le Lépreux de la Cité D'Aoste. By G. MASSON, B.A. 2s.

IV. GERMAN.

Ballads on German History. Arranged and annotated by WILHELM WAGNER, Ph.D. 2s.

Benedix. Doctor Wespe. Lustspiel in fünf Aufzügen. Edited with Notes by KARL HERMANN BREUL, M.A. 3s.

Freytag. Der Staat Friedrichs des Grossen. With Notes. By WILHELM WAGNER, Ph.D. 2s.

German Dactylic Poetry. Arranged and annotated by WILHELM WAGNER, Ph.D. 2s.

Goethe's Knabenjahre. (1749—1759.) Arranged and annotated by WILHELM WAGNER, Ph.D. 2s.

—— **Hermann und Dorothea.** By WILHELM WAGNER, Ph.D. Revised edition by J. W. CARTMELL, M.A. 3s. 6d.

Gutzkow. Zopf und Schwert. Lustspiel in fünf Aufzügen. By H. J. WOLSTENHOLME, B.A. (Lond.). 3s. 6d.

Hauff. Das Wirthshaus im Spessart. By A. SCHLOTTMANN, Ph.D. 3s. 6d.

Hauff. Die Karavane. Edited with Notes by A. SCHLOTTMANN, Ph.D. 3s. 6d.

Immermann. Der Oberhof. A tale of Westphalian Life, by WILHELM WAGNER, Ph.D. 3s.

Kohlrausch. Das Jahr 1813. With English Notes by WILHELM WAGNER, Ph.D. 2s.

Lessing and Gellert. Selected Fables. Edited with Notes by KARL HERMANN BREUL, M.A., Lecturer in German at the University of Cambridge. 3s.

London: Cambridge Warehouse, Ave Maria Lane.

Mendelssohn's Letters. Selections from. Edited by JAMES SIME, M.A. 3s.

Raumer. Der erste Kreuzzug (1095—1099). By WILHELM WAGNER, Ph.D. 2s.

Riehl. Culturgeschichtliche Novellen. Edited by H. J. WOLSTENHOLME, B.A. (Lond.). 4s. 6d.

Uhland. Ernst, Herzog von Schwaben. With Introduction and Notes. By the same Editor. 3s. 6d.

V. ENGLISH.

Ancient Philosophy from Thales to Cicero, A Sketch of. By JOSEPH B. MAYOR, M.A. 3s. 6d.

Bacon's History of the Reign of King Henry VII. With Notes by the Rev. Professor LUMBY, D.D. 3s.

Cowley's Essays. With Introduction and Notes, by the Rev. Professor LUMBY, D.D. 4s.

More's History of King Richard III. Edited with Notes, Glossary, Index of Names. By J. RAWSON LUMBY, D.D. 3s. 6d.

More's Utopia. With Notes, by Rev. Prof. LUMBY, D.D. 3s. 6d.

The Two Noble Kinsmen, edited with Introduction and Notes, by the Rev. Professor SKEAT, Litt.D. 3s. 6d.

VI. EDUCATIONAL SCIENCE.

Comenius, John Amos, Bishop of the Moravians. His Life and Educational Works, by S. S. LAURIE, A.M., F.R.S.E. New Edition, revised. 3s. 6d.

Education, Three Lectures on the Practice of. Delivered under the direction of the Teachers' Training Syndicate. 2s.

Locke on Education. With Introduction and Notes by the Rev. R. H. QUICK, M.A. 3s. 6d.

Milton's Tractate on Education. A facsimile reprint from the Edition of 1673. Edited, with Introduction and Notes, by OSCAR BROWNING, M.A. 2s.

Modern Languages, Lectures on the Teaching of. By C. COLBECK, M.A. 2s.

Teacher, General aims of the, and Form Management. Two Lectures delivered in the University of Cambridge in the Lent Term, 1883, by F. W. FARRAR, D.D. and R. B. POOLE, B.D. 1s. 6d.

Teaching, Theory and Practice of. By the Rev. E. THRING, M.A., late Head Master of Uppingham School. New Edition. 4s. 6d.

Other Volumes are in preparation.

London: Cambridge Warehouse, Ave Maria Lane.

The Cambridge Bible for Schools and Colleges.

GENERAL EDITOR: J. J. S. PEROWNE, D.D.,
DEAN OF PETERBOROUGH.

"It is difficult to commend too highly this excellent series."—
Guardian.

"The modesty of the general title of this series has, we believe, led many to misunderstand its character and underrate its value. The books are well suited for study in the upper forms of our best schools, but not the less are they adapted to the wants of all Bible students who are not specialists. We doubt, indeed, whether any of the numerous popular commentaries recently issued in this country will be found more serviceable for general use."—*Academy.*

"Of great value. The whole series of comments for schools is highly esteemed by students capable of forming a judgment. The books are scholarly without being pretentious: information is so given as to be easily understood."—*Sword and Trowel.*

NOW READY. Cloth, Extra Fcap. 8vo.

Book of Joshua. By Rev. G. F. MACLEAR, D.D. With Maps. *2s. 6d.*

Book of Judges. By Rev. J. J. LIAS, M.A.. *3s. 6d.*

First Book of Samuel. By Rev. Prof. KIRKPATRICK, M.A. With Map. *3s. 6d.*

Second Book of Samuel. By Rev. Prof. KIRKPATRICK, M.A. With 2 Maps. *3s. 6d.*

First Book of Kings. By Rev. Prof. LUMBY, D.D. With 3 Maps. *3s. 6d.*

Second Book of Kings. By Rev. Prof. LUMBY, D.D. With 3 Maps. *3s. 6d.*

Book of Job. By Rev. A. B. DAVIDSON, D.D. *5s.*

Book of Ecclesiastes. By Very Rev. E. H. PLUMPTRE, D.D. *5s.*

Book of Jeremiah. By Rev. A. W. STREANE, M.A. *4s. 6d.*

Book of Hosea. By Rev. T. K. CHEYNE, M.A., D.D. *3s.*

London: Cambridge Warehouse, Ave Maria Lane.

Books of Obadiah and Jonah. By Arch. PEROWNE. 2s. 6d.

Book of Micah. By Rev. T. K. CHEYNE, M.A., D.D. 1s. 6d.

Books of Haggai and Zechariah. By Arch. PEROWNE. 3s.

Gospel according to St Matthew. By Rev. A. CARR, M.A. With 2 Maps. 2s. 6d.

Gospel according to St Mark. By Rev. G. F. MACLEAR, D.D. With 4 Maps. 2s. 6d.

Gospel according to St Luke. By Archdeacon FARRAR. With 4 Maps. 4s. 6d.

Gospel according to St John. By Rev. A. PLUMMER, M.A., D.D. With 4 Maps. 4s. 6d.

Acts of the Apostles. By Rev. Professor LUMBY, D.D. With 4 Maps. 4s. 6d.

Epistle to the Romans. Rev. H. C. G. MOULE, M.A. 3s. 6d.

First Corinthians. By Rev. J. J. LIAS, M.A. With Map. 2s.

Second Corinthians. By Rev. J. J. LIAS, M.A. With Map. 2s.

Epistle to the Ephesians. By Rev. H. C. G. MOULE, M.A. 2s. 6d.

Epistle to the Hebrews. By Arch. FARRAR, D.D. 3s. 6d.

General Epistle of St James. By Very Rev. E. H. PLUMPTRE, D.D. 1s. 6d.

Epistles of St Peter and St Jude. By Very Rev. E. H. PLUMPTRE, D.D. 2s. 6d.

Epistles of St John. By Rev. A. PLUMMER, M.A., D.D. 3s. 6d.

Preparing.

Book of Genesis. By Very Rev. the Dean of Peterborough.

Books of Exodus, Numbers and Deuteronomy. By Rev. C. D. GINSBURG, LL.D.

Books of Ezra and Nehemiah. By Rev. Prof. RYLE, M.A.

Book of Psalms. By Rev. Prof. KIRKPATRICK, M.A.

Book of Isaiah. By W. ROBERTSON SMITH, M.A.

Book of Ezekiel. By Rev. A. B. DAVIDSON, D.D.

Epistle to the Galatians. By Rev. E. H. PEROWNE, D.D.

Epistles to the Philippians, Colossians and Philemon. By Rev. H. C. G. MOULE, M.A.

Epistles to the Thessalonians. By Rev. W. F. MOULTON, D.D.

Book of Revelation. By Rev. W. H. SIMCOX, M.A.

London : Cambridge Warehouse, Ave Maria Lane.

The Cambridge Greek Testament for Schools and Colleges,

with a Revised Text, based on the most recent critical authorities, and English Notes, prepared under the direction of the General Editor,

J. J. S. PEROWNE, D.D., DEAN OF PETERBOROUGH.

Gospel according to St Matthew. By Rev. A. CARR, M.A.
With 4 Maps. 4s. 6d.

Gospel according to St Mark. By Rev. G. F. MACLEAR, D.D.
With 3 Maps. 4s. 6d.

Gospel according to St Luke. By Archdeacon FARRAR.
With 4 Maps. 6s.

Gospel according to St John. By Rev. A. PLUMMER, M.A.
With 4 Maps. 6s.

Acts of the Apostles. By Rev. Professor LUMBY, D.D.
With 4 Maps. 6s.

First Epistle to the Corinthians. By Rev. J. J. LIAS, M.A. 3s.

Second Epistle to the Corinthians. By Rev. J. J. LIAS, M.A.
[*Preparing.*

Epistle to the Hebrews. By Archdeacon FARRAR, D.D.
[*In the Press.*

Epistle of St James. By Very Rev. E. H. PLUMPTRE, D.D.
[*Preparing.*

Epistles of St John. By Rev. A. PLUMMER, M.A., D.D. 4s.

London: C. J. CLAY AND SONS,
CAMBRIDGE WAREHOUSE, AVE MARIA LANE.
Glasgow: 263, ARGYLE STREET.
Cambridge: DEIGHTON, BELL AND CO.
Leipzig: F. A. BROCKHAUS.

CAMBRIDGE: PRINTED BY C. J. CLAY, M.A. AND SONS, AT THE UNIVERSITY PRESS.

FSC
www.fsc.org

MIX

Papier aus ver-
antwortungsvollen
Quellen

Paper from
responsible sources

FSC® C141904

Druck:
Customized Business Services GmbH
im Auftrag der KNV-Gruppe
Ferdinand-Jühlke-Str. 7
99095 Erfurt